I0779723

Evil Returns

Cynthia Hickey

The Sheriff of Misty Hollow, Book 3

To all my readers. You are precious!

Chapter One

Deputy Trevor Bolton trusted his instincts. Always. Trusting his instincts had kept him alive more times than he could count. But the last few days...something felt...off. A creeping sense of unease settled in his bones. Someone was watching.

He glanced at Heidi, Shea's German shepherd. The dog lay with her head on her paws, ears up, dark eyes focused on something Trevor couldn't see or hear through the falling rain. The shepherd's body remained tense, coiled like a spring ready to release. In the three months he'd been watching her while Shea was on vacation, Trevor had learned to read the dog's moods. This wasn't her usual evening alertness. This was something else entirely.

It had all started a few nights ago during his evening run. The sensation of eyes tracking him from the tree line near his property. Then, the moving shadows appeared—dark figures just beyond his line of sight. Every time he turned to take a deeper look, they disappeared. The feeling had been so strong, so visceral, that he'd cut his run short and jogged back to the house with his hand resting on his service weapon.

At first, he'd convinced himself it was nothing. A side effect of missing Shea, a trick of the light, an overactive imagination. God knew he'd been on edge since taking over as acting sheriff. The responsibility weighed on him differently than his regular deputy duties. Every decision felt magnified, every choice scrutinized. But when his motion-detector front porch light came on at three in the morning, then the next two mornings after that, he knew he wasn't dealing with an animal. At least not the four-legged kind.

Trevor had checked the recordings from his security cameras each morning, but whoever was out there knew exactly where to stand to avoid detection. The blind spots around his property weren't accidental—they were being exploited by someone who understood surveillance, someone who had studied his home with methodical precision.

The last two days had offered a little respite because of the rain, but now there was no doubt someone was watching him. Trevor set his empty tea glass on the small iron table next to his patio chair and moved to the porch railing. He squinted through the dark. Nightfall and rain made visibility nonexistent a few yards from the house. The familiar sounds of his neighborhood—dogs barking in the distance, the occasional car engine, the rustle of wind through leaves—all seemed muted by the steady percussion of raindrops against metal and wood.

When his skin crawled, he glanced at the dog again. Heidi still seemed to be on alert but not agitated. Her ears twitched at sounds he couldn't detect, but she hadn't started the low growl that usually preceded her protective stance. Whatever was out there, she sensed it but didn't perceive it as an immediate threat. Yet.

"Come on, girl. Let's go inside. I'll bring you back out later." Hopefully, the rain would've stopped by then.

Trevor spent the next hour trying to watch an action movie on the television. The familiar comfort of explosions and one-liners should have been a distraction, but his training wouldn't let him relax. Instead, his gaze kept flicking to the window. Every shadow seemed to move independently of the swaying tree branches. Every sound outside made his muscles tense. He found himself reaching for his weapon twice before forcing his hand back to the remote.

A creak sounded outside. Then, a crash of thunder. He relaxed, chalking up any unusual sounds to the storm. The old farmhouse had weathered decades of Arkansas storms, and its wooden bones always protested during heavy weather. After a while, the combination of exhaustion and the rhythmic drumming of rain lulled him into an uneasy sleep.

Heidi's barking at the front door startled him awake. The sharp, urgent sound cut through his consciousness like a blade. The dog's hair stood on end, her hackles raised in a ridge along her spine. She scratched at the door with desperate intensity, her claws leaving marks in the wood.

Trevor grabbed his pistol from the coffee table and peered out the window. The rain had stopped. A full moon played peek-a-boo with the clouds, casting intermittent pools of silver light across his yard. The silence felt oppressive after hours of rainfall. He put a restraining hand on the dog's head, feeling the tremor of tension in her muscles, then he carefully opened the front door.

Heidi dashed off the porch and into the woods, her dark form disappearing into the tree line within seconds. Trevor took a step to follow her, but stopped dead in his tracks.

A knife lay in the center of the porch, its blade catching the light of the moon. Rust clung to the handle like dried blood, but he recognized it immediately. The wooden grip, worn smooth by countless hands. The particular curve of the blade. The distinctive notch near the hilt where it had struck stone years ago.

It was identical to the one his brother, Troy, had used twenty years ago. The same blade that had cut into Trevor's flesh when his brother stabbed him five times, leaving him to bleed on the forest floor. When he'd bent over him, Troy had whispered, "You won't be the favored one anymore." The memory of those words, spoken in a voice so like his own yet filled with such malice, still had the power to make Trevor's blood run cold.

Trevor's hand clenched at his side, his pulse hammering against his ribs. The scars along his torso, five parallel lines that had faded but never disappeared, began to ache with phantom pain. His gut told him this wasn't a message. This was a warning. From whom? Who would've known where Troy had hidden the knife he'd used not only on Trevor but on a handful of others? The weapon had been evidence in his brother's trial, but it had disappeared from the police station years ago during a move between facilities.

Frowning, Trevor forced himself to think like a deputy instead of a victim. He needed to preserve any potential evidence. He entered the kitchen and pulled a rubber glove from a drawer, his hands steady despite the adrenaline coursing through his system. Then, he returned to the porch and picked up the knife.

The weight felt wrong in his hand—too light, too familiar. It brought back memories of hunting trips with his father, back when they were just boys and Troy hadn't yet revealed the darkness that lived inside him. They'd used knives like this to field dress deer, their father teaching them to respect both the tool and the life it had taken. Trevor wondered if his father had ever suspected what Troy would become, if there had been signs even then that they'd all missed.

Troy was still in prison. Trevor had checked last week—something he did regularly, a ritual that helped him sleep at night. The knowledge that his twin brother was locked away behind bars had been one of the few constants in his life since the attack. Why would someone leave the knife now? There were always crazies, people fascinated by violent crime. A fan of his brother's?

After whistling for Heidi for several minutes with no response, worry began to gnaw at him. The dog was well-trained and rarely strayed far from the property. But she had sensed something out there, something that had sent her racing into the darkness. He entered the house and placed the knife on the kitchen table where he studied it for several long minutes. The rust wasn't just age—there were dark stains that could have been anything. Or everything.

Realizing he'd get no answers so late at night, he locked up the house, checking each window and door twice. Sleep, when it finally came, was filled with nightmares of running through dark woods while something pursued him, always just out of sight but close enough that he could hear its breathing.

After a sleepless night, he sat at his desk, or rather Shea's desk, at the sheriff's office. The knife, now in an evidence bag, rested on the desk, the rusted blade as familiar as the scars in his side. Five deep wounds, five moments of agonizing clarity before he had collapsed. He'd been fifteen years old, still believing that his brother could be saved, that the darkness in Troy's eyes was just a phase he'd grow out of.

His jaw tightened. The fact that someone had found the knife Troy had hidden all those years ago scared him more than he wanted to admit. It meant someone had been researching his brother's crimes, following the old trails, perhaps even visiting the original crime scenes. The level of planning and dedication required suggested this wasn't a random prank or a crime of opportunity.

Coffee. He needed coffee. Leaving Heidi sleeping on a dog bed in the corner—she'd returned just before dawn, her fur damp with dew and carrying scents of the deep woods—he headed to the break room and poured a cup of sludge, which the department called coffee. The familiar routine helped center him, gave his hands something to do while his mind worked through possibilities. Hoping to make it palatable, he added a healthy dose of cream and sugar, then returned to the office.

He paused in the doorway, his heartbeat speeding up.

Shea whipped around to face him. "What is this?" She pointed at the knife.

Her presence filled the room with an energy he hadn't realized he'd been missing. Sheriff Shea Callahan had a way of making everything seem manageable, even the impossible cases. Her auburn hair was pulled back in its usual practical ponytail, and her green eyes held the sharp intelligence that had made her the youngest sheriff in the county's history.

~

Shea's stomach had tightened the moment she saw the knife. Rusted. Worn. Used. Something about it felt wrong, like a discordant note in a familiar song. The blade seemed to absorb light rather than reflect it, and she found herself instinctively stepping back from the desk. Her gaze locked with Trevor's. "What is this?"

"Something someone left on my porch last night." He sat in a chair across from her, and she noticed the exhaustion etched in the lines around his eyes. "Welcome back. You're early."

"Only a day. Vacation is nice, but a week is more than enough time to spend following my friend to soccer games and swim lessons." She set her bag on the floor, noting how Trevor's shoulders remained rigid, how his eyes kept darting back to the evidence bag. "You look like you haven't slept in days."

"I haven't. Not much, anyway." He leaned forward, his voice low and controlled. "This is the same kind of knife my brother used to stab me twenty years ago."

The words hit her like a physical blow. She'd read Trevor's file when she'd first been elected sheriff, had seen the police reports and medical records from the attack. But hearing him say it aloud, seeing the recognition in his eyes as he stared at the weapon, made it real in a way that paperwork never could.

"Are you sure?" She frowned, her mind already racing through possibilities. "What's its normal purpose?"

"My father used one like this to skin deer. It's perfectly balanced for close work, holds an edge well." Trevor's voice took on the flat, professional tone he used when discussing cases, but she could hear the underlying tension. "Troy always preferred it to the newer knives Dad bought."

She tapped her fingers against the desk, a nervous habit she'd developed during her early days in law enforcement. "Your brother is still locked up, isn't he?"

"Last I checked. But, that's the next thing on my to-do list. Call the prison and make sure." Trevor's jaw clenched. "Though if someone's playing games, they certainly know how to get my attention."

She exhaled, leaning back in her chair. The implications were already forming in her mind, each one worse than the last. "Could be a prank, but…" Her voice trailed off. She knew better than to keep on talking. The weight in Trevor's gaze told her he had already gone through every possible rational explanation. None of them set right with him. Which meant a phone call needed to be made ASAP. "I'll call the prison now. We need to know what we're dealing with."

She dialed the number, identified herself, and asked to speak to the warden. The bureaucratic runaround that followed confirmed her worst fears about the state of their correctional system.

"Warden Mills."

"Sheriff Callahan from Misty Hollow. I'm calling in regard to an inmate by the name of Troy Bolton."

"That inmate was moved to a maximum-security psychiatric hospital a month ago for shanking a fellow inmate over a game of cards."

She narrowed her eyes at Trevor, watching his face go pale. "Why wasn't his brother, Deputy Bolton, notified of this?"

"The hospital should've done that."

"Deputy Bolton checked on his brother a week ago. Are you telling me he'd already been transferred and no one thought to let him know?" She heard the ice in her voice and didn't care. Incompetence in the system put lives at risk, and Trevor's life was one she wasn't willing to gamble with.

"I'm sorry. We're behind in updating our reports." He gave her the phone number to the hospital.

"What?" Trevor asked the moment she hung up.

"Troy was transferred a month ago." She dialed the new number and once again identified herself. Few things bothered her as much as incompetence, but the growing dread in her stomach suggested this was about to get much worse.

News from the hospital was far worse than Trevor not being told. "Inmate Bolton escaped earlier this week en route to medical," the doctor stated. "We believe he had outside help."

Shea's heart plummeted. "Say that again?"

"Troy Bolton escaped our facility. We've been working feverishly to locate him. I fear he may be headed back to Arkansas."

"He's already here." She slammed the phone down and took a deep breath, forcing herself to remain calm when everything inside her wanted to scream. "Your brother escaped earlier this week."

Trevor's face darkened, but she also saw something else there—a flicker of the frightened fifteen-year-old boy who had nearly died at his brother's hands. "No one thought to inform me or this department? It doesn't take a genius to know he's headed back here. No, he's already here. That explains the knife."

Troy had had plenty of time to retrieve the weapon and locate Trevor. His brother had been on his porch. Watched him for days. The systematic stalking, the psychological torture of leaving the knife—it all fit the profile of someone who wanted to savor his victim's fear before making his final move. He'd returned to finish what he'd started.

Clearing her throat, Shea stared at the knife. The evidence bag couldn't contain the malevolence that seemed to emanate from the weapon. "You aren't safe staying alone." This time it wasn't her life in danger but his, and the thought of losing Trevor made her chest tight with panic. "You'll stay in my guest room." She moved her gaze back to his. "We'll find him, Trevor. I promise."

"What a way to welcome you home." He gave a wry smile, but she could see the gratitude in his eyes.

"Fill me in on what else happened while I was gone." She listened as he listed everyday things like car accidents and vandalism, but her mind kept returning to the knife on her desk. When he mentioned one of the elementary teachers being stalked, she straightened, wondering if there could be a connection.

"The man and his wife are both locked up now. No one died, and Deputy Harris has fully recovered."

"You did a good job as acting sheriff, Trevor." She couldn't have left things in better hands. The department had run smoothly in her absence, and she knew that was due to Trevor's steady leadership. "And thank you for watching Heidi."

"She provided company, but she missed you a lot." His smile widened. "I'm great and all, but I'm not you."

She slid the evidence bag across her desk. "Send that to forensics. See what they can pull from it, then lock it up once we have it back. I'll put out an APB on your brother and post his photo everywhere. Someone will see him."

"If they do, he'll kill them. My brother has no regard for life." Trevor marched from the room, his shoulders set with grim determination.

Shea booted up her computer and located the police report on Trevor's attack. The details made her stomach churn. The young boy hadn't been expected to survive the attack, but he did. They'd found Troy hiding in a neighbor's barn among dead livestock—animals he'd killed for practice, according to the psychiatric evaluation. How could one brother turn out so good and the other so evil? Same blood, same parents, same upbringing…twins.

She stared at Troy's mug shot. A handsome young man with dead eyes that seemed to look right through the camera and into her soul. Not an identical twin. No one would even mistake the evil Bolton son with his brother. Where Trevor's eyes held warmth and compassion, Troy's were empty vessels that reflected nothing but darkness.

Six people, all under the age of eighteen, had died at the hands of Troy Bolton. All were stabbed seven times. What significance did the number seven have?

"He claimed it was his lucky number," Trevor said from the doorway.

She hadn't realized she'd asked the question out loud. "He only stabbed you five times."

"I fought back. Hit him in the head with a rock. A hunter heard the commotion and fired a warning shot in the air. Troy disappeared in the forest and wasn't seen again until they found him a week later hiding in a barn."

"So, he wants to finish the stabbing he hadn't been able to finish on you."

Trevor shrugged, but she could see the tension in

his shoulders. "I doubt he'll be satisfied with two stabs unless he goes for the heart. Otherwise, he'll start over and try for seven again."

"Six people before you. You were to be his last."

"I doubt he would've stopped." He sat across from her again. "You didn't see the look in his eyes. He enjoyed the killing."

And now he was in Misty Hollow. Evil had returned, and it wore the face of someone Trevor had once trusted completely. The knife on her desk seemed to pulse with malevolent energy, a promise of violence yet to come. But this time, Troy Bolton wouldn't catch them unprepared. This time, they were ready for him.

Chapter Two

Twenty years ago.

Trevor stretched and yawned as he entered the kitchen after finishing his job at the gas station. The digital clock on the microwave glowed 9:03 PM in harsh green numbers. His shift had run late again. Old Mr. Henderson needed help changing a flat tire, and Trevor couldn't bring himself to leave the elderly man stranded on the side of Highway 12. The house seemed eerily quiet even for nine p.m. His parents had gone to see a movie, and Troy might not have returned from his job at the supermarket, but everything still seemed off.

The silence felt wrong, like the moment before a storm broke. Trevor had lived in this house his entire seventeen years, knew every creak of the floorboards, every groan of the settling foundation. This wasn't the comfortable quiet of an empty home. This was something else entirely.

"Hello?" he called out, his voice echoing strangely in the familiar space. The unlocked back door didn't bother him—it never had before. No one locked their door in the small town of Pea Ridge. At least not until the rash of killings in town. Six people dead so far, their bodies found in various locations around the county. The youngest victim had been only fourteen, just a freshman at the high school. For the first time in his life, Trevor turned the deadbolt behind him and headed to his bedroom upstairs. Better safe than sorry. Wrong.

The stairs creaked under his weight as he climbed, each step seeming louder than usual in the oppressive quiet. His mother had left the hallway light on, casting long shadows that seemed to reach for him with skeletal fingers. Trevor shook his head, annoyed at his own paranoia. The killings had everyone on edge, but this was his home. He was safe here.

Before he could close his bedroom door, a masked figure shoved him backward with brutal force. Trevor slammed against his dresser, the corner driving into his spine like a sledgehammer. Pain shot through his ribcage, stealing his breath. Picture frames scattered across the floor, glass shattering. The Pea Ridge Killer was in his house!

Terror flooded his system, but beneath it, something else stirred. Anger. Determination. He refused to be the seventh victim. This monster had taken enough from his community, from families who would never be whole again. Head down, he roared and charged, pushing his attacker back into the hall. The momentum carried them both down the stairs in a tangle of limbs and fury.

Breathless, Trevor lay at the bottom of the staircase, his head spinning from the impact. Every bone in his body screamed in protest. When the person beside him struggled to his knees, Trevor rolled, ignoring the sharp pain in his ribs, then lunged upright, fists clenched. His father had taught him to box when he was twelve, said every man needed to know how to defend himself and others.

The masked man laughed, a sound like breaking glass, then pulled the ski mask over his head. Troy?

Trevor's world tilted. The face staring back at him was his own, yet twisted by something malevolent. They'd shared a womb, shared a childhood, shared everything brothers were supposed to share. But the eyes looking at him now held no trace of brotherhood, no hint of the boy who'd built forts with him in the backyard and shared secrets under blanket tents.

"What kind of game are you playing?" Trevor dropped his hands to his side, confusion overriding his defensive instincts. This had to be some twisted joke, didn't it? Until his twin smiled. A cold smile devoid of humor, bereft of humanity.

"The best kind of game, brother of mine." He pulled a knife from the pocket of the black hoodie he wore. The very knife their father used to skin deer with, its blade worn smooth by years of use.

Trevor's stomach dropped. He recognized that knife as well as he knew his own reflection. "That's Dad's knife."

"Not anymore." Troy's voice carried a sing-song quality that made Trevor's skin crawl. "This knife slices through human flesh as smoothly as it does venison. Maybe even smoother." Troy's smile widened, stretching his features into something inhuman. "You're lucky, bro. Lucky number seven."

It took a minute for the full horror to sink in. Trevor frowned and took a step back, his mind struggling to process what he was seeing, what he was hearing. "You're the killer?" The words felt foreign on his tongue. It couldn't be. Sure, Troy was always in trouble with school or the authorities—fighting, skipping classes, that incident with the neighbor's cat that everyone pretended hadn't happened. But a murderer? A serial killer?

The brother he'd shared every day of his seventeen years with had been systematically hunting and killing their neighbors, their classmates, people they'd grown up with. Trevor thought about Sarah Martinez, the first victim. Troy had asked her to prom just last month. She'd turned him down gently, kindly, the way Sarah did everything. Had that rejection signed her death warrant?

Trevor shook his head and took another step back, his heel hitting the bottom stair.

Troy moved forward with predatory grace, his

movements fluid and purposeful. The blade of the knife glinted under the fluorescent lights of the kitchen. "I want you dead before Mom and Dad get home. Then, I'll delight in their grief over losing their precious Trevor."

The words hit like physical blows. Their parents had never played favorites—at least, Trevor had never thought they did. They'd supported both boys equally, attended every game, every school event. Where had this poisonous jealousy come from? "This is about jealousy?"

"Not all of it." Troy's grin never faded, stretching wider with each word. "Just your death! I like killing. It gives me a power rush like nothing else in this world."

Trevor's blood ran cold. The casual way Troy spoke about murder, the genuine pleasure in his voice when he described killing—this wasn't his brother anymore. This was something wearing his brother's face.

His brother lunged forward with inhuman speed. A sharp, searing pain erupted in Trevor's side, just below his ribs.

The world tilted as he staggered backward, his hand flying to the wound in time to feel the warm gush of blood spilling through his fingers. The metallic scent filled his nostrils, making him dizzy. His vision blurred, his breath hitched. He stared into Troy's soulless eyes, searching for any trace of the brother he'd loved.

"One."

Trevor frowned through the haze of pain. Was he going to count the strikes like some demented game?

"I thought about you being my first victim." Troy's voice dripped with malice, each word carefully enunciated like he was savoring the taste. "But then, I thought it only fitting that the one I shared a womb with should be number seven. After all, you were born seven minutes after me. Seven has always been my lucky number."

His knees buckled under the combined weight of blood loss and horror. Grabbing the kitchen counter kept him from falling. Trevor inched his way toward the back door, never taking his gaze off his twin. Every step sent fresh waves of agony through his torso, but he forced himself to keep moving.

"Seven victims, seven minutes, seven stab wounds each," Troy continued conversationally, as if discussing the weather. "There's a beautiful symmetry to it all, don't you think?"

Trevor's hand found the door handle. He tumbled down the back porch steps, his shoulder slamming into the wooden railing. For the first time in his life, he wished his parents hadn't bought a house on this lonely country road where the nearest neighbor was at least a football field's distance away. The isolation that had always felt like privacy now felt like a death sentence. Calling for help wasn't an option—his phone upstairs in his bedroom, might as well be on the moon.

Another stab, this one sliding between his ribs,

almost sent him to his knees. Troy was toying with him, drawing out the kill like a cat with a mouse.

"Two!" Troy's laughter echoed across the empty fields.

Swallowing a cry that wanted to tear from his throat, Trevor forced himself forward. His stomach clenched as nausea roiled, and pain flared through his body with each heartbeat. Adrenaline kept him moving when logic told him to lie down and accept his fate. He pushed past low-hanging branches, ignoring the sting as they scraped his already torn skin. Running became his entire focus, his entire world narrowed to the simple act of putting one foot in front of the other. He had to get to the neighboring farm, had to find someone, anyone.

Not hearing his brother behind him anymore, he stopped, ears straining against the symphony of night sounds. Where was he? A shadow shifted between the trees to his left, and Trevor spun around. Too late. Troy struck again, this time the blade sliding through Trevor's stomach like butter.

"Three!" His brother laughed, the sound bouncing off the trees. "How many stabs can you endure, dear Trevor? How long before you beg me to finish it?"

The taste of copper filled Trevor's mouth. He threw himself sideways, his shoulder slamming into a massive oak trunk. Stars exploded across his vision, but the tree also provided momentary cover. He kicked out blindly, his foot connecting solidly with Troy's shin. His twin fell back, snarling like an animal.

A moment of opportunity presented itself. Trevor seized it, lunging forward with every ounce of strength he had left. His fists, slick with his blood, slammed into Troy's face, once, twice, knocking him off balance. The satisfying crunch of cartilage under his knuckles gave him a surge of savage satisfaction. But his brother was stronger, uninjured, and had been planning this moment for God knew how long.

Troy grabbed Trevor by the front of his blood-soaked shirt and shoved him against another tree with enough force to rattle his teeth. The knife blade flashed in the moonlight filtering through the canopy.

"Help!" Trevor barely twisted away in time. The knife slashed across his ribs instead of plunging into his heart. He gasped, his hands scrabbling desperately against Troy's iron grip.

"Four." Troy's voice had taken on an almost orgasmic quality. "We're past the halfway point now, brother. How does it feel to know you're going to die in the same woods where Dad taught us to hunt?"

One more desperate shove and Trevor ran, lurching his way across a moonlit meadow. His legs felt like water, his vision kept graying at the edges, but pure terror kept him upright. "Help me!" He spotted the blessed sight of the Henderson farmhouse in the distance, yellow light spilling from its windows like salvation itself.

Troy tackled him from behind, driving him face-first into the cold earth. Dirt filled Trevor's mouth, his nose, but he managed to roll to his back and press his hands against his brother's chest.

"Please." The word came out as barely a whisper. "Don't."

"But I'm not finished." The knife plunged into his gut for the fifth time, deeper than the others. "I still need two more."

"Hey!" A gunshot rang out across the meadow. "Get off him!"

Through his blurry vision, Trevor spotted old Mr. Henderson with his shotgun, the same one he'd been carrying for forty years of hunting seasons. The man fired another warning shot into the air.

"This isn't over, brother." Troy jumped to his feet with inhuman grace and sprinted back into the trees, disappearing like a wraith. "I'll be back to finish what I started!"

That was the last time Trevor saw him.

His rescuer leaned over him, and Trevor could see the terror in the old man's eyes. "Hold on, son. Help's coming."

Blackness overtook him, merciful and complete.

~

While he hadn't had the dream in a long time, it was always the same when he did. A perfect, horrifying play-by-play of that awful night twenty years ago. Every detail remained crystal clear—the smell of his own blood, the sound of Troy's laughter, the feeling of life draining from his body with each heartbeat. Trevor sat up and hung his legs over the side of the bed in Shea's guest room. His breath came in ragged gasps, the old scars on his body searing as if the wounds were fresh. His watch told him the time was three a.m. There'd be no more sleep tonight.

He rubbed his hands down his face, feeling the stubble and the cold sweat that always followed the nightmare. The dream had been coming more frequently since Troy's escape, his subconscious preparing him for the reunion neither of them had asked for.

He headed for the guest bathroom's shower. Trevor had spent three weeks in the hospital recovering from that night and underwent four surgeries to repair the damage Troy had inflicted. Every time he looked at himself shirtless in the mirror, he was reminded of how close he'd come to dying. Five scars, five reminders that evil could wear a familiar face. He traced the raised lines with his fingers, each one a testament to his survival.

Now, Troy had returned to finish the job. The question that haunted Trevor was whether his brother would start over by killing others first, working his way up to the grand finale, or come straight for the target he'd been denied two decades ago.

He let the shower run as hot as he could stand, then stood under the scalding spray, one hand plastered flat against the tiled wall. The nightmare had left him covered in a sheen of perspiration, his heart still pounding as if he'd actually been running for his life again. The hot water helped wash away the phantom sensations, the feeling of blood on his hands, the taste of terror in his mouth.

From the bedroom came the faint sound of his phone ringing. They could leave a message. He wasn't ready to face the world yet, wasn't ready to pretend that he was the composed deputy sheriff everyone expected him to be.

Thank the good Lord above his parents weren't alive to relive the nightmare of their son being the infamous Pea Ridge Killer. They'd barely survived learning the truth the first time. His mother had never been the same after Troy's arrest, jumping at shadows and refusing to be alone in the house. His father had aged ten years in the span of a month. Finding out that one's child killed for the pure love of it would mess with anyone's head, but for his parents, it had been a special kind of hell.

His phone rang again as he dried off with one of Shea's fluffy towels. He wrapped it around his waist and went to answer, dread pooling in his stomach.

Unknown number.

His stomach twisted into knots. Only one person would be calling him from an unknown number at three in the morning.

He hesitated before answering, his thumb hovering over the screen. Part of him wanted to ignore it, to maintain the illusion of safety for just a few more hours. But the deputy in him, the part that had sworn to protect and serve, made him press the phone to his ear. "Deputy Bolton."

A long silence filled only with the sound of breathing, then a chilling voice he knew as well as his own. "I should've finished the job that night."

The line went dead with a soft click.

He stared at the phone's screen for several minutes, watching the call timer tick upward even though the connection had ended. Troy had managed to get his number, had been close enough to make the call. How long had he been watching? How much did he know about Trevor's current life, his routines, his weaknesses?

Trevor placed the phone back on the nightstand with hands that trembled slightly. What he needed to focus on now was finding out where his brother could be hiding. It wouldn't be in town where he would be spotted by someone who remembered the old case. It would be somewhere isolated, somewhere like the barn he'd been hiding in twenty years ago.

Trevor donned his deputy uniform, the familiar weight of his service weapon providing some comfort. The badge on his chest felt heavier than usual, a reminder of how much he had to lose if Troy succeeded this time. He headed to Shea's home office to pull up an aerial map of Misty Mountain on her computer. The screen showed a vast expanse of wilderness—plenty of places to hide for someone who didn't want to be found.

Abandoned cabins, hunting lodges, caves carved into the limestone cliffs, old mine shafts from the area's industrial past...it would take a month of Sundays to search them all. But Trevor had a feeling he wouldn't have to wait long for Troy to come to him. His brother had never been patient, and twenty years of confinement would have only made him more eager to complete his interrupted work.

Trevor was no longer a frightened seventeen-year-old boy, shocked at discovering the monster wearing his brother's face. This time, he would be prepared. This time, he would be ready.

After two cups of strong coffee and a breakfast of eggs and bacon that tasted like cardboard, he locked Shea's house and headed to his truck parked in her driveway. A piece of paper fluttered from under the windshield wiper like a white flag of surrender. His hand trembled as he removed it, unfolding the simple message written in Troy's familiar handwriting.

"I'm coming for you."

He wadded up the note, anger replacing fear. "Well, come on then, brother. I'm waiting." He tossed the crumpled paper onto the passenger side floor and climbed into the driver's seat.

Again, Troy had been within reach, had stood right next to Trevor's truck while he slept. The violation of it, the casual demonstration of how easily his brother could get to him, sent ice through his veins. Trevor needed to set a trap, lure him closer on Trevor's terms instead of constantly reacting to Troy's moves.

He backed out of Shea's driveway and headed down the highway toward the sheriff's office. In his rearview mirror, he caught sight of a figure standing in the middle of the road, motionless as a scarecrow. Trevor hit the brakes and threw the truck in reverse, backing up as fast as the transmission would allow. The man darted into the trees with inhuman speed.

Trevor shoved the truck into park and jumped out, his hand instinctively moving to his weapon. "Troy! Come face me like a man!"

No answer other than a crow angry at the disturbance, its harsh call echoing through the morning air.

He waited several tense minutes to see whether his brother would emerge from the tree line, but the forest remained still. When Troy didn't appear, Trevor climbed back into the truck and drove toward town, checking his mirrors constantly.

Shea glanced up from her desk as he entered the sheriff's office, and her expression immediately shifted to concern. "What is it?"

"Troy paid me another visit last night." He plopped into the chair across from her, exhaustion weighing him down like a lead blanket. "Left me a note letting me know he's coming. As I pulled away from your house this morning, he was watching me leave from the middle of the road. I tried to confront him, but he ran off."

Her features hardened, and he could see the protective anger flashing in her green eyes. "Do not face him alone, Trevor. I'm serious. He almost killed you once."

"That was a long time ago. I'm not that scared kid anymore."

She folded her hands on her desk and leaned forward. "You were courageous from what I've read in the reports. You fought him and survived when six others couldn't. Both of you are men now. Stronger, faster, more dangerous. What if he's stronger than you? What if you don't survive this time?" She shook her head firmly. "We'll find him and face him together."

"Haven't you faced enough evil in your life?" He tilted his head, studying her face. Shea had seen her share of darkness in her years in law enforcement.

She smiled, but it didn't reach her eyes. "What's one more time?"

The casual way she said it made Trevor's chest tighten with dread. It wouldn't be just him who might not survive his brother's return. Troy had already demonstrated he had no qualms about killing innocent people to get to his target. And if Shea got in his way, she would become just another obstacle to eliminate.

The thought of losing her, of being responsible for her death, was almost worse than the prospect of his own demise.

Chapter Three

"Trevor, you always were the weaker one."

Trevor bolted upright in bed, his eyes searching the dimly lit room for his brother. The familiar weight of dread pressed against his chest as his gaze swept across every shadow, every corner where a figure might be lurking. Nothing. Another dream. But the voice had sounded so real, so close that he could swear he felt breath against his ear.

Last night, Shea had insisted on moving her and Heidi to his place until his brother was caught. She'd arrived with a duffel bag and her service weapon, her jaw set in that determined way that meant arguing would be futile. He'd known better than to argue with the headstrong sheriff, but having her here put her directly in danger. The thought of Troy turning his attention to Shea, of her becoming collateral damage in his brother's twisted game, made Trevor's stomach churn. He hated that more than anything—more than the fear, more than the memories, more than the scars that would never fully fade.

He listened intently for sounds from down the hall—footsteps that shouldn't be there, the creak of floorboards under an intruder's weight, a warning growl from the dog. When none came, just the peaceful sounds of a house at rest, he padded barefoot to the bathroom to brush his teeth. The mundane act of his nighttime routine helped ground him, reminded him that he was safe in his own home, protected by security systems and a trained law enforcement officer sleeping just down the hall.

"I'm still here, little brother."

Trevor whirled around, his heart hammering against his ribs like a caged bird. The toothpaste fell from the brush onto the bathroom floor with a wet plop. Was he losing his mind? There was no way Troy could be in the house. Not with the comprehensive security measures Trevor had installed during Shea's time away—motion sensors, cameras, alarms on every door and window. The system was state-of-the-art, designed to detect even the smallest breach.

No one stood behind him in the bathroom. The mirror reflected only his pale face, eyes wide with terror and confusion. But the hairs on the back of his neck refused to lie back down, standing at attention like soldiers sensing an approaching enemy. His skin prickled with the unmistakable sensation of being watched. He startled when Shea appeared in the doorway of his bedroom, her hair tousled from sleep but her eyes alert and concerned.

"Trevor? Are you talking to someone?" Her hand rested instinctively on the service weapon she kept on the nightstand, even in sleep.

"You heard it?" Relief that he wasn't going insane flooded through him like cool water. If Shea had heard the voice too, then he wasn't losing his grip on reality. The alternative—that Troy had somehow found a way inside his secure home—was terrifying, but at least it was real.

"I heard voices." She narrowed her eyes as she scanned the room with the practiced gaze of someone who'd spent years assessing threats. "What's going on?"

"I keep hearing Troy's voice. It's like he's right here in the room with me, but when I turn around..." Trevor gestured helplessly at the empty space behind him.

Darting from the room with the quick efficiency that had made her sheriff at such a young age, she returned seconds later with her gun in hand and Heidi at her side. The German shepherd's ears were pricked forward, her dark eyes scanning the room for threats her superior senses might detect. Shea stopped at the window and peered out through the blinds, her body tense and ready for action. "I don't see anything out there, but I'll patrol the area with Heidi. She'll pick up any scent trail if someone's been around."

"Not without me, you won't." The words came out

more forcefully than he'd intended, but the thought of Shea facing Troy alone made his blood run cold. "Give me two minutes to get dressed."

He closed the bathroom door and quickly pulled on jeans and a T-shirt, his hands shaking slightly as adrenaline coursed through his system. The face in the mirror looked haggard, aged beyond his years by stress and sleepless nights. Dark circles shadowed his eyes, and the scar along his jawline—a souvenir from that night twenty years ago—seemed more prominent in the harsh bathroom lighting.

Less than two minutes later, he joined Shea in the front room. She was checking her weapon, her movements sure and practiced. "Ready?" she asked, looking up at him with those steady green eyes that always made him feel like everything might be okay.

Not really. The last thing he wanted was to go stumbling around in the dark, potentially walking into one of Troy's traps. "Yes."

"Heidi, go." She commanded the dog, who immediately moved to the front door. "It's safer to let her lead the way. Her nose will pick up anything we might miss." She pulled her inhaler from her pocket and took a puff, the medication hissing softly in the quiet room.

"You okay?" He studied her face, noting that her lips were a bit too pale for his liking. The stress of the situation was affecting her too, though she'd never admit it.

She smiled, but he could see the exhaustion around her eyes. "I'm fine. You aren't the best housekeeper, is all. The guest room is quite dusty. I'll take care of that later."

"No, I will. You don't need to stir up the dust when you're already squeaking like a screen door." The protective instinct surprised him with its intensity. When had Shea's wellbeing become so important to him?

"Bossy." Shea grinned and stepped onto the porch, but her humor faded as she surveyed the darkness beyond the porch light's reach. She paused, every sense alert, then followed Heidi, who had her nose to the ground and was heading purposefully toward the woods.

The search took them in a wide circle around Trevor's property. Heidi led them through areas where the underbrush was trampled, where someone had clearly been moving through recently. They found cigarette butts that weren't Trevor's brand, footprints in the soft earth near the creek that ran behind his house, and broken branches at eye level—clear signs that someone had been watching, waiting, moving through the darkness like a predator stalking prey.

After searching for an hour with no sign of the intruder, they returned to the house where they sat in his home office and viewed the camera footage on his computer. Trevor's security system was comprehensive, with cameras covering every approach to the house and motion sensors scattered throughout the property.

The footage cut out at exactly 3:07 a.m. The screen glitched, flickered with static, then turned black as if someone had thrown a switch.

Trevor rewound it to watch again, his jaw clenching with frustrated anger. Right before the camera died, a shadow moved outside his front door—too quick and fleeting to make out many details, but definitely human in shape and movement.

"Someone was here," Shea said, leaning forward to study the screen more closely.

"Not someone. Troy." He rubbed his hands down his face, feeling the stubble and the weight of exhaustion from too many nights of little sleep. "He knew exactly how to cut the feed. Probably watched me install the system and figured out the weak points."

"People learn all kinds of things in prison. Electronics, security systems—it's not uncommon for inmates to pick up technical skills."

"Hmm." Trevor reset the system, his mind already working on ways to make it more secure. He needed redundancies, backup systems that Troy wouldn't know about. "This still doesn't explain his voice. How is he getting into the house to talk to me?"

"He must've gotten inside at some point and placed listening devices so he can haunt you remotely. Maybe even small speakers hidden throughout the house." She clapped a hand on his shoulder, the contact warm and reassuring. "I'll have a tech team out here to sweep the place for electronic devices."

"Hire a maid service while you're at it. I don't want you to get sick. I need you." The admission slipped out before he could stop it, more honest than he'd intended to be.

"Sweetest thing I've heard in a long time." She pulled her phone from her pocket and placed the calls, first to the tech team and then to a cleaning service.

By late afternoon, his cabin was clean of both electronic devices and dust. The tech team had found three small speakers hidden in various rooms and a listening device in his bedroom—sophisticated equipment that would have cost serious money. Troy had either stolen it or had help from someone with resources.

The next morning, Trevor stepped onto his back deck with his first cup of coffee, looking forward to a few minutes of peace before facing another day of hunting his brother. He tripped over something soft and warm, nearly spilling the hot liquid down his front. A rabbit lay at his feet, its throat slashed with surgical precision. His stomach lurched as he stared at the clean cut across its neck, the blood still relatively fresh. This wasn't an animal attack or the work of a predator seeking food.

His brother used to do things like this when he was a kid, leaving mutilated animals in the backyard or on a neighbor's doorstep like some twisted calling card. Small animals at first—mice, birds, the occasional squirrel—then bigger ones before eventually moving on to humans. His way of testing the limits, seeing how much violence people would tolerate before they pushed back. It had been one of the early warning signs that their parents had chosen to ignore, explaining it away as a phase, as boys being boys.

"Company again?" Shea joined him on the deck, her hair still damp from her morning shower. Heidi approached the dead animal cautiously, her hackles raised as she caught the scent of death and violence.

"Soon, Troy will move on to people again. This is just him letting me know he's getting impatient." Trevor's voice was flat, emotionless, but inside he was screaming. How many more innocent people would die because his brother was obsessed with him?

~

"We'll do our best to make sure that doesn't happen. I will have a patrol do regular passes by your house for the next few nights." Shea's voice was firm, professional, but he could hear the underlying worry. "Don't worry, Trevor. We'll get him before he hurts anyone else."

"I want to believe you, but Troy is clever. He's had twenty years to plan this, to think about every detail." He grabbed a shovel from the side of the house and carried the rabbit a few yards away before digging a hole in the soft earth. "It won't be easy to catch someone who's been studying us while we've been trying to forget him."

The simple act of burying the animal felt like a ritual, a small gesture of respect for something that had died for no other reason than Troy's need to send a message. When he finished, patting down the soil with the back of the shovel, Shea drove them both to the office.

Trevor headed for the bullpen while she went to her desk and stared at the pile of messages waiting for her. Work still had to be done while they searched for Troy—other crimes didn't stop just because they had a serial killer on the loose. But it was hard to focus on routine police work when she knew that somewhere out there, Troy Bolton was planning his next move.

The man was like a ghost, able to move through their community without being seen. He was close enough to watch Trevor's house, to leave messages and dead animals, yet no one had caught so much as a glimpse of him. The man had to eat and sleep somewhere. Where was he hiding that gave him such easy access to Trevor's property while remaining completely invisible to law enforcement?

She studied the aerial map Trevor had hung on the wall of her office, marking potential hiding spots with red pins. Far too many places to search effectively with their limited resources. But they had to try. There wasn't much money in the budget, but she'd hired a helicopter to fly several deputies around the mountain in grid patterns. Who knows? They might get lucky and spot some sign of him from the air.

"Sheriff?" A worried Doris stood in the doorway, her usual calm demeanor replaced by obvious distress. "We've got a body found near the lake. A couple of kids ditching school found it. They're pretty shaken up and waiting for you."

Shea's heart sank. She asked Trevor to go with her, dreading what they would find but knowing they had to face it. Two teenage boys who smelled strongly of marijuana leaned against a battered sedan in the parking area near the lake. She ignored the fact that they reeked of something they had no business smoking—there were bigger problems to deal with today—and asked them what they'd found.

"There's a man over there." One of the boys pointed toward the bank with a shaking hand. "He's covered with blood. We didn't touch nothing, I swear."

Seconds later, Shea and Trevor stood over the dead body of a man who looked to be in his early thirties. He was well-dressed, probably a tourist who'd been enjoying the scenic beauty of the lake when he'd encountered Troy. The man had died of multiple stab wounds, each one precise and deliberate. "Is it Troy's work?"

"I count seven stab wounds, so I'm saying yes." Trevor's shoulders slumped as he stared at the victim. "He's starting over. Fresh slate, new count."

"Which means you'll be number seven again." The thought made her blood run cold. She couldn't let that happen. Troy wasn't going to get his knife in

Trevor again, not while she drew breath.

Shea slowly moved around the crime scene, carefully examining the area for clues. Finally, she found a footprint near the water's edge that didn't match the victim's shoes—larger, with a distinctive tread pattern that would help them identify Troy's boots if they ever caught him. She frowned as she studied the muddy ground. "What did he do? Lie in wait in the water like an alligator?"

"I wouldn't put it past him." Trevor stood next to her, his face grim as he surveyed the scene. "This is all a game to him. He'll do whatever he can to make it more challenging, more fun. The harder it is, the more he enjoys it."

"That's sick." Further exploration showed disturbed vegetation in the tall reeds near the water's edge, suggesting that Troy had indeed hidden there, possibly for hours, waiting for the right victim to come along. She had no other explanation for how he'd managed to attack someone in such an open area without being seen.

After taking the boys' statements and lecturing them on smoking illegal substances, though her heart wasn't really in it given the circumstances, she sent them home with a warning. Then she stood back as Trevor and another deputy processed the scene, photographing everything and collecting what little evidence there was.

Early the following morning, while Trevor slept

fitfully in his bedroom, she sat in front of the monitor in his office, watching the feeds from his security cameras. The new system was working perfectly, the footage was clear, the motion sensors responsive. But the feeling of being watched made her skin crawl, as if eyes bored into her back even through the walls of the house.

Shea picked up her gun from the desk and moved carefully to the window. She slowly pulled the curtain aside, her heart hammering as she peered out into the pre-dawn darkness.

There. Just beyond the tree line, a shadow stood motionless among the pines.

Her skin twitched with the primal recognition of danger. Shea's grip on the gun turned her knuckles white as she fought the urge to shoot first and ask questions later. The figure was too far away to reveal his features clearly, but she knew with absolute certainty that it was Troy. Watching. Waiting. Planning his next move in the deadly game he was playing with his brother's life.

For a long moment, nothing happened. Hunter and hunted stared at each other across the darkness, separated by perhaps fifty yards of forest. Then, as if he'd made his point, the man stepped back into the deeper shadows and disappeared like smoke.

She raced for the door and swung it open, gun raised and ready. With Heidi at her side, growling low in her throat, she ran toward where she'd seen the figure. Her flashlight sliced through the night, illuminating tree trunks and undergrowth but finding no trace of the intruder. The only sound was the wind whispering through the trees and her labored breathing. It occurred to her, too late, that she was alone in the woods with a deranged killer who had every advantage in this terrain. "Come on, Heidi." She quickly returned to the house and locked the door, then moved from room to room to make sure Troy hadn't somehow circled and gotten inside.

Not seeing Trevor in his bed sent her heart into her throat until she heard the toilet flush from the bathroom.

He frowned as he emerged, instantly reading the tension in her posture. "He was here again, wasn't he?"

"Yes. Watching from the tree line. Bold as brass, like he wanted me to see him." She holstered her weapon but kept her hand near it. "He's gone now, but he'll be back."

"We need something out there to alert us when he approaches. Motion sensors, trip wires, an alarm system around the perimeter of my property." He grabbed a shirt from the back of a chair and pulled it on. "I won't be caught off guard again."

Shea nodded, her mind already working on the logistics. "Tomorrow, I want to visit the hospital where he'd been detained. See what anyone has to say about your brother. Maybe he bragged about his plans for you, or maybe someone there knows more about how he escaped." She looked at him. "Up for a field trip?"

"Absolutely. It's time we stopped reacting to Troy and started getting ahead of him."

~

So, the pretty sheriff thought she could protect Trevor. Troy chuckled to himself as he made his way through the forest, moving with the silent grace of someone who'd spent countless hours learning to hunt both animals and humans. Not a chance in hell. All she was doing was putting herself in the lineup, making herself part of the game. He'd already decided—he would make her number six. Kill her while his brother watched, let Trevor see what happened to people who tried to interfere with destiny.

He marched down the barely visible logging road to the truck he'd stolen from a gas station shortly after his escape. The owner had been an old man working the night shift, too trusting for his own good. Troy had almost felt sorry for him. Almost. The cabin he was staying in wasn't far from here, but it was far enough off the beaten path not to be easily located by law enforcement helicopters or search teams. He'd seen the helicopter circling earlier, its rotors beating the air like mechanical insects. The thick canopy of pine and oak made perfect cover from prying eyes .

He eyed the still-damp clothes on the passenger seat and laughed, remembering how easy it had been to slip into the lake and wait for his first victim. What did they make of his stealth? His ability to strike without warning and disappear like morning mist? There was absolutely no way anyone could best him this time. He wasn't the angry, impulsive teenager he'd been twenty years ago. Prison had hardened him, refined his skills, turned him into something far more dangerous than the boy who'd first tasted blood in these same woods.

The psychiatric hospital they'd transferred him to had been a joke. Maximum security? More like a kindergarten run by bleeding hearts who thought they could cure him with therapy and medication. It had been pathetically easy to get one of the aides to help him escape when he'd threatened the man's family. People were so predictable when you knew which buttons to push.

People were weak. Caring for another person made them vulnerable, gave him leverage to use against them. Troy didn't know that feeling and never wanted to. He cared for no one, felt genuine affection for nothing except the hunt itself. Not even his twin brother meant anything to him beyond being the perfect final victim. All Trevor was good for was to be Troy's lucky number seven, the culmination of everything he'd worked toward for two decades.

He parked behind the hunting cabin where he'd been staying, hidden among the trees where even aerial surveillance would have trouble spotting the stolen vehicle. Since it wasn't close to hunting season, the cabin should remain undisturbed while he finished what he'd started so long ago. The owners probably wouldn't return until October, giving him months to play his game.

He had everything he needed here—canned food lifted from various stores, bottled water, camping supplies. The weather didn't require a fire, which was good since smoke might give away his position. He cooked over a small kerosene stove and drew water from the well behind the cabin. The rustic accommodations were luxury compared to the sterile room and tiny cell he'd spent the last twenty years in, dreaming of this moment.

Troy popped the tab on a can of beer he'd taken from someone's cooler and sat on the porch's top step, enjoying the absolute silence of the forest. He loved the night, the quiet, the darkness that concealed his movements, the way fear tasted in the air when people realized they weren't alone. Daytime was for sleeping or procuring supplies when necessary. It was easy enough to do business with the small mom-and-pop stores scattered throughout the rural area. So far, none of them had posted his mug shot where customers could see it. If he walked into a place and saw his face staring back at him from a wanted poster, he'd have to kill the proprietors—a waste since he couldn't count them as part of his sacred seven. No, the seven had to be people he stalked, people who challenged his skills and made him think creatively.

He downed the beer in long gulps and crushed the can in his hand before tossing it into the bushes. The metallic crunch was satisfying, like the sound bones made when they broke. Yep, only those victims that made him plan and strategize could count toward his goal. Troy grinned, his teeth white in the darkness. He could hardly wait to reach numbers six and seven. The grand finale was going to be worth the twenty-year wait.

Chapter Four.

"Sheriff, there's a man here to see you." Doris's lips curled in distaste as she spoke through the intercom. "Says he has some info on Troy Bolton."

Shea looked up from the stack of incident reports she'd been reviewing, her pulse quickening at the mention of Trevor's brother. Any information about Troy could be crucial, even if it came from questionable sources. She arched a brow. "Really?" This would put them behind schedule for their planned trip to Little Rock, but she wouldn't turn away a potential lead. "Put him in the conference room, please, and have Deputy Bolton meet us there."

She turned off her computer and grabbed a small digital recorder from her desk drawer, along with a notepad and pen. The conference room was the most secure place in the building for sensitive interviews, with reinforced walls and no windows that could be compromised by outside surveillance. If this man truly had information about Troy, she wanted to make sure they captured every detail.

She joined their visitor in the conference room moments later, immediately taking note of his nervous energy and the way his eyes darted around the space as if looking for escape routes. "I'm Sheriff Callahan. Can I bring you something to drink? Coffee, water, or soda?"

"I'd love a coffee." The wiry man with sunken cheeks and a permanent smirk that didn't reach his eyes put out a cigarette directly in the metal trash can, the acrid smoke curling toward the ceiling.

"I'm sorry, Mr…" She waited for him to fill in the blank while mentally noting his disregard for basic courtesy.

"Tate. Russell Tate." His voice carried the rough edge of someone who'd spent years smoking and drinking hard.

"No smoking is allowed inside the building, Mr. Tate." She frowned, her tone carrying the authority of someone accustomed to being obeyed. She motioned for Doris to bring the man a cup of coffee, hoping the caffeine might help settle his obvious nerves.

Tate didn't apologize for breaking the no-smoking rule. Instead, he grinned wider and crossed his arms in a gesture that seemed designed to show he wasn't intimidated by law enforcement. The attitude immediately put Shea on guard—most people seeking police protection showed more deference.

Trevor entered the room a few minutes later, carrying a steaming cup of coffee which he set in front of Tate with careful precision. His movements were controlled and professional, but Shea could see the tension in his shoulders.

"You sure can tell you're Troy's brother," Tate said, studying Trevor's face with uncomfortable intensity. "Got the same look about you, only he's harder. Meaner looking. Prison'll do that to a man."

Shea and Trevor sat across from the man at the polished conference table. The fluorescent lights overhead cast harsh shadows across Tate's weathered features, making him look older than his probable forty-something years. "Why are you here, Mr. Tate? I hope you don't mind if I record our conversation." Shea pressed the red button on the digital device she'd placed in the center of the table. "This is Sheriff Callahan and Deputy Bolton interviewing Russell Tate on..." She glanced at her watch and noted the date and time.

The man shrugged, his shoulders moving in a casual gesture that didn't match the fear Shea could see in his eyes. "Makes no never mind to me. I'm here because I need protection. If Troy finds out I came to you—" He let the sentence hang in the air like a threat.

"Why did you come?" Trevor asked, leaning forward slightly. "You know what my brother is capable of."

"Sure do. He never shut up about you during the years we were locked up together. It was like he had one thing keeping him going in that place. Trevor this, Trevor that. How he was gonna finish what he started." Tate took a sip of his coffee, his hands trembling slightly around the ceramic mug. "Honestly, it got old real fast, but you don't tell Troy Bolton to shut up about nothing."

"You were incarcerated with him?" Shea pulled out her notepad and began taking notes in addition to the recording.

"Yep. Same block for three years before they transferred him to that psych hospital. Got released last year on good behavior." He laughed bitterly. "Good behavior. That's a joke if I ever heard one. When I heard on the news that he escaped, I wanted to leave the country, head to Mexico or somewhere they'd never find me. But I ain't got the money for that kind of disappearing act. So, I'm here asking for protection."

"Why do you need protection, Mr. Tate?" Shea folded her hands on the table, adopting the patient but firm tone she used with reluctant witnesses. "What makes you think Troy would come after you specifically?"

Tate took his time taking several more sips of his coffee, clearly organizing his thoughts or perhaps working up the courage to speak. "Better than the swill they serve in lockup," he muttered. He drummed his fingers against the table in a nervous rhythm. "Troy didn't escape from that hospital for freedom, Sheriff. He escaped for revenge. It's all he talked about for years.

That his brother was the only one who got away, the only one who survived when he was supposed to be number seven."

The words settled in the air like smoke from his extinguished cigarette. A muscle ticked in Trevor's jaw, and Shea imagined his hands clenched into fists beneath the table.

"He showed me pictures," Tate continued, his voice dropping to barely above a whisper. "Pictures he'd somehow gotten of you, Deputy Bolton. Your house, your routine, places you went. He had it all mapped out, even from inside prison. Said he had people on the outside keeping tabs on you."

Trevor's face went pale. "What kind of people?"

"Didn't say exactly, but Troy's got a way of making folks do what he wants. Fear's a powerful motivator, and your brother knows how to use it better than anyone I ever met."

"I thought you should know that Troy is coming for you," Tate said, meeting Trevor's eyes directly for the first time since entering the room.

Trevor pushed to his feet, the chair scraping loudly against the floor. "He's already here."

"Are y'all going to protect me or not?" Tate lunged to his feet as well, his earlier cockiness completely replaced by a look of genuine terror. "If he finds out I warned you, he'll skin me alive. Literally. I've seen what he can do with that knife of his."

"We'll find you a safe house," Shea said, standing

as well. "For now, you're welcome to stay in this room until we can arrange proper protection. It's reasonable to believe that Troy doesn't know you're here yet."

"He knows everything," Tate said, his voice hollow with despair. "You don't understand what kind of monster you're dealing with. He's got eyes and ears everywhere."

A chill crawled down Shea's spine, and she glanced at Trevor's pale face. "He can't possibly know everything, Mr. Tate. You're being paranoid."

"Am I? He knew when I got out of prison before the paperwork was even processed. He knew when I moved to a new apartment, when I changed jobs. The man's got a network you wouldn't believe." Tate fell back into his seat heavily. "He's like Satan himself, I'm telling you. Evil incarnate. When he shanked that guy in prison over a card game, he laughed while the man bled out on the floor. Laughed! Who does that?"

"My brother," Trevor said grimly, then marched from the room without another word.

"If you need anything, Mr. Tate, please let our receptionist know. Don't leave this building without talking to me first." Shea followed Trevor to his desk in the bullpen, where he was staring blankly at his computer screen. "You okay?"

"More people are going to die, Shea. That man in the conference room will probably be one of them, and there isn't anything we can do about it." His voice was flat, defeated in a way that scared her more than Troy's threats.

"We can do our best to prevent that from happening. I'll enforce a town-wide curfew, increase patrols, maybe even call in the state police for backup."

"That won't stop him. He's a ghost who can strike anywhere, anytime." Trevor slumped into his chair, looking older than his years. "You heard what Tate said. Troy's been planning this for decades."

"Don't give up, Trevor. He wins if you do." The thought of facing this alone terrified her, though she'd never admit it. Shea had faced enough evil in her lifetime to know that monsters were real and they often wore human faces. "Let's head to Little Rock like we planned. Maybe the doctors at the hospital can tell us something useful. You up for it?"

"Might as well." He grabbed his gun holster from his desk drawer and strapped it on with mechanical precision, then brushed past her toward the exit.

"Trevor." She called after him, concerned by his detached manner.

"Let's go." He kept moving without looking back, his shoulders rigid with tension.

"Wait for me." She needed to retrieve some files from her desk and ensure Doris knew where they were going.

"He won't kill me yet," Trevor said as she caught up to him in the parking lot. "Troy still has five more victims to go before he gets to his lucky number seven." His words fell like an anvil, striking to the very center of her heart.

~

Four hours later, Trevor stared at the imposing three-story red brick building that housed Arkansas's most dangerous criminally insane patients. The place gave him the creeps with its institutional architecture and the way it seemed to absorb light rather than reflect it. High walls topped with razor wire surrounded the complex, and guard towers stood sentinel at each corner.

Inside, the atmosphere was even more oppressive. The walls were painted a faded yellow that had probably once been cheerful but now looked sickly under the harsh fluorescent lighting. The air was thick with the smell of industrial-strength antiseptic mixed with something stale and unidentifiable—despair, perhaps, or the accumulated weight of human suffering.

A nurse in scrubs that had seen better days led them down a long corridor past rooms where patients sat motionless in chairs, staring at walls with vacant expressions, or paced the floor like caged animals. Some called out as they passed, their words either incomprehensible or disturbingly lucid. Trevor tried not to look too closely through the reinforced glass windows, but he couldn't help wondering if this was what his brother had become during his time here.

The nurse stopped in front of a door marked "Dr. Mason - Chief of Psychiatry" and pushed it open without knocking. "Dr. Mason will see you now. Don't leave this room until I return for you." Her tone suggested that wandering the halls unescorted would be both dangerous and strictly forbidden.

They entered a small, sterile visitor's room where an older man sat behind a metal desk, flipping through what appeared to be a thick patient file. His white hair was neatly combed in an apparent attempt to hide his advancing baldness, and wire-rimmed glasses perched on his nose. He lifted a weary gaze their way, and Trevor could see the exhaustion of someone who'd spent too many years dealing with the worst of humanity. "You're here about Troy Bolton?"

"Yes, sir." Trevor squared his shoulders, unconsciously adopting a more military bearing.

"Have a seat. I knew this day would come sooner or later." The doctor's voice carried a resigned quality that suggested he'd been dreading this conversation. "I tried to warn the review board that Troy wasn't ready for any kind of reduced security, but budget constraints and overcrowding won out over common sense."

"How did he escape?" Shea took a seat in one of the uncomfortable plastic chairs, then Trevor settled beside her.

"We're chronically understaffed and severely underfunded—a dangerous combination when dealing with patients like your brother." The doctor removed his glasses and cleaned them with a tissue, buying time before continuing. "He had to have had help from someone on the inside, but despite a thorough investigation, I haven't been able to identify who. What kind of person would help a man like Troy escape? It's mind-boggling."

Trevor gripped the arms of his chair until his knuckles went white. "What can you tell us about his time here? His mental state, his behavior patterns, anything that might help us predict his next move?"

The doctor folded his hands on the desk, his expression becoming even more grave. "Your brother was one of my more…difficult patients during his stay here. Oh, he could be charming when it suited his purposes, even likeable when the mood struck him. He was intelligent, articulate, and had an uncanny ability to read people's weaknesses. But that was all a carefully constructed mask. Underneath, he was something else entirely."

"Go on," Shea prompted when the doctor paused.

The doctor exhaled heavily, as if reluctant to continue but knowing he had no choice. "He didn't feel remorse for his crimes. Ever. Not even a flicker of regret or empathy for his victims. However, he felt something else very strongly. Fixation, obsession—once he set his mind on someone or something, he never let go." His gaze turned directly to Trevor. "You were his primary obsession, Deputy Bolton."

The man's words settled on Trevor's shoulders like a lead blanket, heavy and suffocating. "What exactly are you saying, Doctor?"

Dr. Mason's lips pressed into a thin line. "I'm

saying that Troy never lost sight of you during his entire incarceration. Not once. You were the center of his universe, the focal point of every plan he made, every hope he harbored for the future."

Silence hung in the room like a physical presence. The air felt suffocating, and Trevor found it difficult to breathe normally.

"Any idea where he might go? Places he talked about, people he mentioned?" Shea broke the oppressive silence.

The doctor flipped several pages in the thick file in front of him, scanning his notes. "I might have some insights. But if I'm right about his psychological state and his level of preparation, you're running out of time faster than you realize."

"We were running out of time the moment he escaped," Trevor said grimly. He gestured toward the file. "May I see that?"

The doctor hesitated for a moment, then slid the folder across the table. "Normally, patient confidentiality would prevent this, but given the circumstances and the danger to public safety..."

Trevor stared at the file for a long moment before flipping it open. The first thing that caught his eye was a grainy black-and-white photograph clipped to the inside cover. A younger version of Troy stared back at him, but the eyes were the same—cold, calculating, completely devoid of human warmth. Below the photo was a case summary filled with psychological evaluations, notes from multiple doctors and therapists, and most unsettling of all, dozens of drawings.

"What exactly am I looking at here?" Trevor asked, though part of him already knew he didn't want to hear the answer.

"That's everything I have documented about your brother's mental state during his time here, including his artistic expressions of his various obsessions."

Shea leaned over to look at the drawings, her breath catching audibly. "These drawings are horrible."

Trevor flipped through them slowly, his stomach churning with each page. Detailed sketches of animal mutilations, graphic depictions of human violence, anatomical studies that showed an intimate knowledge of how to inflict maximum damage with minimal effort. One section in particular made his blood run cold—a comprehensive list of names written in Troy's precise handwriting. At the top of the list was his own name. Next to "Trevor Bolton" were the words "not finished" repeated over and over in an increasingly frantic script until they filled the entire sheet.

Shea sucked in a sharp breath. "My Lord."

Trevor kept flipping through the file, his fingers growing tense against the paper. More notes revealed the depth of Troy's obsession—detailed information about Trevor's daily routines, his work schedule, his home address, even the names and addresses of people he associated with regularly. Troy hadn't just been harboring resentment during his incarceration. He had been conducting a systematic study of every detail he could gather about Trevor's life.

Then came more drawings, sketch after sketch rendered in disturbing detail despite their crude execution. One showed a man bound to a chair with rope, and the facial features strongly resembled Trevor's. Another depicted a hunting knife buried to the hilt in the bound man's stomach, with careful attention paid to the blood patterns. There was even a surprisingly accurate drawing of Trevor's house, complete with details about window placement and entry points.

But the worst drawing was saved for last—a detailed sketch of a woman with long dark hair and a sheriff's badge prominently displayed on her chest. Written across the page in large, bold letters was the number 6.

"This was all found in his room?" Trevor tore his gaze away from the disturbing image that represented Shea.

"Yes, hidden behind a loose tile in his bathroom wall. He doesn't just hate you, Deputy. He's completely obsessed with the idea of finishing what he started twenty years ago. It's become the sole purpose of his existence." The doctor's voice carried a professional detachment that didn't quite hide his disgust. "This is why I warned the prison review board not to consider any reduction in his sentence or security level. He hasn't gotten better during his incarceration. If anything, the man has become more focused, more determined, and infinitely more dangerous. Now someone helped that monster escape, and he's out there with twenty years of pent-up rage and carefully laid plans."

"You mentioned you might know where he could be hiding?" Shea's voice shook slightly as she spoke.

The doctor flipped to another section of the file, revealing visitor logs and correspondence records. "Before he escaped, Troy had one visitor that I found particularly concerning. An old associate of his from the Pea Ridge area—a man named Frank Hutchinson. He runs a remote hunting lodge just outside of your jurisdiction, Sheriff Callahan."

"Hutchinson?" Trevor narrowed his eyes, searching his memory. "I know that name from somewhere. Wasn't he locked up a few years back?"

"He was incarcerated for illegal weapons trafficking and served four years before being released about twelve months ago. If Troy looked for someone to help him once he escaped, he'd naturally gravitate toward someone who operated outside the law, someone who could provide both shelter and weapons if necessary."

Trevor shook his head slowly. "My brother's weapon of choice has always been a hunting knife. He can get one of those almost anywhere—sporting goods stores, pawn shops, even gas stations."

"Perhaps, but Hutchinson represents more than just access to weapons. He's someone who lives off the grid, who understands how to avoid law enforcement detection. That kind of expertise would be invaluable to an escaped patient."

"It's worth investigating. We'll track down this Hutchinson and see what he can tell us." Shea stood and extended her hand to the doctor. "Thank you, Dr. Mason. You've been tremendously helpful. Please let us know immediately if you discover who aided Troy in his escape."

"I won't stop looking until I find out who's responsible. Someone in this facility committed a terrible crime by helping that monster get free, and I intend to see them prosecuted to the fullest extent of the law." He pressed a call button on his desk.

Within minutes, the same stern-faced nurse who had escorted them to the office appeared to lead them out of the hospital. With a curt nod and no words of farewell, she locked the heavy front door securely behind them.

"Guess working in a place like that sucks any joy you might have right out of you," Shea observed as they walked toward their vehicle. "You okay, Trevor?"

"I will be once we catch him." Trevor slid into the driver's seat, his jaw set with grim determination. "I want to talk to this Hutchinson character. The hunting lodge isn't too far out of our way home."

"You think he'll be there when it's not hunting season?" she asked as she climbed into the passenger seat.

"I'm hoping the man lives there year-round. Remote hunting lodges often serve as permanent residences for their owners."

An hour's drive past Misty Hollow, following increasingly narrow and poorly maintained roads, Trevor finally turned down a dirt road that led to the lodge. A battered pickup truck and a bush hog sat parked in front of a large log cabin that had seen better days. Smoke curled from the chimney, and several hunting dogs lounged on the front porch. "Looks like we're in luck," Trevor said as he parked their cruiser.

He led the way up the wooden steps and knocked firmly on the front door. After several minutes, it opened to reveal a man in his fifties wiping his hands on a piece of flannel fabric. His clothes were work-worn but clean, and his eyes held the wariness of someone who didn't receive many unexpected visitors.

"What can I do for you folks?" he asked, his gaze taking in their uniforms and badges.

Trevor studied the man's face carefully. "You don't recognize me, Mr. Hutchinson?"

Shock registered clearly on the man's weathered features as he took a closer look at Trevor's face. "Well, I'll be damned. There's enough of a family resemblance for me to know whose brother you are."

"I'm Sheriff Callahan and this is Deputy Bolton. We'd like to ask you some questions regarding your time in prison with Troy Bolton, and more specifically, about your recent visit to see him at the psychiatric hospital."

Hutchinson's expression became guarded. "Not sure what I can tell you that would be helpful, but I suppose you'd better come inside." He led them through a rustic, but clean common room decorated with mounted deer heads and fishing trophies, then into a small dining area with a handmade wooden table. "We can talk privately here. The lodge doesn't open for business until deer hunting season starts in October, so I'm the only one around for miles."

"You visited my brother at the hospital?" Trevor sat down and crossed his arms, adopting an intimidating posture.

"Figured I might be the only friend he had left in the world. Prison changes a man, but it doesn't have to destroy him completely."

"My brother is incapable of making genuine friends, Mr. Hutchinson. He uses people until they're no longer useful, then discards them. Try again."

The man's facade of innocent concern cracked slightly, and he managed a rueful smile. "You're every bit as smart as Troy said you were. Fine, I'll level with you. I wanted to know where he'd hidden the money I trusted him with when I got locked up years ago. A substantial sum that I needed to get my life back on track."

"Did you get your money back?" Shea asked.

"I'd rather not answer that specific question if I don't have to, Sheriff."

"Fair enough, for now." Instead of sitting, Shea remained standing to Trevor's right, maintaining a position of tactical advantage. "Have you heard from or seen my brother since his escape from the hospital?"

The man's smile faded completely, replaced by genuine fear. "I hadn't heard about any escape until just now." Hutchinson jumped to his feet, nearly knocking over his chair. "Jesus Christ, I've got to get out of here. If Troy finds out that the two of you came here asking questions about him…well, I won't be long for this world."

Shea's brow furrowed with concern. "How would he possibly find out about our visit?"

"He always does, Sheriff. Troy's got a network of people who owe him favors or are too scared to refuse him. Word travels fast in certain circles." The man rushed toward the front of the lodge, clearly panicking. "I strongly advise you both to watch yourselves. You especially, Sheriff Callahan. Since you work closely with Trevor here, you won't be just a bystander in Troy's plans. You'll be a target."

Trevor already knew that, had seen the drawing with the number 6 written across Shea's likeness. He pulled a business card from his wallet and offered it to Hutchinson. "If you hear from him or see any sign of him, please call me immediately."

"Deputy, I'm going somewhere that no one can find me, somewhere without phone service or any connection to the outside world. If I were you, I'd seriously consider doing the same. Not that Troy would ever give up his hunt, but you might buy yourself some time, maybe even live a little longer." He opened the front door and gestured for them to leave.

A loud click sounded as soon as they stepped outside, followed by the sound of window blinds falling into place throughout the cabin.

"Folks around here act like your brother is the worst thing to ever walk this earth," Shea observed as they walked back to their cruiser.

Trevor paused at the driver's door and looked back at the now-shuttered lodge. "If he isn't the worst thing, Shea, then he's definitely running a close second."

Chapter Five

Shea rushed into the bullpen, her face flushed with urgency and her radio crackling with dispatcher chatter. "911 call about a fire on the mountain. My gut tells me it's more than what it appears." Especially with Troy Bolton prowling their territory like a predator marking his hunting grounds.

Trevor didn't hesitate to follow her toward the exit, grabbing his service weapon and radio from his desk. "I've learned to trust your instincts, Shea. They've kept us both alive so far."

"A passing motorist heading to his campsite spotted the fire from the main road and went to investigate. Said it's a hunting cabin that's only used during deer season." She turned on the siren and sped after the fire truck that was already racing up the mountain road, its red lights cutting through the late afternoon gloom. "The caller said the flames were too intense to be accidental."

"Could be where Troy was holed up," Trevor said, his jaw clenching as he considered the implications. His brother had always been methodical, careful to cover his tracks. If he was abandoning a hideout, it meant he was either moving to a new location or eliminating evidence.

She glanced at Trevor, noting the tension in his shoulders and the way his hand rested near his weapon. "My thoughts exactly. At this point, we can't afford not to check out every lead, no matter how small." It might be the only way to save innocent lives before Troy reached his twisted goal of seven victims.

The mountain road twisted through dense forest, and the smell of smoke grew stronger with each mile. By the time they reached the remote cabin location, flames completely engulfed the structure. The roof had already collapsed, sending a shower of sparks high into the sky like deadly fireworks. The heat was so intense they could feel it from fifty yards away.

Shea marched directly to Fire Chief Martinez, who was coordinating his crew's efforts to contain the blaze and prevent it from spreading to the surrounding forest. "Chief, do you know what caused this?"

He pulled off his helmet and wiped sweat from his brow, his face grim with professional concern. "Haven't had time for a full investigation yet, but considering the speed and intensity of this burn, I'm going to hazard a guess that an accelerant was used. Probably gasoline or kerosene, judging by the smell and burn pattern."

"Chief!" A fireman shouted from the other side of the cabin, his voice urgent even over the roar of the flames. "Got a body over here!"

Shea and Trevor exchanged a meaningful look—they both knew this wasn't going to be good news. They followed Chief Martinez around the burning structure, their boots crunching on debris and ash that had fallen like deadly snow.

A badly burned body lay in the dirt approximately twenty feet from the cabin, positioned as if the person had fallen while trying to escape the flames. From what Shea could determine through the damage, it appeared to be a male victim. He lay on his back, and despite the extensive burns, she could make out two distinct knife wounds in his stomach—precise, deliberate stabs that had been inflicted before the fire started. Drawn in the dirt next to the body, as clear as a signature, was the number 2. Troy had definitely done this.

She sighed heavily, the weight of another senseless death settling on her shoulders. "We'll need a positive ID as soon as possible. Get an ambulance out here." She jumped back in shock as the man's fingers suddenly twitched. "ASAP! Dear God, he's still alive!"

With obvious effort, one finger pointed weakly toward something lying several feet away in the scorched earth. Trevor quickly pulled a rubber glove over his right hand and carefully plucked a leather wallet from the dirt, its edges charred but contents still readable. "Dale Kearns," he announced, reading from the driver's license inside.

"See what you can find out about his background and any connection to Troy," Shea instructed as she knelt down beside the dying man. "Help is coming, Mr. Kearns. Try to stay with us."

But help didn't arrive in time. Despite the paramedics' best efforts, when they finally reached the remote location, Kearns drew his last labored breath just moments after they'd learned his identity. His final words were barely audible whispers that sounded like "he promised" and "couldn't run far enough."

"Kearns was incarcerated at the same facility as Troy," Trevor said, showing Shea his phone screen after running a quick background check. "Served three years for armed robbery and was released eight months ago. Once we're finished processing this scene, I'll call the prison and see what the warden can tell us about their relationship."

Shea nodded grimly and pulled on a pair of latex gloves. A methodical search of the victim's pockets revealed a partially melted plastic keycard from the Pineview Motel, a rundown establishment on the outskirts of town. She'd bet her badge that the motel was Kearns' last known address, the kind of place that rented rooms to ex-cons and people trying to stay under the radar.

After leaving the crime scene to the arriving paramedics and forensics team, she instructed Chief Martinez to keep her informed of any developments, then headed toward town with Trevor. It wasn't difficult to determine which motel the key card belonged to. There were only two lodging establishments in Misty Hollow: the respectable Mountain View Inn where tourists stayed, and the Pineview Motel where the staff didn't ask questions and didn't care who rented a room.

Shea approached the manager's desk in the dingy lobby and rang the tarnished bell with authority.

"We're full up," a gravelly voice called from a back room. A man who desperately needed a shower and should have thrown away his stained tee-shirt months ago poked his head through a beaded curtain.

"Sheriff Callahan," she announced, displaying her badge prominently. "I'd like to ask you some questions about one of your guests."

The man muttered something profane under his breath, then reluctantly shuffled to the desk, his bare feet slapping against the worn linoleum. "We pride ourselves on giving our guests the privacy they pay for. No questions asked, no information shared."

Shea slid Kearns' driver's license across the scarred desk surface. "This man was one of your guests?"

The manager barely glanced at the photo. "Yep. Quiet guy, paid in cash, minded his own business."

"I need to know which room he was staying in, and I need access to it immediately."

"Not without a warrant, lady. I don't care if you're the sheriff or the governor." He crossed his beefy arms across a protruding belly that strained the fabric of his shirt.

"The man is dead, sir. Murdered. We're trying to find out why and prevent more deaths." She kept her voice level and professional, though her patience was wearing thin.

The manager's defiant expression faltered slightly as he processed this information. After a long moment of consideration, he reached under the counter and produced a magnetic keycard. "Fine. Room number four. Bring that back to me when you're done, and don't take nothing that ain't evidence."

"Much obliged." She spun on her heel and marched toward the guest rooms with Trevor close behind her.

The door to room four opened to reveal a space that was shabby but relatively clean. There didn't appear to have been much attempt at hiding anything suspicious. A prepaid burner phone sat prominently on the small table next to the window, and when Shea checked its call log, she found that the last outgoing call had been made just hours earlier. A notepad from the motel sat beside the phone, with a time written in blue ink—3:15 PM—along with a set of GPS coordinates that she suspected would lead them right back to the burned cabin.

"Look at this," Trevor said, turning over a pillowcase he'd found on the bed. Cash fluttered down to the faded paisley bedspread like green confetti— mostly twenties and fifties, several thousand dollar's worth. "Either he owed someone a substantial amount of money, or this was everything he had left to live on after getting out of prison."

Shea powered on the burner phone and scrolled through the text messages. The last exchange was brief but telling: an incoming message that read simply "I have something for you." Kearns' response was equally short: "I'll be right there." The final mistake the man would ever make.

A loud bang suddenly echoed from the room next door, followed by the sound of something heavy falling. Shea immediately drew her weapon and motioned for Trevor to follow her lead. They pressed themselves against the wall on either side of the slightly ajar door to room number five.

At Shea's silent countdown, Trevor shoved the door open with his shoulder and announced loudly, "Sheriff's department! Come out with your hands visible!"

This room was in complete contrast to Kearns' neat space. The mattress had been flipped over and slashed open, drawers were pulled out and their contents scattered across the floor, and a cell phone lay smashed into pieces near the bathroom door. Someone had been searching for something specific and hadn't cared about being subtle.

A creaking sound came from the bathroom, followed by the slam of what sounded like a window. "I'll cover the front," Shea called out as she sprinted toward the parking lot.

She arrived just in time to see a figure in dark clothing hop into a beat-up pickup truck and speed away, tires squealing against the asphalt. Mud had been deliberately smeared across the license plate, making it impossible to read, so the description of an old Ford with a dented tailgate would have to suffice for the APB she'd put out.

"He climbed out the bathroom window," Trevor reported when she returned. "Probably been hiding in there since we arrived, waiting for a chance to escape."

"And drove away before I could get a clear look at him." She exhaled heavily, frustrated by their continued inability to get ahead of Troy's network. "We're always one step behind."

"Maybe not entirely." He handed her a cocktail napkin from Hank's Bar with a single name scrawled on it in pencil: "Gordy."

Shea glanced from the napkin back toward the motel office. "So, who was registered in room number five?"

The manager's response was predictably unhelpful: a wry smile and a shrug. "Tom Jones. But honestly, I don't check IDs or ask for real names. We aren't that kind of establishment, if you catch my meaning."

Obviously not. Outside in the parking lot, she turned to Trevor with renewed determination. "Let's head to Hank's Bar and find out who this Gordy character is and what he knows."

"I know the place well—they have excellent

buffalo wings and don't ask too many questions about their clientele. We can grab some food while we're there." He managed a tired grin as he climbed into the driver's seat of their cruiser.

En route to the bar, she used her radio to call the office and request a complete forensics team to process both motel rooms. If Troy's network was using these locations as safe houses or meeting points, there might be fingerprints, DNA evidence, or other clues that could help them identify his accomplices.

Hank's Bar sat off Highway 9 about five miles outside Misty Hollow's city limits, a deliberately isolated location that catered to people who preferred to drink away from prying eyes. The building itself was a converted house with blackened windows and a gravel parking lot filled with motorcycles and pickup trucks. When they entered through the heavy wooden door, Shea paused to allow her eyes to adjust to the dim lighting, then approached the bartender—a thick-set man with tattoos covering both arms.

"We're looking for someone called Gordy," she announced, showing her badge.

The bartender barely glanced at her credentials before jerking his head toward a corner table. "Came in about half an hour ago, ordered two beers, and drank them both really fast. Seems pretty shaken up about something, keeps looking at the door like he's expecting trouble."

"Do you know his full name?" she asked.

"Only know him as Gordy. He's what you might call a freelancer. He'll do anything, and I mean anything, for the right price. Not the kind of guy you want to owe money to, if you understand my meaning."

When they started walking toward the corner table, the man immediately spotted them and jumped to his feet, knocking over his chair in his haste to reach the back exit. Trevor bolted after him with impressive speed, catching him just outside the rear door and slamming him against the brick wall hard enough to knock the wind out of him.

"Where are you going in such a hurry?" Trevor demanded, maintaining his grip on the man's shirt.

"The bathroom," Gordy gasped, his eyes darting around frantically as if looking for an escape route. "Just needed to use the bathroom, that's all."

"Do you know who I am?"

"Yeah, you're Trevor Bolton. You're Troy's twin brother." The admission came out in a rush, as if he'd been holding it back.

~

Trevor narrowed his eyes and tightened his grip. "How exactly do you know my brother?"

"He…" Gordy took a deep, shuddering breath, clearly terrified. "Come on, man. If I say anything about Troy, he'll kill me. You don't understand what he's capable of."

"He'll probably kill you anyway, whether you talk or stay quiet. That's who Troy is. So you might as well answer my questions and maybe help us stop him before he kills more innocent people."

Gordy's shoulders sagged in defeat. "He paid me five hundred dollars to lure Kearns away from his motel room and search the place for some cash that was supposed to be hidden there. Y'all showed up before I could find the money. Kearns kept bragging that him and Troy were working on something big, some score that would set them up for life. I suspect that was just talk to get me to do what they wanted."

"Is my brother armed with anything besides his knife?"

Gordy shrugged nervously. "I ain't actually seen Troy in person. Everything's been done through phone calls and text messages. He's real careful about not showing his face."

A gunshot suddenly shattered the large front window of the bar, sending glass shards flying across the interior. Patrons screamed and dove for cover as more shots followed in rapid succession.

Trevor gave Gordy another hard shove against the wall, then burst through the back door into the parking lot. He arrived just in time to see a man in black leather gear speed away on a motorcycle, the engine roaring as he disappeared down the highway. They'd lost their quarry again, and Trevor couldn't be certain whether Troy had been the shooter, the motorcycle rider, or if he'd simply orchestrated the distraction to help his network of accomplices escape.

How many people did his brother have helping him, and why would they risk their lives for someone as dangerous and unpredictable as Troy? What could they possibly get out of the arrangement? Troy had never shown loyalty to anyone in his entire life. These men were far more likely to end up as victims than to receive any promised rewards.

By the time they finally returned to Trevor's house several hours later, processing the crime scenes and filing reports, exhaustion made his legs feel like lead weights. He flipped on the interior lights out of habit and immediately froze in place. The television was on, but it wasn't tuned to the local news channel he always watched.

The screen displayed grainy black-and-white security footage that appeared to have been taken from inside the sheriff's station parking lot. The timestamp in the corner showed it had been recorded just one hour earlier. The video showed him and Shea walking to their patrol car after their shift, completely unaware they were being watched. In the far corner of the frame, barely visible in the shadows cast by the building, Trevor could make out the silhouette of a man standing motionless, observing their every movement.

He turned to point this out to Shea when his phone buzzed with an incoming text from an unknown number. He read the message aloud: "You're not as careful as you think you are. I'm everywhere, watching everything."

"I don't like this at all," Shea said, sinking onto his sofa with obvious fatigue. "How is he managing to move around town without being seen by anyone else? It's like he's invisible."

His phone buzzed again, this time with a set of GPS coordinates. Trevor quickly looked up the location on his phone's mapping application. "It's an abandoned airstrip about fifteen miles north of here. Hasn't been used in at least fifty years, according to county records."

She stood up with renewed purpose, though he could see the exhaustion in her movements. "Doesn't look like we're getting any sleep tonight. I'll call for backup to meet us there—we're not walking into another one of Troy's traps without reinforcements." She disappeared into the guest room to make the call, and when she returned, she'd changed from her uniform into dark jeans and a black T-shirt. "We stand out like targets in our official uniforms. Better to blend in."

"Good thinking." He rushed to his bedroom to change into similar dark clothing. Five minutes later, accompanied by Heidi for added security, they sped through the night toward the coordinates Troy had provided.

Deputies Harris and Butler were already waiting when they arrived at the overgrown airstrip, their patrol car positioned to provide cover and a quick escape route if necessary.

"Haven't seen any movement or activity," Butler

reported as they approached. "But we haven't done any exploring yet. With a psychopath like Troy on the loose, we figured it was smarter to wait for you two. Safety in numbers and all that."

"I don't blame you for being cautious," Shea replied, surveying the area with a tactical eye. She moved a few feet away from the group and knelt down. "Fresh tire tracks here that are not fifty years old. Multiple vehicles, by the look of it."

Trevor stepped to her side and followed the tracks with his flashlight beam. "They lead toward that old storage shed at the far end of the strip." He drew his service weapon, and the others immediately followed suit.

"Harris, Butler, you two watch our backs and cover our retreat if this goes sideways. Come on, Heidi." Shea took point and led their small formation toward the dilapidated building.

The storage shed's door stood ajar, creaking in the night breeze. Inside, they found a metal burn barrel in the center of the space, filled with half-burned documents and photographs. The papers were too damaged to read, but Trevor could make out fragments of what appeared to be official prison correspondence and medical records from the psychiatric hospital.

A clear set of footprints in the thick dust led from the barrel to a back door that opened toward the dense woods. A few yards beyond the shed, they discovered a second set of prints—smaller and narrower than the first, suggesting a woman's shoes.

They followed a rough trail of trampled leaves and broken branches through the forest to a small clearing where someone had built a makeshift fire pit surrounded by logs arranged as seating. The ashes were still warm, indicating the site had been used within the last few hours, but whoever had been there was long gone.

Then Trevor spotted something that made his blood run cold. A single piece of paper, carefully folded and placed on one of the log seats where it couldn't be missed. Scrawled across it in black ink were the words: "Too slow, brother. You'll have to do better than that."

Realization slammed into him like a physical blow to the stomach. Troy had led them here deliberately, using them like pieces in some twisted chess game. This was all planned, orchestrated to waste their time and resources while he moved his real pieces into position. Trevor whipped around as a twig snapped somewhere in the darkness behind them.

Heidi immediately went on alert, her hackles rising as she growled low in her throat.

Shea raised her weapon toward the sound. "Whoever is out there, come out now with your hands visible. This is Sheriff Callahan."

A man wearing full camouflage hunting gear stepped carefully out of the tree line, holding a rifle high over his head. "Don't shoot! I'm not armed—well, except for this, but it's not loaded."

"Who are you and what are you doing here?" Shea demanded, taking the rifle from him and quickly checking to confirm it was indeed unloaded.

"James Weston. I was just doing some night hunting—I know it's not exactly legal, but I wasn't hurting nobody. Just trying to put some meat on the table."

"Did you see anyone else pass through this area tonight?" Trevor asked urgently.

The man nodded vigorously. "A man and a woman, maybe an hour ago. They were arguing about something, but I couldn't hear what. They went that way, deeper into the woods." He pointed toward a narrow game trail that disappeared into the darkness.

"Did you hear anything they said? Any details about why they were here?" Shea pressed.

Weston scratched his head nervously. "The woman said something about following him anywhere, that it was worth everything she'd risked to help him escape from some kind of hospital or prison. She seemed real devoted to him, if you know what I mean. Is he some kind of dangerous convict? Am I in danger here?"

"Yes, extremely dangerous. My strong suggestion is that you get in your vehicle and drive as far away from here as possible, right now." Shea handed his rifle back to him and motioned toward the parking area. "Don't come back to this area for any reason."

They didn't have to tell Weston twice. The man grabbed his rifle and sprinted through the woods toward his truck as if his life depended on it—which it very well might.

Trevor swallowed hard against a suddenly dry throat as he followed Shea and Heidi deeper into the forest along the trail Weston had indicated. The sounds of the night settled around them like a heavy blanket, the soft whisper of wind through pine needles, the distant hoot of an owl, the rustle of small animals in the underbrush. Then, cutting through the peaceful night sounds like a knife, came the shrill, terrified scream of a woman.

The pounding of their boots against the forest floor joined the nighttime symphony as they ran toward the source of the scream, flashlight beams dancing wildly through the trees. Shea grabbed Trevor's arm and stopped him just before he would have burst into a moonlit clearing.

"Check the perimeter first," she whispered urgently. "This could be a trap. Troy might be using her as bait to draw us into an ambush."

Feeling like a rookie who'd almost made a fatal tactical error, Trevor nodded and forced himself to think like a trained law enforcement officer rather than a man desperate to save an innocent life. When they didn't detect any movement or hear any other sounds after several tense minutes of observation, they slowly and carefully entered the clearing with weapons drawn.

Heidi immediately ran to where a woman lay motionless on the forest floor, her sightless eyes staring up toward the star-filled sky while a dark pool of blood slowly spread beneath her body. Trevor stared down at the face and felt his heart sink with recognition—it was the stern-faced nurse from the psychiatric hospital, the one who had escorted them through the facility and locked the door behind them.

"I guess we know who helped my brother escape," he said grimly, though the knowledge brought no satisfaction. Drawn clearly in the dirt next to her body, as precise as a signature, was the number 3.

Troy was moving toward his goal of seven victims at a much quicker pace than he had twenty years ago. The game was accelerating, and Trevor realized with growing dread that they were running out of time to stop his brother's methodical march toward the final number. Seven.

Chapter Six

Shea pored over reports at her desk, having stayed later than all the deputies to catch up on paperwork that had been neglected during their frantic search for Troy. The fluorescent lights flickered overhead with their usual erratic rhythm, casting intermittent shadows across the scattered files and crime scene photographs. The hum of electronics—computers, printers, the ancient coffee machine in the break room—was the only sound in the otherwise empty building.

Then, cutting through the electronic white noise, came the creak of a door. Slow, deliberate, the groan of metal hinges stretching into the stillness like a warning. She frowned and looked up from the forensics report she'd been reviewing. The office doors were all heavy-duty steel with well-oiled hinges—they did not make that particular sound.

Boots clomped on the tile floor outside her office.

Steady. Controlled. Measured. Each step purposeful and unhurried, like the person knew exactly where they were going and that Shea couldn't get past them. A shadow loomed just beyond her peripheral vision, too large and too dark to be cast by the flickering fluorescent lights.

She reached for her service weapon, but her hand moved like it was trapped in molasses. Her muscles wouldn't respond to her commands, wouldn't obey the urgent signals her brain was sending. The footsteps grew closer, echoing in the empty hallway with the rhythm of a funeral march.

Fingers trailed down her neck. Light, almost hesitant at first, like someone testing the texture of her skin. Then the touch became cold, possessive, claiming ownership of her body with casual intimacy that made her skin crawl.

Shea wrenched herself awake with a sharp gasp, her heart pounding so hard she could feel it hammering against her ribs. Darkness pressed in around her like a living thing, and for a moment she couldn't remember where she was. The guest room at Trevor's house slowly came into focus as her eyes adjusted to the dim light filtering through the curtains.

Shea rarely remembered her dreams with any clarity, but this one lingered like a physical presence, the sensation of those fingers on her neck still making her skin twitch. She touched her throat reflexively, half-expecting to find marks there.

Heidi whimpered softly from her bed on the floor and padded over to lick Shea's face, the dog's warm breath and familiar scent helping to ground her in reality. The German shepherd had an uncanny ability to sense when humans were distressed, and her gentle ministrations helped slow Shea's racing heartbeat.

A quick glance at the bedside clock showed four a.m. in glowing red digits. There'd be no more sleep tonight—the dream had been too vivid, too real to shake off and return to unconsciousness. She groaned and climbed from the bed, her legs still shaky from the adrenaline surge of the nightmare.

She padded barefoot to the attached bathroom, hoping that the familiar routine of her morning preparations would help dispel the lingering effects of the dream. Hopefully, a hot shower would wash away the imaginary chill that seemed to have settled into her bones, the phantom sensation of those possessive fingers still trailing along her skin.

She turned the water to the hottest temperature she could handle and stepped under the spray. At first, her muscles tensed reflexively at the heat, but gradually they began to relax as the steam filled the small bathroom. She stood there with her head bowed for several long minutes, letting the water cascade over her shoulders and back, before finally reaching for the shampoo and beginning to wash away the sheen of perspiration that the nightmare had left on her body.

By the time she finished her shower and wrapped

herself in a towel, the rich aroma of brewing coffee was already hanging in the air. Trevor must be awake as well—insomnia seemed to be contagious in this house. She pulled her damp hair into a practical ponytail and headed to the kitchen, drawn by the promise of caffeine and human companionship.

Trevor looked up from the stove with a tired smile when she entered the kitchen. Dark circles shadowed his eyes, and his hair stuck up at odd angles, suggesting he'd been running his hands through it—a nervous habit she'd noticed him developing. "Hungry?"

"Famished. Did I wake you?" She poured a steaming cup of coffee from the pot and wrapped her hands around the warm ceramic, savoring both the heat and the familiar ritual.

"No, I don't sleep much lately." He scooped fluffy scrambled eggs and crispy bacon onto a plate with the practiced efficiency of someone who'd been cooking for himself for years, then handed it to her. "Bad dreams keeping you up too?"

She shook her head, though they both knew it was a lie. "I'll catch up on my sleep once your brother is behind bars again." She hoped that was true, though part of her suspected the nightmares might linger long after Troy was recaptured.

"Yeah, he haunts my dreams too." Trevor carried his plate to the small kitchen table and sat down heavily, moving like a man much older than his years. "Has since I was fifteen years old."

Shea sat across from him at the familiar oak table, noting how he pushed his eggs around on his plate without actually eating them. The stress was taking its toll on both of them, but Trevor bore the additional burden of knowing that he was Troy's ultimate target. "We'll catch him, Trevor. I promise you that."

"Hmm." He continued moving food around his plate in abstract patterns, his mind elsewhere.

"We will," she repeated with more conviction, needing him to believe it as much as she needed to convince herself.

Trevor's phone suddenly buzzed against the table, the vibration abnormally loud in the quiet kitchen. His entire body tensed as he looked at the screen. "It's him again."

"How can you be so certain?"

"Unknown number. It's always him when it shows up that way." He picked up the phone with obvious reluctance, as if the device might bite him. "Deputy Bolton."

Silence stretched across the connection at first, filled only with the sound of breathing that seemed deliberately controlled. Then came a familiar voice that made Trevor's blood run cold. "Feels good, doesn't it? The hunt. Gets your heart racing, makes you feel alive in a way normal life never could. For a while at least, you get to enjoy the same thrill I feel every single day."

"Where are you, Troy?" Trevor's tortured gaze locked with Shea's across the table, his knuckles white where he gripped the phone. "What do you want?"

The line went dead with a soft click that seemed to echo in the sudden silence.

"He hung up," Trevor said unnecessarily, staring at the phone as if it might provide answers.

"Let's get to the office." Shea pushed away the untouched portion of her breakfast and filled two travel thermoses with coffee, her movements quick and efficient. "Come on, Heidi. We've got work to do."

They'd no sooner stepped through the front door of the sheriff's station when Doris intercepted them with an expression that suggested their day was about to get more complicated.

"Don't get comfortable," she announced, waving a handful of message slips. "Got a vagrant outside Lucy's Diner that refuses to leave. She wants y'all over there ten minutes ago, and she's getting more agitated by the minute."

Shea frowned, already mentally rearranging her morning priorities. "Why didn't you send one of the other deputies? This doesn't exactly require the sheriff's attention."

"No one else is available right now. They're all tied up on calls—domestic disturbance on Pine Street, fender-bender out on Highway 9, and Deputy Martinez is dealing with a break-in at the hardware store."

Shea sighed and spun around, heading back toward the exit. "Come on then. Let's go deal with our vagrant." Trevor and Heidi fell into step behind her, their brief breakfast forgotten.

The scene outside Lucy's Diner was exactly what Shea had expected. A man in soiled, tattered clothes sat with his back against the brick wall of the building, mumbling incoherently to himself. The smell of alcohol was so overpowering that Shea found herself hoping no one would light a cigarette anywhere nearby. Empty bottles scattered around him suggested he'd been there for some time.

"Sir, why don't you come with us?" Shea said gently, crouching down to his eye level. "We've got hot coffee at the station, and you can take a shower, get something to eat, maybe find you a warm place to sleep."

He lifted bloodshot, unfocused eyes in her direction, struggling to bring her face into focus. "Food? I'd rather have another beer, if it's all the same to you."

"We'll talk about that later." She forced what she hoped was a reassuring smile, then motioned for Trevor to take the man's other arm. "Let's get you cleaned up first."

Together, they hauled the unsteady man to his feet and guided him toward their patrol car. He moved with the careful, exaggerated precision of someone trying very hard not to fall down, and it took considerable effort to get him settled in the backseat next to Heidi.

"Will the dog bite me?" he asked, shrinking back against the door as far as the confined space would allow.

"Not unless I tell her to," Shea replied, adjusting the rearview mirror to keep an eye on their passenger.

"Please don't tell her to." He sat rigidly upright, maintaining maximum distance from the German shepherd, who regarded him with mild curiosity.

Back at the station, Trevor escorted the man to the small shower facility they maintained for situations exactly like this, while Shea hunted through their supply closet for clean clothes that might fit him and microwaved a burrito from the break room vending machine. Basic human dignity demanded they at least try to help the man get back on his feet.

They put him in the interview room twenty minutes later, and both officers sat across from him while he devoured the burrito with the desperate hunger of someone who hadn't eaten a proper meal in days.

"What's your name, sir?" Shea asked, trying not to grimace as he ate with apparent relish but questionable table manners.

"Deacon Brown. I know it's a common name—got teased about it in school." He grinned, revealing several missing teeth and others in desperate need of dental attention. His smile faded abruptly, and a haunted expression crossed his weathered features. "He showed me where it was…said he wanted it ready for when the time came. Made me dig it with my own hands."

"What did he want ready?" Shea felt her blood chill as she asked the question, though she suspected she already knew the answer.

The man's eyes widened with remembered terror. "The grave. He made me dig a grave and told me exactly what it was for." He rattled off a set of GPS coordinates with surprising accuracy, given his condition.

"Excuse us for just a moment, please." She jerked her head toward the door, and Trevor immediately followed her into the hallway. "Find out everything you can about this man—background check, criminal history, when and where he was incarcerated. I'll keep him occupied with more food and see what else I can get out of him."

'Already on it. I'll also get the exact GPS location mapped out so we know where we're going." Trevor was already pulling out his phone to run preliminary checks.

Shea bought a ham and cheese sandwich and a bag of chips from the vending machine, then rejoined Deacon in the interview room. "Figured you might still be hungry," she said, setting the food in front of him. She sat down and crossed her arms, adopting what she hoped was a non-threatening but authoritative posture. "This devil you mentioned—who exactly are we talking about here?"

"No, no, no." He tore into the sandwich with enthusiasm. "You won't get me to say his name out loud. Names have power, and saying his name might call him here. But he looks exactly like your deputy out there. That should tell you all you need to know about who we're dealing with."

A soft knock interrupted them, and Trevor motioned through the window for her to step outside. "Deacon Brown was incarcerated at the same facility as Troy," he reported quietly. "Served time for multiple DUI offenses over the past decade. Unlike my brother, Deacon isn't a violent criminal. He's just a man with a serious drinking problem who made some very poor choices."

"What was his scheduled release date?"

"That's the interesting part. He wasn't supposed to be released for another two years, but there's been some kind of early release program due to overcrowding."

"Let's head to the location he gave us and see what Troy's left for us this time." Shea paused at the door of the interview room. "Hold on a minute—I want to ask him about the early release."

She ducked back into the room where Deacon was finishing his sandwich. "When were you originally scheduled for release, Mr. Brown?"

"Not for another two years, minimum." He didn't look up from his food, as if the question made him uncomfortable.

"So why were you released early?"

"They said the prison was too crowded for non-violent offenders like me, that they needed the space for more dangerous criminals. I ain't complaining about getting out early, mind you, but I'd catch this other guy real quick if I was you. He ain't right in the head."

~

"Are we headed toward your place?" Shea asked as they drove through the familiar countryside, Heidi alert in the backseat.

Trevor shook his head, his jaw tight with tension. "Not exactly, but close. The GPS coordinates are taking us about half a mile down a dirt road that branches off just past my driveway." He had a horrible feeling about what they were going to find, but he kept that thought to himself.

Twenty minutes later, they stood at the edge of a clearing where someone had been doing some digging. A shallow grave had been carefully excavated, and lying inside was a store mannequin dressed in what appeared to be an old deputy's uniform. A tarnished badge was pinned prominently to the chest, and someone had written "TREVOR BOLTON" across the mannequin's plastic forehead in black permanent marker.

"Not exactly subtle about who's supposed to end up in that grave," Trevor said, exhaling heavily. The proximity to his own home wasn't lost on him—Troy was making it clear that he planned to kill his brother on familiar ground.

At the bottom of the shallow grave, wedged firmly into the dirt, was a playing card with a detailed drawing of a hangman's gallows. "What do you think the card means?" Shea frowned as she studied the image. "That he's leaving us hanging as to clues? Some kind of riddle we're supposed to solve?"

"It doesn't have to make logical sense. It's all just an elaborate game to him, and we're the unwilling players." Trevor studied the ground around the grave site, looking for any additional clues or evidence Troy might have left behind.

"Wait—I think there's more." Shea pulled on a pair of latex gloves and picked up a shovel that had been left leaning against a nearby tree. "I think he's left us another message, and we need to keep digging to find it."

Trevor took the shovel from her hands. "I'll do the digging. You supervise and watch for any signs that we're not alone out here."

"I'm perfectly capable of manual labor, Trevor."

"I know you are, but I need to do something physical right now. If I don't keep my hands and mind occupied, I'm going to lose what's left of my sanity." The repetitive motion of digging helped channel his nervous energy and growing anger into something productive.

He'd worked up a considerable sweat by the time his shovel struck something solid. "Got something down here. Looks like actual human remains this time."

"Any idea who it might be?" Shea reached carefully into the hole and retrieved a faded photograph—the kind taken annually at elementary schools across the country. She turned it so Trevor could see the image.

"That's Billy Reynolds," Trevor said, his voice thick

with emotion. "He disappeared one night without a trace when we were kids. Everyone in town suspected he might be one of Troy's early victims, but he was the only person to go missing during that time period. Troy always left his other victims where they could be found easily."

"Why would Troy want you to discover this boy's remains now, after all these years?"

Trevor shrugged, though his casual gesture didn't hide the pain in his eyes. "Just another way of taunting me, showing me that he's always been in control. We didn't find Billy when it mattered, and Troy doesn't think we'll be able to stop him now either. Not until he decides he wants to be caught."

Shea stepped away from the grave site and made the necessary call to get a complete forensics team to the location. The remains would need to be properly excavated and processed as evidence, though after all these years there probably wouldn't be much helpful information to be gleaned.

Leaning heavily on the shovel handle, Trevor stared down into the hole at the skeletal remains of the boy who had once been his closest friend. Law enforcement at the time had suspected that Billy might have been Troy's first victim, killed in a moment of rage or experimentation before Troy had developed his more systematic approach to murder. If Troy had wanted to hurt his twin brother emotionally, taking away his best friend would have been an effective way to do it.

"Did Troy only target children back then?" Shea asked, slipping her phone back into her pocket.

"No, but he focused on young people exclusively. No one over twenty-one, as far as we could determine. I always figured he preferred victims who were close to his own age, but I never understood the psychology behind that choice."

"Maybe because they were easier to lure into vulnerable situations? Young people at that age often think they're invincible, that nothing bad could ever happen to them."

Shea's phone suddenly rang with the sharp, urgent tone she'd assigned to emergency calls. Her expression grew grim as she listened to the voice on the other end. "We'll be right there," she said curtly before hanging up. She turned to Trevor with reluctance. "We've got body number four."

"Who is it this time?" He let the shovel fall to the ground with a dull thud.

"The bartender from Hank's Watering Hole. The one who helped us identify Gordy."

~

Troy crouched in the dense underbrush at the edge of the bar's parking lot, watching with predatory patience as his brother and the sheriff entered through the front door of Hank's establishment. The bartender's body lay in the alley behind the building, positioned where it would be discovered quickly but not so obviously that it would seem staged.

As soon as they disappeared inside, he sprinted to a new vantage point that would allow him to observe their exit into the alley. The bartender had been ridiculously easy to kill—disappointingly so. The man had simply been taking out the evening's trash, not even slightly suspicious when he spotted Troy standing in the shadows with a knife in his hand. Instead of running or calling for help like a sensible person would have done, the fool had tried to fight him.

It had been a waste of what could have been an interesting kill. Troy preferred when his victims understood precisely what was happening to them, when they had time to experience the full terror of their situation before he ended their lives. Most people were terrified when they realized who he was and that he would be the last person they would ever see. The anticipation of that moment, watching the light slowly fade from his brother's eyes, was what had sustained him through twenty years of imprisonment.

After Trevor was dead, Troy would need to find a new quest, a new purpose to give meaning to his existence. He'd figure out the details when the time came, but he had no doubt that he would succeed this time. Despite Trevor knowing he was coming and despite having law enforcement protection, his brother was still predictable, still emotionally driven in ways that could be exploited.

Troy lit a cigarette—a vice he'd acquired during his years in prison—and leaned casually against the trunk of a large oak tree while his brother and the attractive sheriff examined the bartender's body. He had to admit, it almost seemed like a shame to kill something so lovely and strong-willed. He'd read extensively about Sheriff Callahan's previous exploits, including her successful investigation of a dangerous criminal network that had been operating in these mountains.

Unfortunately for her, Trevor cared about the woman, which meant she had become an automatic target. It would be a fitting end to his brother's life to watch someone he cared about die in front of him, helpless to prevent it. The psychological trauma would be exquisite.

Troy found himself wondering if things might have been different if their parents hadn't so obviously favored one twin over the other. Had he always been the "bad twin," born with some fundamental flaw that made violence inevitable? Was his thirst for killing something genetic, hardwired into his DNA from birth? Perhaps it was, but it no longer mattered. He had long ago embraced the path he'd chosen, and he genuinely enjoyed the power that came with taking lives.

Why had he chosen the number seven as his goal? Initially, it had been because their mother had told him it was the number of completion in the Bible, the number that represented divine perfection. Seven days of creation, seven deadly sins, seven virtues, the number appeared throughout scripture as a symbol of wholeness. It had seemed fitting that his own quest for completion should follow the same pattern.

There was also the fact that Trevor had been born exactly seven minutes after Troy, making him technically the younger twin despite their identical appearance. Seven had become Troy's lucky number, his signature, his brand.

The problem was that he was beginning to suspect he wouldn't be able to stop with his brother's death. The killing had become more than just revenge—it was a compulsion, a need as fundamental as breathing. He would probably start the count over again and again, moving from town to town, creating new games and new challenges for himself. Who could stop him? He didn't play by anyone's rules except his own.

The sheriff suddenly lifted her head and sniffed the air like the German shepherd at her side. Did she detect the smell of his cigarette smoke? Did she somehow sense how close he was to them at that very moment?

As if responding to some primal instinct, she turned those remarkable green eyes in his direction, scanning the tree line where he stood concealed.

With a cold smile, Troy ground his cigarette out carefully with the heel of his boot and stepped deeper into the shadows of the forest. The game was accelerating toward its inevitable conclusion, and he was very much looking forward to the final act.

Chapter Seven

Shea cut off the ignition and turned to Trevor, studying his profile as he stared at the familiar houses lining the street where he'd grown up. The tension in his jaw was visible, and she could see his hands trembling slightly where they rested on his knees. "You sure you want to dig up old memories? Isn't it enough that your past has come back to haunt you without voluntarily subjecting yourself to more pain?"

"I guess it might seem that way to an outsider." Trevor's voice was quiet, thoughtful, as if he was still working through his own motivations. "Since I didn't know my brother as well as I thought I did, I want to try and understand what turned him into a killer. Maybe there were signs I missed, warning signals that could have prevented all this tragedy."

He shoved open the car door with more force than necessary, the metal groaning in protest. "Mrs. Marshall is the oldest person I know who's still mentally sharp, and she was one of my mother's closest friends for decades. If anyone would remember the details from our childhood that might shed light on Troy's transformation, it would be her."

"Okay." Shea climbed out of the driver's seat, her instincts telling her that returning to Pea Ridge was a mistake that could only cause Trevor more emotional pain. But if he genuinely thought this pilgrimage might help them understand Troy's psychology well enough to anticipate his next moves, she'd follow his lead.

The neighborhood looked much the same as it had twenty years ago, though the houses showed their age and the trees had grown taller. Several properties appeared abandoned, their windows boarded up and yards overgrown with weeds. The economic impact of having a serial killer emerge from this community had been devastating—property values had plummeted, families had moved away, and the town had never fully recovered from the stigma.

Trevor marched up the cracked concrete walkway to Mrs. Marshall's front door and rang the bell, his shoulders squared with determination. An elderly woman in a cheerful flowered robe answered after several moments, her white hair neatly styled despite the early hour.

"Yes? Can I help you?" she asked, peering at them through wire-rimmed glasses.

"I'm Trevor Bolton, Mrs. Marshall. Do you remember me?" His voice carried a mixture of hope and uncertainty.

A genuine smile crossed her deeply wrinkled face, transforming her entire expression. "Of course, I remember you, dear boy. What a wonderful surprise to see you after all these years." Her gaze dropped to the badge prominently displayed on his chest. "Law enforcement, I see. Your parents would be so proud."

"Yes, ma'am. This is Sheriff Callahan from Misty Hollow." Trevor gestured toward Shea with obvious respect.

Shea stepped forward and extended her hand. "Pleased to meet you, Mrs. Marshall."

The elderly woman returned the handshake with a grip that was surprisingly firm for someone her age, then stepped back to allow them entry. "Please, come inside. I'm quite curious to know what brings you back to Pea Ridge after so many years. Have a seat wherever you're comfortable. I've got fresh tea brewing in the kitchen."

She bustled away with the energy of someone half her age, leaving them alone in a living room that seemed frozen in time. The furniture was clearly from decades past but well-maintained, and family photographs covered every available surface.

"She seems remarkably spry for her age," Shea observed, running her fingers along the intricate crocheted afghan that covered a forest-green sofa.

"Always has been. Even when I was a kid, she could outwork people half her age." Trevor sat down on the sofa and patted the cushion next to him, inviting Shea to join him.

Shea settled beside him just as Mrs. Marshall returned carrying an ornate silver tea set that looked like a family heirloom. The delicate china cups and saucers seemed almost absurdly formal for their grim purpose, but the ritual of serving tea appeared to give the elderly woman comfort.

Mrs. Marshall arranged herself carefully in a high-backed wing chair that had probably been her favorite spot for decades. "Now then, tell me exactly what I can do for you children."

Trevor accepted a cup of tea, holding the delicate china with obvious discomfort, as if he were afraid his large hands might shatter the fragile porcelain. He cleared his throat nervously before speaking. "I'm here to ask you about Troy, Mrs. Marshall. About our childhood and anything you might remember that seemed... unusual."

A flicker of genuine fear crossed the woman's eyes, and she involuntarily pulled her robe tighter around her frail frame. "Why on earth would you want to bring that evil man back to mind? Some memories are better left buried."

"Because he's returned to finish what he started twenty years ago," Shea said gently, adding sugar to her tea with deliberate calm. "He's already killed four people, and he's targeting Trevor specifically. We're hoping that understanding his psychology might help us predict his next moves."

Mrs. Marshall gasped audibly, her cup rattling against its saucer. "Dear Lord. What number is he working toward?"

"Seven," Trevor said grimly. "Same as before."

"Then there isn't much time left." She set down her tea with shaking hands and pulled her robe even tighter around her thin shoulders. "Troy was always an odd child, even as a toddler. Born with something missing inside him, I always said. The complete opposite of you in every way that mattered."

She paused to collect her thoughts, her expression growing distant as she recalled painful memories. "He would often try to mimic you—dressing the same way, attempting to befriend the same boys at school, even trying to copy the way you spoke and moved. But it never seemed natural with Troy. It was like watching someone trying to impersonate a human being without understanding what made them human."

"I don't remember him doing that," Trevor said, leaning back against the sofa cushions with a puzzled frown.

Mrs. Marshall nodded sadly. "Because your parents were so concerned about Troy's behavior problems at school, they made the mistake of constantly praising you in front of him, hoping it would encourage him to model your behavior. All it accomplished was making Troy more resentful and withdrawn. The jealousy was eating him alive from the inside."

She struggled to her feet with apparent difficulty. "Wait here, dear. I have something your mother left with me before she passed away. She somehow knew that someday you might come back looking for answers, and she wanted to make sure you could find them."

The elderly woman hurried from the room as quickly as her age would allow, returning several minutes later carrying a large cardboard box that was heavy for her to manage.

Trevor immediately jumped to his feet to relieve her of the burden, setting the box carefully on the coffee table between them. "What exactly is this, Mrs. Marshall?"

"Open it and see for yourself," she said, settling back into her chair with obvious relief.

Shea scooted closer to Trevor so she could examine the contents alongside him. Inside the box were dozens of disturbing drawings, a small leather-bound notebook, and a thick photo album with a cracked spine.

Shea picked up one of the drawings from the top of the pile. It showed two young boys standing side by side, but one of the figures had a large X drawn through his face in what appeared to be red crayon. The artistic skill was crude but the message was unmistakably clear—Troy had wanted to eliminate his twin brother even as a child.

The small notebook proved even more disturbing.

Page after page contained detailed daily observations about Trevor's activities, written in increasingly erratic handwriting that suggested growing obsession. What Trevor wore to school, which friends he spoke to during recess, what time he returned home each afternoon—his brother had meticulously documented every aspect of his life.

"The last entry is dated our fourteenth birthday," Trevor observed, his voice tight with suppressed emotion. "I guess that's when Troy decided he would be better off without me in the picture permanently."

With apparent reluctance, he opened the photo album. The first half appeared relatively normal, with typical childhood photographs showing family gatherings, neighborhood events, and school activities. Both boys appeared in many of the early pictures, and a casual observer might have thought they were documenting a happy family life.

But as Trevor continued flipping through the pages, the photographs became increasingly disturbing and invasive. The later images were exclusively of Trevor, taken without his knowledge or consent. Candid shots of him playing with friends in the backyard, riding his bicycle through the neighborhood, walking to school alone. The photographer had been following him systematically, documenting his daily routines with the patience of a predator studying its prey.

Then the photographs became even more sinister

and violating. Pictures of Trevor sleeping in his bed, obviously taken through his bedroom window during the night. Shots of him crying at their parents' funeral, with Troy's unmistakable shadow visible in the background of the image. The final page contained no photographs at all, just a message scrawled in red ink: "If I can't be you, I'll be better without you."

Trevor slammed the album shut with enough force to rattle the tea service. "So I was right about his motivations. This was never about sibling rivalry. This was about complete replacement."

Shea placed a comforting hand on his shoulder, feeling the tension radiating through his muscles. "Come on. We should probably go before this gets more overwhelming."

"I always hoped he wanted to be like you," Mrs. Marshall said, wiping tears from her weathered cheeks. "But now it's clear that he wanted to replace you entirely. To eliminate you and take over your identity somehow. I'm so very sorry, dear."

Trevor took a slow, uneven breath, struggling to maintain his composure. "Thank you for showing us this, Mrs. Marshall. I know it wasn't easy."

"There's one more thing I should probably tell you, something that still haunts me after all these years." She glanced toward the windows as if expecting to see Troy's face peering in at them. "This was about a month before Troy tried to... you know. Kill you. I was having trouble sleeping one night and heard strange noises outside—the rustling of leaves, then hurried footsteps across my yard."

She paused, clearly reliving the disturbing memory. "When I peeked through my bedroom curtains, I saw Troy standing perfectly still in your backyard, just staring up at your bedroom window. He must have been there for at least an hour, completely motionless, like he was deep in thought about something."

"Yeah, probably thinking about the best way to murder me in my sleep," Trevor said, his words cutting through the room like a blade. "He failed then, and he'll fail again now."

~

Trevor stopped beside their car to compose himself before continuing their journey. The contents of that box had been disturbing but not entirely surprising—they had simply confirmed his worst suspicions about how his twin brother had always viewed him. The obsession had run much deeper than he'd realized, but the basic dynamic had been precisely what he'd feared.

"We don't have to speak with anyone else if this is too difficult for you," Shea said, her voice filled with genuine concern as she studied his pale features.

He raised his head to meet her worried eyes, drawing strength from her steady presence. "I want to continue. I need to visit the families of Troy's victims. I owe them that much, at least."

Their next stop was the modest home of Beth and Daniel Caldwell, whose teenage son Kyle had been Troy's third victim. The house felt frozen in time, as if the family had stopped living the day their child died. The yard was overgrown, paint was peeling from the shutters, and several newspapers lay scattered on the front porch.

Beth Caldwell answered the door after Trevor's second attempt at knocking. She had aged decades in the twenty years since her son's death, her hair now completely gray and her frame frighteningly frail. Recognition flickered in her hollow eyes as she took in Trevor's face.

"Trevor Bolton," she said, her voice carrying a mixture of pain and accusation. "The brother of the serial killer who destroyed our lives."

Trevor nodded, swallowing past the lump that had formed in his throat. "I'm so sorry for what Troy did to your family, Mrs. Caldwell. Words can't express how deeply I regret the pain he caused."

The grieving mother studied both of them for a long moment, her gaze lingering on their badges and uniforms. Finally, she stepped aside to allow them entry. "I'm not entirely sure why you're here after all these years, but I suppose you'd better come in."

The interior of the house was as frozen in time as the exterior. Kyle's school photographs still hung on the walls, his trophies from Little League baseball still lined the mantelpiece, and his bedroom door remained closed as if he might return home at any moment.

"My brother has escaped from custody and returned to the area," Trevor explained, taking a seat in an uncomfortable wooden chair while leaving the small sofa for Shea. "I'm trying to gather as much information as possible about his past behavior patterns to help us stop him permanently this time."

"I don't know what I could tell you that would be helpful after all this time," Mrs. Caldwell said, settling into her husband's empty recliner. "But there was something deeply wrong with your brother, even before he started killing. My son never liked Troy, said there was something creepy about the way he acted around other kids."

Mr. Caldwell entered the room at that moment, moving with the slow gait of someone much older than his actual years. The loss of their child had broken both parents in fundamental ways. "Kyle once told us that Troy had asked him a very disturbing question," he said without preamble. "He wanted to know if Kyle had ever wondered what it would feel like to be genuinely terrified."

Trevor exchanged an uneasy glance with Shea, both of them recognizing the predatory nature of such a question.

Mrs. Caldwell gripped the armrest of her chair so tightly that her knuckles turned white. "At the time, we thought maybe Troy was just socially awkward, that he didn't understand appropriate boundaries when talking to other children. I can see now that it was much more calculated than that."

She struggled to her feet and disappeared into another room, returning with a yellowed piece of paper that had been handled many times over the years. "Kyle wrote this in his journal just a few days before his murder. I've read it so many times I have it memorized."

Trevor accepted the page with trembling hands and read the childish handwriting aloud: "Troy won't stop staring at me at school. It's like he's waiting for something to happen, but I don't know what. He makes me feel scared even when he's not doing anything wrong."

The words made Trevor's blood run cold. Troy had indeed been waiting—waiting for the perfect opportunity to isolate Kyle and make him the third victim in his twisted game.

Their next stop was the home of the Holloways, an elderly couple who had lived just a few houses down from the Bolton family. Mrs. Holloway almost slammed the door in their faces when she recognized Trevor, her expression filled with fear and barely contained anger.

Trevor quickly blocked the closing door with his foot. "Please, ma'am. I only need a few minutes of your time. It's important."

"We left town specifically because of that monster you call a brother," she said through the partially open door. "Sold our house at a loss and moved three states away."

"Please," Trevor repeated, his desperation evident.

She reluctantly allowed them inside, though she remained standing near the door as if ready to flee at a moment's notice. "We only came back to Pea Ridge because we were told Troy was locked away permanently. If we'd known he might escape..."

"He's not just free," Shea informed her gently. "He's actively killing again, targeting people in my jurisdiction now."

The color drained from Mrs. Holloway's face. "You can't kill something that evil. It's not human anymore."

Trevor silently agreed with that assessment, though he kept the thought to himself.

The elderly woman had no intention of offering them seats or refreshments. "I caught Troy digging a hole in the woods just past your family's property line one afternoon. When I asked him what he was doing, he looked up at me with those dead eyes and smiled. Said he was 'practicing' for something important."

She glanced around nervously, as if Troy might be listening from the shadows. "My husband found a dead dog in those same woods a few days later. The poor animal's body had been arranged in an unnatural position, almost like it was posed for some kind of sick photograph. Harold never told anyone but me about it, but now I wonder if that wasn't more of Troy's 'practice.'"

She lowered her voice to barely above a whisper. "A neighbor girl came running home in tears one day because Troy had asked her a horrible question. He wanted to know if she thought people could still scream after their throats were cut."

The woman shuddered visibly at the memory. "One night, I saw your brother standing in our backyard in the middle of the night, just watching our house. When I stepped outside and turned on the porch light, he didn't run or try to hide. He just stood there staring at me for several minutes. Then he smiled and waved, like we were old friends."

She wrapped her arms around herself protectively. "It felt like he was trying to mimic normal human behavior rather than expressing genuine emotion. Like someone pretending to be human without understanding what that meant."

Their final stop was the home of Amber Simpson, now a woman in her thirties who had been forced to carry the burden of her younger brother's murder throughout her adult life. When Trevor started to exit the car, Shea placed a restraining hand on his arm.

"I'm not sure I want to hear any more details about how evil your brother was," she admitted, her voice tight with strain. "I thought I'd encountered true evil in my previous cases, but nothing I've faced compares to what Troy represents."

"We're doing this so that no one else will have to

suffer what these families have endured," Trevor replied, though his emotional reserves were nearly exhausted. He exited the car and waited for Shea to join him on the sidewalk.

Amber Simpson's initial reaction was hostile when Trevor introduced himself and requested an interview about her deceased brother Seth. "Why would I want to relive that nightmare? Are you here to ease your survivor's guilt over being the twin who lived? Or do you enjoy digging up other people's pain?"

Trevor remained silent, recognizing the validity of her anger and allowing Shea to take the lead in the conversation. His survivor's guilt was indeed one of the reasons he felt compelled to make these visits, though he hoped there might be practical benefits as well.

After studying Shea's sheriff's badge for several moments, Amber took a deep breath and stepped aside to let them enter her small apartment. "My brother wasn't a random target," she said without preamble. "Troy used to sit in his car outside our house for hours at a time, just watching our daily routines. Seth tried to laugh it off and act like it didn't bother him, but I could see that he was genuinely frightened."

She paused to rub her hands along her arms, as if trying to remove the memories from her skin physically. "Troy asked Seth a question once that still gives me nightmares. He wanted to know if Seth had ever woken up in the middle of the night with the feeling that someone was in the room with him, watching him sleep."

Trevor stiffened at those words, recognizing the scenario from his own childhood experiences. He had awakened with exactly that sensation many times during his early teenage years, though he'd always attributed it to ordinary nightmares.

Amber's voice broke with emotion as she continued. "Seth told me once that he thought Troy was conducting some kind of psychological experiment, testing to see how frightened he could make someone before moving in for the kill. Maybe if I'd told an adult about those conversations back then, my little brother would still be alive today."

"That wouldn't have stopped Troy," Trevor said with quiet certainty. "Once he had chosen his victims, nothing could have changed his mind. The selection process was part of his ritual."

"Seth wrote a note to your brother during his final week of life," Amber revealed, tears flowing freely down her cheeks. "It was the last thing he ever wrote that I'm aware of. The message was simple and desperate: 'I don't know what you want from me, but please stay away.'"

Trevor's jaw tightened with suppressed rage, and he gave Amber a respectful nod before marching back to their car without another word.

Shea followed him, studying his expression over the hood of their vehicle. "Troy was never just your brother," she observed with sudden clarity. "He was your stalker from childhood. All those other victims were simply practice sessions, preparation for when he finally came after his real target."

"Then what are the people dying now for?" Trevor asked, his eyes burning with unshed tears and barely contained fury.

"It's all still a game to him. Troy feeds off fear and psychological torture. With each new death, he knows your terror is growing stronger." Her features hardened with determination. "You have to find a way to push that fear down as deep as possible. Don't let him see even a hint of how much he's affecting you. Don't give him that kind of power over your emotions."

"I don't know if I'm capable of that kind of control," Trevor admitted, his voice raw with honesty. "The terror fills every moment of my existence, both waking and sleeping. Every time I look in the mirror or take off my shirt, I'm reminded of what he did to me and what he's planning to finish."

"Then don't take off your shirt," Shea said with a slight grin, attempting to inject some lightness into the oppressive atmosphere. "Although I have to admit, it would be a shame to deprive the world of that particular view."

Trevor arched an eyebrow in surprise. "Is the Ice Queen making a joke at a time like this?"

Her grin faded quickly. "You really think I'm that cold and unapproachable?"

"Not cold, just intensely serious most of the time.

But the world becomes a brighter place when you smile, Shea. You should do it more often."

"I haven't had many reasons to smile in recent years," she replied, climbing into the driver's seat as her brief moment of levity disappeared entirely.

As they pulled away from Amber Simpson's apartment building, Trevor directed them back toward Misty Hollow. He'd asked enough questions and heard more than enough disturbing details about his brother's psychology to last several lifetimes.

"I won't let him kill you," Shea whispered as they drove through the gathering dusk. "I promise you that."

Trevor appreciated the sentiment, though he knew it was a promise that might be impossible to keep. If their roles were reversed, he would move heaven and earth to honor such a vow. But with Troy methodically working his way toward the final number, Shea might very well find herself directly in the line of fire, and Trevor wasn't sure he could live with himself if she became another casualty in his brother's twisted game.

Chapter Eight

Trevor woke to the faint, golden light of the sun filtering through the blinds, painting warm stripes across his bedroom floor. For the first time in weeks, he'd slept heavily without the nightmares that usually plagued his rest. The absence of dreams felt like a small miracle, and for a moment, he allowed himself to enjoy the sensation of being genuinely rested.

Still groggy from the deep sleep, he sat up slowly and rubbed his hands down his face, feeling the stubble that had grown overnight. His body felt stiff from sleeping in one position for so long, but it was a good kind of stiffness—the kind that came from actual rest rather than the tense, fitful dozing he'd become accustomed to.

He stretched his arms above his head and yawned deeply before swinging his legs over the side of the bed. The hardwood floor was cool against his bare feet as he stood and moved to make the bed, a habit ingrained since his military service years ago. He reached for the top of the blanket to pull it over his pillow, but his hand froze in midair as his gaze locked on an object that absolutely should not have been there.

A hunting knife lay on the pillow next to the one where he'd rested his head all night. The blade was identical to the one Troy had used twenty years ago, the same worn wooden handle, the same distinctive curve of steel that had been designed for skinning deer but had proven equally effective on human flesh. A folded piece of paper was pinned beneath the knife's point, held in place like a butterfly specimen.

His hand trembling despite his efforts to remain calm, Trevor carefully slipped the note free from under the blade. The paper was ordinary notebook stock, but the message written in Troy's distinctive handwriting made his blood turn to ice: "You should've died that night twenty years ago. See how close I can get to you without you even knowing I'm there? Watch for me, brother. I'm always closer than you think."

Ice water seemed to surge through his veins as the implications hit him with full force. His heart hammered against his ribcage so violently he could hear it in his ears as he frantically scanned the room for any sign of his brother's presence. The bedroom door was closed exactly as he'd left it before going to sleep. The window was still latched securely from the inside, with no broken glass or any other sign of forced entry.

Yet somehow, impossibly, Troy had gotten inside

the house. He'd managed to enter Trevor's bedroom, place the knife inches from his sleeping head, and leave again without waking either Trevor or Shea. The security system showed no signs of tampering, the dog hadn't raised an alarm, and Trevor himself was usually a light sleeper who woke at the slightest unusual sound.

The realization that his brother had been standing over him while he slept, close enough to touch him, close enough to complete his deadly mission if he'd chosen to, sent waves of nausea through Trevor's system. Troy could have ended everything right then and there, but he'd chosen psychological torture instead. This was all part of his sick game.

Trevor quickly pulled on jeans and a t-shirt, his movements jerky with adrenaline and barely controlled panic. He needed to find Shea immediately, needed to make sure she was safe and unharmed. He knocked urgently on her bedroom door, listening for any response that would indicate she was alive and well.

"Shea?" he called out when no answer came. The silence from her room sent his panic spiraling even higher. He pushed the door open without waiting for permission and felt his heart stop when he saw that her bed didn't look as if it had been slept in at all. The covers were still neatly arranged, the pillows undisturbed.

Terror gripped him with iron claws, and he thundered down the stairs, taking them three at a time in his haste to search the rest of the house. Had Troy taken her during the night? Was she already dead somewhere, victim number five in his brother's twisted countdown?

Just as he reached the bottom of the staircase, Shea and Heidi entered through the front door. She was carrying a coffee cup from the sheriff's station and had been up for hours, but she was alive and unharmed. Relief flooded through him so powerfully that his knees nearly buckled.

Her experienced eyes immediately took in his disheveled appearance and the obvious distress on his face. "What happened? You look like you've seen a ghost."

"Where were you?" The words came out more harshly than he'd intended, but the fear for her safety was still coursing through his system.

"I went into the office early to catch up on some paperwork that's been piling up, but I left you a note explaining where I'd gone." She moved to the small table near the door and retrieved a yellow Post-it note that she'd placed there before leaving. "I always leave word when I go somewhere."

"I hadn't made it that far yet. When I saw your bed looking unslept in, I thought..." He couldn't finish the sentence, couldn't voice his worst fears about what Troy might have done to her.

Her gaze dropped to the piece of paper clutched in his trembling hand. "What is that?"

"A note from Troy. He got into the house while

we were sleeping." The words felt surreal as he spoke them, but the evidence was undeniable.

Shea's expression grew grim as she read the threatening message. "The alarm system was armed when I left the house at midnight. I woke up around then and couldn't get back to sleep, so I decided to be productive. It's seven now, which means he knew you were here alone and vulnerable."

Her eyes flickered with a mixture of anger and concern. "If he was already close to reaching his target number of seven victims, you'd be dead right now. The only reason you're still breathing is because he's not ready for the grand finale yet."

"If he was that close to completing his mission, you never would have left me alone in the first place," Trevor replied, recognizing the truth in his own words. "I know you better than that."

"True, but I still don't like how easily he's manipulating our movements and decisions. I won't leave you alone again, not even for a few hours. Troy is becoming increasingly unstable and unpredictable. He might decide not to wait until he's killed two more victims before coming for you directly. I don't like the rules of this game he's created."

Trevor padded to the kitchen to start the coffee maker, needing the familiar routine to help calm his shattered nerves. "How does this situation compare to that case you handled on the mountain?" He was referring to the time she'd taken on a group of men who had turned hunting people into a deadly sport, luring victims to a remote cabin before torturing and killing them for entertainment.

"I honestly thought this case would be easier to resolve," Shea admitted, settling into a chair at the kitchen table. "It's one man, after all, regardless of how dangerous he might be. On the mountain, I was dealing with an entire network of killers, all of them heavily armed and working together in a coordinated fashion."

Trevor turned to face her, studying her expression. "Because of the skill and courage you demonstrated up there, I have complete faith that you'll find a way to win this confrontation as well."

"We'll win it," she corrected firmly. "I'm not facing this alone, and neither are you. We're in this together."

He wished desperately that she wasn't involved at all, that he could somehow face his brother's threat without putting anyone else in danger. "Troy left his knife on the pillow right next to where my head was resting all night. He could have killed me in my sleep if that's what he'd wanted."

Her eyes widened with a mixture of horror and professional curiosity. "How is he managing to get past our security measures? We have motion sensors, cameras, and a state-of-the-art alarm system."

"He's been watching us constantly, studying our routines and our defenses. Every move we make, every precaution we take, he's observing and learning how to counter it. He knows exactly how to get around the alarm system." Trevor handed her a steaming cup of coffee, then poured one for himself before sitting at the table across from her. "I never thought Troy was particularly intelligent when we were growing up. Cunning, maybe, but not genuinely smart. He's certainly proving me wrong now."

"Like I said before, people learn all kinds of skills during long prison sentences that they didn't possess before their incarceration," Shea said, adding vanilla-flavored creamer to her coffee. "Electronics, security systems, lock picking—these are common areas of study among inmates."

"I thought you always took your coffee black." Trevor was grateful for any topic that didn't involve his psychotic brother, even something as mundane as coffee preferences.

"I usually do, but I've already had two cups at the office this morning. My stomach can't handle any more straight caffeine." She stared into her cup for several long minutes, clearly lost in thought. "I hate to admit this, but I'm not sure what our next move should be. Troy is pulling all the strings in this situation, and we're essentially dancing to his tune."

"You mean we wait for someone else to die before we can react," Trevor said grimly, gripping the handle of his coffee cup so tightly that the ceramic might crack under the pressure.

"Unfortunately, that seems to be the pattern he's

established." She raised tortured eyes to meet his gaze. "According to his established methodology, he only needs to kill one more person before he comes for me."

"Before he makes you victim number six," Trevor corrected, his voice thick with emotion he was struggling to control.

"Yes. And then..." She didn't need to finish the sentence. They both knew that Trevor was intended to be the final victim, the culmination of everything Troy had been working toward for the past twenty years.

Trevor reached across the table to take her hand, intertwining their fingers in a gesture that was both comforting and possessive. "Whatever happens, we've got each other's backs. That has to count for something."

"Look who's trying to be the optimistic one today," Shea said, managing a smile that didn't quite reach her eyes.

"I guess we'll have to take turns keeping each other's spirits up and morale high," Trevor replied. "If we let despair and hopelessness take over, then Troy has already won."

~

They were talking about him again. Troy crouched in the dense shrubbery just outside the kitchen window, close enough to see their expressions and body language even if he couldn't make out every word they were saying. Wasn't he just the most fascinating and important thing in their lives right now? Everything they did, every decision they made, revolved around him and his plans.

He held his breath as the German shepherd suddenly lifted her head, ears pricked forward as if she'd detected something unusual. For a moment, he thought he'd been discovered, but then the dog relaxed and lowered her head back to her paws. The animal was the biggest obstacle to his plans. There was no security code for his brother's alarm system that he couldn't eventually figure out with enough time and patience. But that dog's superior senses presented a much more challenging problem.

Unless he found a way to neutralize the canine threat, he wouldn't be able to get close enough to the sheriff when the time came to take her as his sixth victim. The dog would alert them to his presence long before he could complete his mission.

A faint smirk tugged at the corners of his mouth as he realized that maybe the problem wouldn't be as insurmountable as he'd initially thought. After all, he was standing right outside their kitchen window at this very moment, and the dog hadn't raised any kind of alarm. Perhaps he was already more of a phantom than he'd realized, able to move through their world without detection when he chose to be careful about it.

Troy was indeed like a ghost, flitting from shadow to shadow, appearing and disappearing at will. When the time was right, he would materialize, grab the sheriff, and use her as bait to lure his brother to whatever location Troy chose for their final confrontation.

A low chuckle escaped his lips as his mind began forming the details of his plan. The beautiful sheriff could be forced to dig Trevor's grave with her own hands before Troy killed her in front of his brother's eyes. Her body would be left on display afterward, positioned where it would be discovered quickly, to show the world that Troy Bolton was the best predator who had ever lived.

He grinned so widely that the expression hurt his facial muscles. His pulse raced with anticipation and excitement. Oh, what delicious fun this was turning out to be. The psychological torture was almost as satisfying as the physical violence would be.

The dog suddenly glanced toward the window again, this time rising to her feet with obvious alertness. Troy's survival instincts kicked in immediately, and he turned and ran toward the safety of the woods before his presence could be confirmed.

~

"Get your weapon, Trevor!" Shea bolted to her feet so quickly that her chair scraped loudly against the floor, simultaneously pulling her service pistol from its holster with practiced efficiency.

"Is he here on the property?" Trevor asked, though he was already moving toward where he'd left his gun.

"Someone is out there. Look at Heidi's behavior."

Shea darted toward the back door, noting how the dog's entire body was tense with alertness. She reached the door just in time to see a male figure sprinting toward the tree line at the back of Trevor's property.

"Troy Bolton!" she shouted at the fleeing man, hoping to stop him through the sheer authority in her voice. When he continued running without even slowing down, she fired a warning shot into the air, then gave chase with Heidi at her side.

"Shea!" Trevor called out behind her, his voice filled with concern and frustration. "Wait for backup!"

"No time!" she called back over her shoulder, focused entirely on the retreating figure. She raised her weapon and fired again, this time aiming to wound rather than warn, but the shot went wide as her target dodged behind a tree.

The morning light vanished almost completely once she entered the dense woods, but the sound of branches breaking and undergrowth being trampled ahead of her provided a clear trail to follow. Trevor's longer legs allowed him to catch up with her quickly, and within moments he had taken the lead in their pursuit.

"No, Trevor!" Shea called out as a sudden realization hit her. "What if this is exactly what he wants? What if Troy is deliberately leading you into some kind of trap?"

"I'm not letting him get away from us again," Trevor replied grimly, increasing his speed even further as adrenaline and determination drove him forward.

Heidi glanced back at Shea as if seeking guidance. "Stay with him, girl," she commanded. "Don't let him go in there alone." The dog immediately rushed forward to keep pace with Trevor.

They burst out of the woods and onto the main highway, causing immediate chaos as car horns blared and vehicles swerved to avoid the sudden appearance of people and a dog in the roadway. Troy jumped into a late-model Chevy pickup truck that had been waiting for him and sped away, tires squealing against the asphalt as he fled the scene.

Shea quickly pulled her radio from her belt and called in the incident. "This is Sheriff Callahan requesting an APB on a navy-blue Chevy pickup truck, 1980s model, license plate number 264YEA. Suspect is armed and extremely dangerous."

She knew that Troy would most likely abandon the vehicle at the first opportunity, but at least putting out the alert gave them some chance of tracking his movements. They desperately needed some kind of luck to break in their favor.

Trevor stood at the edge of the highway, every line of his body rigid with frustration and barely contained rage. "This is ridiculous. He's playing with us like we're amateur hour."

"The fact that he won't stay away from us is going to be how we eventually catch him," Shea said with more confidence than she felt. "His obsession with you makes him predictable in some ways." She called Heidi back to her side. "Let's head back to the house. We have serious work to do."

She began the return journey at a much slower pace than their frantic pursuit had required. The lack of sleep from the previous night, combined with an adrenaline-fueled sprint through dense woods, had left her feeling drained and slightly dizzy.

Her phone rang just as they reached Trevor's back door. "Sheriff Callahan."

"The license plate number you provided belongs to a vehicle that was reported stolen over a week ago," Deputy Harris informed her. "The truck has been located abandoned at mile marker 108 near the state liquor store. No sign of the driver, but we're processing it for fingerprints and other evidence."

"Thanks for the quick work," she replied, then repeated the information to Trevor. They couldn't seem to catch even the smallest break in this case. Every lead turned into a dead end, every opportunity slipped through their fingers.

It wouldn't be much longer before they were forced to confront pure evil face to face, and that prospect scared her more than she cared to admit. The fear that was slowly building inside her meant that Troy was already winning part of his psychological war. He fed on terror, thirsted for it like other people craved food or water. He'd demonstrated that tendency even as a teenager, asking potential victims about their capacity for fear before moving in for the kill. Now, instead of simply asking people about being scared, he actively created that fear, watching with pleasure as the life drained from their eyes at the point of his knife.

She turned to Trevor when they were safely back inside the house. "There has to be something stored in that head of yours that will help us anticipate his next move. No one in the world knows Troy better than you do—you're his identical twin, you shared a childhood with him, you understand his psychology in ways that no one else possibly could."

Trevor's brow furrowed with frustration. "If I knew something useful, don't you think I would have shared it already? I'm not holding back information that could save lives."

"Maybe you don't realize that you know it," Shea suggested. "Sometimes the most important insights are things we take for granted or dismiss as unimportant."

"Oh, right. What do you want me to do? Get hypnotized by some television psychic?" He crossed his arms defensively. "What I do know for certain is that he's completely fixated on me and the number seven. Everything he does revolves around those two obsessions."

His eyes suddenly widened as a new thought occurred to him. "I was born exactly seven minutes after Troy, which made me technically the younger twin even though we were identical in appearance."

"And immediately upon your birth, you took the

place in your parents' hearts that he felt rightfully belonged to him as the firstborn," Shea said, seeing the psychological pattern. "That's the source of his resentment and his need to eliminate you. See? You did know something important."

"Nothing that will help us catch him before he kills more innocent people," Trevor said grimly. "I'm going to take a shower and try to clear my head. Maybe the hot water will help me think more clearly."

He paused at the hallway entrance and turned back to face her. "Don't take off after him like that again without me by your side. We need to stick together from now on, no matter what. I couldn't live with myself if something happened to you because I wasn't there to help."

"Okay," Shea replied, though they both knew she was being deliberately vague in her response.

Trevor narrowed his eyes, clearly recognizing that she hadn't made the promise he was looking for. "Hrnm." He marched toward the bathroom with obvious dissatisfaction.

The truth was that Shea couldn't make that promise, much as she might want to ease Trevor's concerns. If she saw a clear opportunity to go after Troy and end this nightmare, she would take it with or without Trevor by her side. The man had to be stopped regardless of the personal cost to herself. Keeping Trevor alive and safe outweighed any danger that might be directed at her in the process.

Rather than attempt to cook breakfast in their current emotional state, they decided to head to the local diner for a meal and a change of scenery. They requested a booth by the large front window, and Shea positioned herself where she could maintain visual surveillance of both the parking lot outside and anyone who might enter through either the front or back doors.

Trevor had remained silent during the entire drive from his house, and his mood hadn't improved since they'd arrived at the restaurant. Instead of engaging in conversation, he kept the oversized menu raised high enough that she couldn't see his face, effectively shutting her out.

"You're angry with me," Shea observed, though it was hardly a difficult deduction to make.

"Nope," Trevor replied curtly, not bothering to lower the menu that was serving as a barrier between them.

"Fine. Sulk like a child then," she said, turning her attention to her own menu and deciding on a ham and cheese omelet with hash browns.

"I specifically asked you not to run off after Troy without me as backup. You didn't give me the response I was hoping for, so yeah, I guess I am upset." He slapped the menu down on the table with enough force to rattle the water glasses. "I thought we were supposed to be partners in this investigation."

"We are partners, but I am still your superior officer," Shea replied, hating that she pulled rank but needing him to understand that she would make the final decisions in dangerous situations.

"Wow, that's really low, even for you," Trevor said, his voice thick with hurt and disappointment.

Shea immediately regretted her words. "Let's not fight with each other when Troy is the real enemy here. Let's focus our anger and frustration on him instead of tearing each other apart."

Trevor's gaze locked with hers for a long, tense moment, then he finally nodded. "I suppose I know when I can't win an argument."

The server arrived to take their breakfast orders, after which they sat in uncomfortable silence. Shea turned her attention to the view outside the window, where Heidi sat alertly in the bed of Trevor's pickup truck. The dog's ears were constantly moving, monitoring the sounds and scents around them, and she would alert them if Troy ventured anywhere nearby. He'd been around their property enough times that Heidi knew his scent, and she would recognize from Shea's previous reactions that the man was decidedly not a friend.

While Shea considered herself to have excellent instincts developed through years of law enforcement experience, she knew she couldn't compete with the superior senses of a well-trained German shepherd.

"I'm sorry," Trevor said softly, breaking the strained silence between them. "I've been letting the stress of this situation get to me, and I took it out on you. That wasn't fair."

Shea turned her attention back to him, seeing the genuine remorse in his expression. "I'm sorry too. I shouldn't have pulled rank on you like that. It was unnecessary and hurtful."

"Well, you are technically my boss," Trevor said with a slight smile.

"That doesn't mean I had to throw it in your face during a personal conversation. We are partners, Trevor. You're honestly the best partner I've ever worked with, and I've been in law enforcement for quite a while now. Don't ever think that you can't speak your mind around me."

"Even if you might not like what I have to say?" He arched an eyebrow.

"Especially then," Shea replied firmly. "Open communication is essential if we're going to be effective as a team."

When the server brought their food, Shea also requested two scrambled eggs to be packaged for takeout. "Those are for Heidi," she explained when Trevor looked curious.

"If you got her registered as an official service dog, you could bring her inside restaurants with us," Trevor suggested.

"I'm not disabled in any way that would qualify me for a service animal," Shea replied.

"Then make her an official police dog. That would give you the legal authority to bring her anywhere you need to go in your professional capacity."

"That's an excellent idea," Shea said, brightening at the suggestion. "I wouldn't mind having her with me at all times. She's the best early warning system either of us could ask for."

Given that Troy was on a deadly mission and growing more unpredictable by the day, they needed all the help they could get.

Chapter Nine

Shea woke to the sharp, insistent ring of her phone cutting through the early morning quiet. The digital clock beside her bed showed 5:47 AM in harsh red numbers. She fumbled for the device with sleep-heavy hands, her heart already racing because calls at this hour were never good news.

She listened with growing dread as dispatch told her that a local merchant had been murdered, stabbed multiple times behind her shop in what appeared to be another of Troy Bolton's methodical killings. The dispatcher's voice was carefully controlled, but Shea could hear the underlying tension that came from knowing they were dealing with a serial killer who was systematically working his way toward a specific goal.

Hanging up with a trembling hand, she yelled down the hall for Trevor to be ready to leave in five minutes. Her voice carried a note of urgency that would wake him instantly, even from the deepest sleep.

Her hands shook so violently that she had trouble buttoning her uniform shirt, the small buttons seeming to slip away from her fingers despite her best efforts. Victim number five. The number burned in her mind like a brand. That meant she was next in Troy's twisted countdown, followed by Trevor as the grand finale. The knowledge sent ice water through her veins, but she forced herself to take several deep breaths to steady her nerves. Panic would only make her ineffective when she needed to be at her professional best.

She went to meet Trevor in the living room, finding him already dressed and checking his service weapon with the automatic efficiency of someone who'd done it thousands of times. His face was grim but determined, and she could see the same mixture of fear and resolve in his eyes that she felt in her chest.

Shea quickly explained what little she knew about the crime scene as they rushed to the car, their footsteps echoing loudly in the pre-dawn stillness. The morning air was crisp and cold, carrying the scent of dew and the promise of another day that would be forever changed by violence. After helping Heidi into the back seat, she climbed behind the wheel and started the engine with hands that were steadier now that she had something concrete to focus on.

Deputy Butler was waiting for them in the narrow alley behind Applewood Mercantile, his usually cheerful demeanor replaced by the serious expression of an officer who'd seen too much death in recent weeks. "Delivery driver named Dave Millwood found her," he reported, consulting his notebook. "He noticed the back door standing wide open and went to investigate, thinking maybe she'd forgotten to lock up the night before. Found the body, lost his breakfast all over the alley, and stumbled back outside in shock."

Butler jerked his head toward where a pale young man in his twenties leaned heavily against a white delivery van, his hands still visibly shaking from the trauma of discovery. "Poor kid's pretty shaken up. Says he's never seen anything like it before."

"I can imagine," Shea replied grimly, glancing in the driver's direction. "Tell him to wait just a bit longer while we process the initial scene, then I'll take his statement, and he can go home to his family."

"My brother has never killed a woman before in any of his previous sprees," Trevor observed as he led the way into the shop through the propped-open back door. "Why would he change his established MO now, especially when he's so close to completing his mission?"

"Just another unpredictable piece of his sick game," Shea sighed, pulling on latex gloves as she studied the body of Millie Applewood, a well-liked middle-aged woman who had owned the mercantile for over fifteen years.

The victim lay sprawled behind the wooden counter that had been the centerpiece of her store, her cheerful blue apron now soaked through with crimson blood. A shattered jar of homemade muscadine jam lay next to her body, its purple contents mingling grotesquely with the spreading pool of blood beneath her. The sweet scent of the fruit preserves mixed with the metallic smell of death created a nauseating combination that made Shea's stomach churn.

The old-fashioned cash register stood open but hadn't been emptied of its contents, suggesting that robbery had never been the motive. Several bills and coins were visible in the drawer, along with credit card receipts from the previous day's business.

Shea frowned as she surveyed the scene more carefully. "She was waiting on a customer when this happened. The register is open for a transaction, and there are items on the counter that haven't been bagged yet."

"Troy wouldn't have approached through the front door like a normal customer," Trevor said, studying the positioning of the body and the evidence around it. "He's always preferred the element of surprise, catching his victims when they're most vulnerable."

She nodded, seeing where his reasoning was leading. "Which means we might have a witness to the crime this time. Someone who was in the store when Troy entered through the back."

A younger woman suddenly burst through the front door of the shop and immediately let out a piercing scream when she saw the body. "Aunt Millie! Oh God, what happened to her?"

Trevor quickly moved to intercept the woman before she could contaminate the crime scene or disturb any evidence. "You'll have to wait outside, ma'am. This is an active crime scene, and we can't allow anyone else inside until we're finished processing it."

"She called me about an hour ago," the woman said through tears that were already pouring down her cheeks. "Said someone suspicious was lurking in the alley behind the store, watching her movements. I told her I'd be here as soon as I could and that she should call the police if she felt threatened."

It appeared the victim hadn't had time to make that call before Troy struck. "Do you work here at the mercantile?" Shea asked gently.

"Yes, I'm her assistant manager. I come in every morning after I drop my daughter off at elementary school, usually around eight-thirty." The woman's voice broke with guilt and grief. "I got caught up talking to the school nurse about my daughter's allergies this morning. I should've been here to help her. Maybe if I hadn't been late..."

"You very well might have ended up dead too," Shea said, though she knew that wasn't entirely true. Troy had never killed multiple victims in a single incident, but as Trevor had pointed out, he'd also never targeted women before. His pattern was becoming increasingly unpredictable as he approached his ultimate goal.

"I'm going to need you to step outside while we

finish processing the scene," Shea continued. "But don't go far—I'll need to take a formal statement from you shortly."

"My name is Trish Duncan," the woman managed between sobs. "Miss Duncan." With another wail of grief, she rushed out the front door and pressed her face against the window, staring in at the scene with horrified fascination.

A small crowd of curious onlookers began gathering around Miss Duncan on the sidewalk, drawn by the presence of police vehicles and the obvious distress of the woman. Shea could see people pointing and whispering, the way communities always did when violence shattered their sense of safety.

"I'm going to see if any of the bystanders witnessed someone entering or leaving the store," Shea announced, squaring her shoulders as she prepared to face the crowd. She frowned when she spotted a news van from the regional television station parked directly in front of the mercantile, its satellite antenna already extended.

Ignoring the shouted questions and requests for comments from the reporter, she approached the gathering crowd with professional authority. "Did anyone see anything unusual this morning? Anyone who might have gone into or come out of the store? Did any of you visit Millie's shop earlier today? Please speak one at a time so I can hear everyone."

She glared at the news reporter who was trying to

edge closer with her microphone extended. "You stay over there by your van. I'll give an official statement when I'm finished with my preliminary investigation."

The reporter flinched at the sharp tone and reluctantly returned to her position by the news van, although she continued to record everything with her camera.

"I saw that young man over there go into the store," an elderly lady said, pointing with a gnarled finger toward a teenager who was slumped against the brick wall of the building next door. "This was maybe thirty or forty minutes ago. I also heard some kind of commotion coming from the alley around that same time, but it turns out that was just the delivery man being sick to his stomach."

"Excuse me," Shea said, pushing through the crowd to reach the teenager. "You were inside the mercantile this morning?"

The boy nodded miserably, his face pale and drawn with obvious trauma. "I was just buying some chips and a soda for breakfast before school. Millie was being real nice, chatting with me about my classes while she rang up my stuff. Then this guy came in through the back door, and as soon as I saw his face, I knew exactly who he was."

The teenager scuffed the toe of his sneaker against the concrete sidewalk. "I should've tried to help her or called for help or something. Instead, I just ran like a coward."

"There's absolutely nothing you could have done against someone like Troy Bolton," Shea assured him firmly. "Running was the smartest thing you could have done. Are you positive it was the man we're looking for?"

"Yes, Sheriff. I'll never forget that face as long as I live." The boy raised tortured eyes to meet her gaze. "Besides, my parents make me watch the evening news every single night. They say it keeps me informed about what's happening in the world. They show his picture every night, warning people to be on the lookout."

"You did the right thing by getting out of there safely," Shea repeated. "Can I let you go now, or do you need someone to call your parents?"

"Can I go? I mean, is he going to come after me now that I saw him?"

Shea wanted to tell him no, that Troy wouldn't bother with him since he didn't fit into the specific countdown that seemed to drive all of the killer's actions. But she didn't want the boy to let down his guard or take unnecessary risks. "I strongly suggest that you don't go anywhere alone until we have Troy Bolton back in custody."

"Yeah, I figured as much. My parents are having breakfast at the diner down the street. I'll go meet them there and tell them what happened." He turned and ran toward the restaurant without looking back.

"The mercantile has a security camera system," Trevor announced as he joined her outside the shop.

"I've made a copy of this morning's footage for us to review when we get back to the station."

"Excellent work. We also have an eyewitness who positively identified Troy as the killer." Shea straightened her shoulders as she prepared to face the media. "I'm going to give a brief statement to the reporters, then we'll head back to the office to analyze what we've learned."

The reporters immediately converged on her when she stepped to the edge of the sidewalk, microphones thrust forward and cameras rolling.

"I will make one brief statement, but I won't be taking questions at this time," she announced in her most authoritative voice. "Time is critical in this investigation. Millie Applewood was murdered this morning by Troy Bolton, the escaped patient we've been searching for. I strongly urge all citizens of Misty Hollow to remain extremely vigilant. Do not go out after dark and avoid being alone anywhere until this dangerous individual is back in custody. Thank you."

She turned and strode back into the store as questions were shouted behind her, ignoring the reporter's attempts to get her attention.

~

Back at the sheriff's station, Trevor inserted the thumb drive containing the security footage into Shea's laptop computer. "This video is actually from the camera system of the store next door to Millie's," he explained as the grainy black-and-white images began playing on the screen.

The timestamp showed that a dark-colored SUV had been idling in the alley for nearly an hour before the actual crime occurred, suggesting that Troy had been conducting surveillance and waiting for the right moment to strike. Then warm light spilled into the previously dark alley as Millie unlocked her back door, most likely to make things easier for the morning delivery driver who was scheduled to arrive.

A man slid out of the passenger side of the waiting vehicle just moments before a white delivery van turned into the alley. Trevor's brother stepped clearly into view of the security camera and smiled directly at the lens before casually entering the shop through the propped-open door.

"He doesn't care at all that we can see him," Shea observed, her voice hardening with anger and frustration. "He's not even trying to hide his identity."

"Nope. He's actively taunting us, showing off how bold he can be." Trevor's jaw clenched as he watched his brother's casual arrogance. "This is all just entertainment to him."

A few minutes later, Troy emerged from the shop still holding the bloody knife he'd used to kill Millie Applewood. He paused to smile and nod directly at the camera again, as if acknowledging an audience, then strolled casually in the opposite direction until he disappeared from view.

"We need to identify whoever was driving that

SUV," Shea said, leaning forward to study the footage. "Find out who else has been recently released from the same prison where your brother was incarcerated. I want the driver of that vehicle to be arrested and behind bars as soon as possible."

Trevor spent the next hour cross-referencing vehicle registrations with recent prison releases, generating several possibilities before narrowing them down to two solid leads. One name in particular caught his attention: Steven Doyd, who had been released from the state penitentiary just two weeks before Troy's escape from the psychiatric hospital.

He wrote down Doyd's current address and employment information before going to inform Shea of his findings. "I think I've got our man. Steven Doyd, age thirty-four, recently released after serving time for armed robbery. He works as an accountant for Greene Construction."

"Perfect." Shea motioned for Heidi to follow as she grabbed her keys and service weapon. "Let's go have a conversation with Mr. Doyd."

They drove several miles outside of town to the construction company's modest office building. The receptionist, a friendly middle-aged woman with graying hair, pointed toward a small trailer parked behind the main office. "Steven is our bookkeeper and accountant. You'll find him working out there in the trailer. He keeps pretty much to himself, but he's good with numbers."

"Is it too much to hope that this Doyd fellow might have a current address where we can find your brother?" Shea asked as they walked toward the trailer.

Trevor gave a sarcastic chuckle. "That would be expecting way too much luck for one day."

"A girl has to maintain some optimism," Shea replied, though her tone suggested she wasn't particularly hopeful either.

She knocked firmly on the trailer door, then pushed it open without waiting for permission, waving Trevor in ahead of her as backup.

A thin, nervous-looking man turned away from a tall filing cabinet, his eyes widening with obvious alarm at the sight of their badges and uniforms. He had the pale, unhealthy complexion of someone who spent too much time indoors, and there was something furtive about his manner that immediately put both officers on alert.

"Are you Steven Doyd?" Trevor asked, his voice carrying the authority of law enforcement.

"Yeah, that's me." The man limped noticeably as he made his way to his desk and sat down heavily, fixing his pale, frightened gaze on both officers. "What can I do for you folks?"

"Do you own a black panel van?" Shea asked directly, not bothering with small talk.

Trevor hadn't thought it was possible, but Doyd's face went even paler at the question, and he nodded reluctantly.

"Did you give Troy Bolton a ride to Millie's Mercantile this morning?" Trevor pressed, studying the man's body language for signs of deception.

Doyd's Adam's apple bobbed nervously as he swallowed hard. "Yeah, I gave him a ride. But I didn't know what he was planning to do there."

"Were you aware that Troy Bolton is a wanted fugitive?" Shea crossed her arms and fixed him with a steely stare. "Did you know you were helping an escaped killer?"

"He... he didn't tell me exactly what he wanted to go to the store for," Doyd stammered. "I just thought maybe he needed to buy something."

"But you knew he was a dangerous wanted man," Shea said, pulling handcuffs from her duty belt. "Steven Doyd, you're under arrest for aiding and abetting in the commission of murder. Things might go considerably easier for you if you can provide me with an address where we can find Troy Bolton."

"Sheriff, you don't understand what kind of man Troy is," Doyd said desperately as she approached with the handcuffs. "When someone like him wants you to do something, you don't have a choice. You do it, or you become a dead man yourself. I don't know where he's staying because he told me he moves around constantly to avoid detection."

"Well, we now have a dead woman on our hands— an innocent woman who was just going about her daily business while a coward like you provided transportation for her killer." Shea clicked the handcuffs around his wrists with perhaps more force than was strictly necessary. "I'm going to put you in the back seat with my dog while Deputy Bolton searches this trailer for additional evidence."

"Who's Heidi?" Doyd asked nervously.

"My German shepherd. She doesn't like people who help murderers."

The man cursed under his breath as Shea marched him outside toward their patrol vehicle.

Trevor immediately began searching the small trailer systematically, looking for anything that might provide a clue to his brother's whereabouts or plans. He spotted a cell phone lying partially hidden under some scattered papers on Doyd's desk. Fortunately, the man hadn't bothered to use a password to lock the device, making it easy to access his text messages and call history.

Trevor scrolled through the recent messages, stopping when he found one that could only have come from his brother: "Need a ride. Pick me up at the corner of Main and Fourth at six a.m. Don't be late."

He understood Doyd's reluctance to refuse Troy's demands—his brother could be highly persuasive when he wanted something, and the threat of violence was always implicit in his requests. But regardless of the circumstances, an innocent woman was still dead because of Doyd's cooperation.

Trevor carefully noted the phone number that the

text had originated from, though he suspected it would turn out to be another burner phone that couldn't be traced. He searched through the rest of the papers on Doyd's desk but found nothing else that seemed relevant to their investigation.

With one final glance around the cramped trailer to make sure he hadn't missed anything important, he joined Shea at their patrol car. "I found a phone number that Troy used to contact Doyd, but I'm betting it's another dead end."

"Go ahead and run a trace on it anyway," Shea said, turning the car's laptop computer in his direction. "We have to check every lead, no matter how unlikely."

It didn't take long for Trevor's suspicions to be confirmed. "You're righ. It's another untraceable burner phone. Just like all the others."

"At least we're taking one more scumbag off the streets," Shea said as she pulled onto the interstate heading back toward town. "Your brother is eventually going to run out of people willing to help him. Did you find any other recent prison releases who might be potential accomplices?"

"Doyd appears to have been the last one released from that particular facility," Trevor replied, glaring at the handcuffed man in the back seat. "Tell me, does Troy have any other friends on the outside who might be willing to help him?"

"He don't have no friends," Doyd said bitterly. "Only people who are too scared to tell him no. And once he's done using you, he don't care what happens to you."

~

Troy strolled down a narrow dirt road several miles outside of Misty Hollow, searching for a suitable vehicle he could steal without attracting too much attention. The occasional isolated farm would provide exactly what he needed, as long as he could take something without being seen by the property owners. He didn't want to kill anyone else right now. That would disrupt his carefully planned count and force him to start over again.

No, the next time he used his knife would be for the sheriff and his brother. Excitement danced in his chest at the prospect of finally completing the mission he'd started twenty years ago. The anticipation was almost as satisfying as the actual violence would be.

He didn't yet know exactly how he would capture both of his final targets, but he was confident that an opportunity would present itself. As a fifteen-year-old boy, he had failed due to inexperience and poor planning. As a mature man hardened by decades of imprisonment, he was essentially invincible.

The rumble of an approaching engine sent him diving into the roadside brush until the vehicle passed, its driver apparently unaware of his presence. Doyd had mentioned that the local news stations were showing his photograph every evening, warning citizens to be on the lookout for him. He couldn't afford to be recognized by anyone, especially not when he was so close to achieving his ultimate goal.

After the road cleared again, he emerged from his hiding place and resumed his purposeful hike. Over the next rise, he spotted a modest farmhouse where no one appeared to be working the fields despite the early hour. An old pickup truck sat parked next to a weathered barn, and he was willing to bet that the keys would be either on the sun visor or in some other easily accessible location. Country folk were notoriously trusting, often leaving their vehicles unlocked with the keys inside.

Keeping low to avoid being spotted from the farmhouse windows, he darted toward the truck and smiled when he noticed a pile of empty burlap sacks in the bed. Perfect. Plenty of material to cover up his prisoners while he transported them to their final resting place.

He slowly opened the driver's door, then paused to listen for any indication that someone had noticed his presence. When no alarm was raised, he climbed inside and began searching for the keys. They weren't on the sun visor as he'd expected, but lay in plain sight on the cracked dashboard. Stupid, trusting people.

A few minutes later, he was bouncing across an empty meadow and away from the farm, staying off the main roads to avoid detection. Once he was safely out of sight of the farm buildings, he stopped to smear mud across the license plate, obscuring the numbers and letters. The truck would eventually be reported stolen, but there were dozens of similar old vehicles scattered throughout the rural areas around Misty Hollow. He would have all the time he needed to complete his mission before anyone connected the theft to him.

Everything was falling into place perfectly. Soon, very soon, he would have his revenge, and his brother would finally pay for being born seven minutes too late to be the favorite son.

Chapter Ten

For three long, torturous days Troy remained utterly silent. No more threatening notes slipped under doors, no more bodies discovered in alleys, no more taunting phone calls in the dead of night. The absence of his presence was somehow more unnerving than his active harassment had been. Time hung heavy for Shea, its passing marked by an audible tick tock, tick tock that seemed to echo in her mind while she waited with growing anxiety for the killer's next inevitable move.

He wasn't gone, though. She could feel his presence like a physical weight pressing down on her shoulders, could sense his cold eyes watching her every time she left the house or stepped outside the sheriff's station. The sensation of being constantly observed began to fray her nerves in ways that direct confrontation never could.

The waiting was slowly driving her toward the edge of sanity. She found herself tapping a pencil against her desk in perfect rhythm with the relentless clock ticking in her head, the sound growing louder and more insistent with each passing hour. Sleep had become elusive, meals had lost their taste, and even simple conversations required tremendous effort to maintain focus.

Not hearing from Troy was simply another calculated move in the elaborate psychological game he was playing with all of them. He didn't just want to kill Trevor—that would be too simple, too quick, too merciful. Instead, he wanted to break his brother emotionally first, piece by methodical piece, slowly unraveling his sanity by using fear and guilt as his primary weapons. Troy knew Trevor better than anyone else in the world, understood his deepest vulnerabilities and the trauma he still carried from that night twenty years ago when he'd nearly died at his twin's hands.

"He's not rushing toward the finale because he's genuinely enjoying this part," Shea said aloud to the empty office, needing to hear her voice to break the oppressive silence. "Every threatening message, every calculated killing, every moment of terror—it's all entertainment to him."

She rose from her desk and went in search of Trevor, hoping to find him in the bullpen or perhaps grabbing coffee from the break room. When she didn't locate him in either of those places, a familiar trickle of dread began working its way through her system. In recent days, neither of them had been comfortable being separated for more than a few minutes at a time.

Relief flooded through her when she finally spotted him sleeping on the narrow cot in their holding cell, his service weapon within easy reach even in unconsciousness. Good. He wasn't sleeping well at his house anymore, and neither was she, really. Both of them had become too focused on watching for Troy's next move, too alert to every small sound and shadow that might signal danger. The sheriff's station was the most secure location they had access to, the safest place to catch a few hours of desperately needed rest.

She backed away quietly from the cell and returned to her office, determined not to wake him unless an emergency call came in that required both of their attention. In the meantime, she would use this opportunity to dig deeper into Troy Bolton's psychological profile. The more she understood about his mind and motivations, the better prepared she would be when their final confrontation inevitably arrived.

A couple of phone calls to various state agencies eventually connected her with Doctor Rachel Woodbrook, a retired psychologist who had worked extensively with Troy during his years in the state penitentiary. Shea introduced herself and explained the urgent nature of her inquiry.

"I know there are strict rules about client-doctor privilege," she began carefully, "but you might be able to help me save innocent lives. Troy has escaped, and he's killing again."

"I have no problem discussing such a dangerous individual with law enforcement," Doctor Woodbrook replied without hesitation. "Please, ask me anything you need to know, although I suspect you've already gathered quite a bit of information from the psychiatric hospital."

"I'm hoping you might have more detailed psychological assessments that could help us predict his behavior patterns," Shea said. "Perhaps you could send me copies of your files on him?"

"Absolutely. I'll scan and email them to you right now." True to her word, Shea's computer chimed with an incoming message just minutes later, containing dozens of pages of psychological evaluations and session notes.

"Bolton is a textbook sociopath with narcissistic tendencies," the doctor continued over the phone. "He barely functions in normal society but can turn on considerable charm when it serves his purposes. He almost fooled me during our first few sessions with his apparent cooperation and insight, but over time, he couldn't maintain the façade. The man has absolutely no conscience or capacity for genuine remorse. Taking human life means nothing more to him than swatting a fly. He cares about exactly one person in this world—himself."

This was information Shea had already figured out through her own observations, but it was helpful to have professional confirmation. "Did Troy ever talk about his relationship with his brother Trevor during your sessions?"

"That subject dominated virtually every conversation we had. His brother and the psychology of fear were his two primary obsessions." Doctor Woodbrook chuckled grimly. "He asked me during every single session what made me feel genuinely scared. I always gave him mundane answers like snakes or spiders, but I think he desperately wanted me to admit that he frightened me. Which he did, but I would never have given him that satisfaction."

"Are you aware that he's begun killing again?" Shea asked.

"No, I don't watch the news much anymore. I found that constant exposure to violence and tragedy was affecting my mental health." The doctor's voice became strained. "What number victim is he working toward now?"

Shea drew a deep breath through her nose, bracing herself for the response. "He just killed his fifth victim."

"Then, according to his established pattern, there's one more death before he goes after his brother again. Do you have any idea who he's selected as number six?"

The words felt like lead in Shea's mouth. "Me."

"Because you're emotionally close to his brother?"

"As close as anyone, I suppose. Trevor is my deputy, and we spend most of our time together, both professionally and personally. Troy sees me as an obstacle to his ultimate goal."

"Is there any possibility that you could distance yourself from Trevor, at least temporarily?" Doctor Woodbrook asked hopefully. "Sometimes these obsessive killers can be thrown off their plans if their intended victims become unavailable."

Shea frowned at the suggestion. "I can't abandon Trevor to face this nightmare alone, Doctor. Besides, it's probably too late for that strategy anyway. If Troy has decided that I'm going to be victim number six, he won't deviate from that plan. You of all people should understand how rigid his thinking patterns are."

"You're absolutely right, of course," the doctor sighed heavily. "I was merely grasping at straws, hoping there might be some way to disrupt his methodology. Is there anything else specific you'd like to know about his psychological profile?"

"I'm open to any insights you might be willing to share."

"As I mentioned, he rarely spoke about anything except his brother during our sessions. Every conversation followed the same obsessive pattern— Trevor's childhood, Trevor's perceived advantages, Trevor's survival of the original attack. I'll be praying for both you and Deputy Bolton, Sheriff. If anything else occurs to me that might be helpful, I'll call you immediately."

The conversation had helped pass some time, but

Shea realized she hadn't learned anything genuinely new about Troy's psychology. Nothing that would give them a tactical advantage or help them anticipate his next move. The man was plowing ahead like an unstoppable locomotive toward his ultimate mission, and all they could do was try to stay out of his way until they could find an opportunity to stop him.

"Sheriff, we've got a situation developing," Doris announced, poking her head through the office doorway. "There's a man with a gun outside Lucy's Diner, and he's not letting anyone enter or leave the building."

"We're on our way," Shea replied, leaping to her feet and rushing toward the holding cell where Trevor was sleeping.

~

"Trevor." She shook his shoulder gently but firmly. "We've got an emergency call."

He bolted upright immediately, his hand instinctively moving toward his weapon before his eyes had fully focused. "What's the situation?"

"Armed individual outside Lucy's Diner. Reports say he's preventing people from entering or leaving the building." Shea took a step back to give him room to gather his equipment. "Are you alert enough to handle this, or should I call Deputy Butler for backup?"

"No, we stick together like we agreed," Trevor said, scrambling to retrieve his service weapon from his desk and check that it was fully loaded. "Remember our rule about not separating?"

They both froze in their tracks when they reached the squad car and spotted a white envelope tucked under the windshield wiper. The sight of it sent ice water through both of their veins, because they knew precisely who had placed it there.

"Looks like Troy's period of silence is officially over," Shea observed grimly, carefully extracting the envelope and handing it to Trevor.

Inside was a faded but unmistakable photograph showing him and Troy as young children, perhaps seven or eight years old, smiling innocently in front of a rusted swing set in what appeared to be a public park. Dark spots that resembled dried blood had stained several areas of the image, lending it a macabre quality that made Trevor's stomach churn.

The innocence still visible on his brother's face in the photograph was heartbreaking. When exactly had that natural childhood joy been replaced by the calculating evil that now defined Troy's existence? What had gone so fundamentally wrong during their development that two identical twins could grow up to be such polar opposites?

Trevor turned the photograph over and immediately recognized the familiar scrawling handwriting as Troy's. The message was brief but loaded with psychological significance: "Remember who you were before you forgot me."

Forgot him? Trevor couldn't forget his evil twin

even if his life depended on it. Troy's presence had haunted every day of the past twenty years, influencing every major decision Trevor had made about his career, his relationships, his entire approach to life. How could Troy possibly think he'd been forgotten?

Trevor shoved the disturbing photograph into his jacket pocket, not wanting to spend more time analyzing its implications. "Let's go handle this situation."

"Are you going to be okay?" Shea asked, studying his face with obvious concern. "This kind of psychological harassment has to be taking a toll on you."

"I'm fine. This isn't anything new for me, and it shouldn't be surprising to you either after everything we've been through. It's just another move in Troy's sick game." He slid into the passenger seat, his jaw set with determination.

The diner was close enough that they could have walked there in just a few minutes, but the drive gave them time to mentally prepare for whatever situation they were about to encounter. When they arrived, they immediately spotted the source of the emergency call.

A man in faded denim overalls was pacing back and forth in front of the diner's main entrance, waving a pistol in one hand and a half-empty bottle of whiskey in the other. Every time someone tried to approach the front door, he would aim his weapon in their direction and shout warnings for them to stay back.

"That's Bob Delaney," Trevor said, exiting the patrol car and studying the man's erratic behavior. "This is not normal behavior for him. Bob's usually one of the most peaceful, law-abiding citizens in town."

"Since you have a personal relationship with him, I'll let you take the lead on this," Shea said, falling into step behind him. "I'll provide backup and crowd control."

She positioned herself several feet away while Trevor moved closer to the agitated man, his hands held out to his sides in a non-threatening gesture.

"Hey there, Bob. What's going on out here?" Trevor kept his voice calm and conversational. "Are you having some kind of problem today?"

"You could say that, Deputy." Bob's words were slurred from the alcohol, and his eyes were red-rimmed with grief. "My wife up and left me."

"Bob..." Trevor said gently. "Your wife has been gone for several years now." Alice Delaney had died of an aggressive brain tumor five years earlier, and the entire community had attended her funeral.

"I know that!" Spittle flew from the man's lips as his voice rose with anger and pain. "Today is the fifth anniversary of her death. The anniversary of when she left me all alone in this world."

"Why are you here at the diner scaring all these innocent people, Bob?" From the corner of his eye, Trevor spotted Shea carefully skirting around the crowd of onlookers with Heidi at her side, positioning herself for a better tactical advantage.

Bob laughed bitterly, the sound harsh and broken. "Didn't want to spend this terrible day grieving all by myself." He fumbled in his pocket and produced another photograph. "Found this sitting on my kitchen table when I woke up this morning. It should have been in our photo album with all the other pictures, but somehow it appeared on the table like Alice had left it there for me to find."

"Do you mind if I come a little closer to take a look at that photograph?" Trevor asked carefully.

"You stay right where you are," Bob warned, gesturing with his weapon. He turned toward a teenage girl who was part of the crowd. "Sweetie, would you mind taking this picture to the deputy for me? I promise I won't hurt you."

Trevor nodded reassuringly to the frightened girl, encouraging her to help.

The teenager darted forward with evident reluctance, snatched the photograph from Bob's outstretched hand, and then practically threw it at Trevor before scrambling back to safety.

Trevor glanced down at the image and saw a much younger, healthier Bob Delaney with his arm lovingly wrapped around his wife Alice. The photograph had been taken several years before Alice's illness, when they were both happy and had no idea what tragedy lay ahead of them.

"Bob, do you normally lock your doors at night?"

Trevor asked, though he suspected he already knew the answer.

"Of course not. I live way out in the middle of nowhere, and I've never had any trouble with break-ins or theft." Bob swayed slightly on his feet. "Oh, and Alice's old pickup truck disappeared from my property a few days ago. I thought some kids or drug addicts had stolen it, but now I'm thinking maybe Alice came back and took it herself."

Trevor's heart skipped several beats as the implications became clear. "Bob, Alice is dead. She can't come back to visit you or take her truck."

He felt certain he knew who had broken into Bob's house, stolen the truck, and strategically placed the photograph where the grieving widower would find it. But why would Troy target Bob Delaney? The answer came to Trevor in a flash of insight—this was all designed to lure him and Shea away from the relative safety of the sheriff's station.

He searched the crowd for Shea, his heart rising into his throat with sudden panic. Relief flooded through him when he spotted her crouched down, speaking quietly to Heidi, then straightening up to assess the tactical situation. Seeing her safe and unharmed allowed Trevor to release the breath he'd been holding.

"Put the gun down, Bob," Trevor said with renewed authority. "Let's get you inside the diner for some hot coffee, and we can talk about Alice properly."

"Coffee doesn't fix everything that's wrong with the world, Deputy," Bob replied sadly.

While Trevor kept the man's attention focused on their conversation, Heidi began moving with the silent precision of a trained police dog. Shea had given her some kind of signal that Trevor hadn't noticed.

"Maybe coffee can't solve everything," Trevor agreed, careful not to look directly at the approaching dog so he wouldn't alert Bob to her presence. "But it usually helps people think more clearly about their problems."

The German shepherd made her move with lightning speed, launching herself through the air to clamp her powerful jaws around the arm that held the pistol.

Bob screamed in surprise and pain, dropping the whiskey bottle, which shattered on the pavement. In his shock, he pulled the trigger reflexively, sending a wild shot into the asphalt near his feet.

Shea and Trevor immediately rushed forward, taking the disoriented man to the ground and securing his weapon before he could fire again.

"Release," Shea commanded firmly. Heidi immediately backed away as both officers hauled Bob to his feet and began escorting him toward their patrol car.

"Looks like you'll be getting that coffee after all, sir," Trevor said as he helped the unsteady man into the back seat. "Though you'll be drinking it at the county jail while you sober up and think about your actions today."

Bob would be spending at least a few days behind bars regardless of his grief, because threatening innocent people with a firearm was a serious crime that couldn't be overlooked.

As they drove back toward the sheriff's station, Trevor filled Shea in on the details of what Bob had told him about the mysterious photograph and the missing truck. "It looks like Troy is back to playing his psychological games, and he's managed to score himself another vehicle in the process."

"Mr. Delaney is very fortunate," Shea observed as she navigated through the downtown traffic. "If Troy wasn't currently focused on making us his final two victims, Bob could very well be dead right now instead of just being used as another pawn in this sick chess game."

She parked in front of the sheriff's station and turned off the engine. "I'm reaching the point where I genuinely want Troy to stop hiding and face us directly. All this waiting and uncertainty is more stressful than the actual confrontation would be. We need to find a way to force his hand."

"Do you have some kind of plan forming?" Trevor asked as he opened his door.

"I'm working on several possibilities," Shea replied grimly. "It's time to stop being reactive and start taking control of this situation ourselves."

Chapter Eleven

Shea waved Trevor into her office when he knocked on the door frame, her expression grave with the weight of what she was about to propose. The late afternoon sun streamed through the blinds, casting long shadows across the scattered case files and crime scene photographs that had become the centerpiece of their investigation.

"I've finally made my plan," she announced without preamble as he settled into the chair across from her desk.

His eyes widened with a mixture of anticipation and apprehension as he folded his arms across his chest in a defensive posture. "I'm listening."

"The plan should work, at least in theory," she said, straightening in her chair and adopting the authoritative tone she used when briefing her deputies. "Troy has been testing us for weeks now, circling us like a boxer in a ring, studying our defenses and probing for weaknesses. With each encounter, he's only getting bolder and more confident."

"I completely agree with that assessment," Trevor nodded, though wariness flickered in his eyes.

"I've compiled everything we've gathered on him into this comprehensive file." She slid a thick folder across the desk toward him. "Psychological reports, crime scene photos, news articles, witness statements, prison records…everything we know about his methods, his motivations, and his psychological profile. We're going to use all of this information to set an elaborate trap, with you serving as the primary bait."

"I figured that's what you had in mind," Trevor said grimly, glancing at the bulky file but not opening it to examine the contents. "How exactly do you plan to make this work?"

Shea took a deep breath, knowing that her following words would trigger immediate resistance. "You're going to leave town. Publicly and visibly, so that everyone knows you've gone."

"Absolutely not." His response was immediate and forceful, his eyes flashing with anger. "I will not leave you here alone to face my psychotic brother. That's not happening under any circumstances."

"Just hear me out before you start objecting," she said, crossing her arms to match his defensive posture. "We're only going to let Troy think that you've left. The official story will be that you were ordered to relocate for your safety by state authorities who were concerned about the escalating threat level. But here's the key part...Troy doesn't know that we suspect I'm his intended sixth victim."

"We don't just suspect anything, Shea," Trevor interrupted harshly. "We know with absolute certainty that you're next on his list. This plan essentially makes you the bait instead of me, and I'm not comfortable with that role reversal."

"Listen to the full strategy before you make your decision," she continued, refusing to be derailed. "Gossip travels incredibly fast in a small town like Misty Hollow, as I've discovered during my time as sheriff. A few carefully placed phone calls from Doris inquiring about safe house procedures, a strategically dropped comment at the diner about your relocation orders—it won't take more than a full day for the entire town to believe that you've been forced to leave for your protection."

She leaned forward, her voice taking on an urgent quality. "Meanwhile, Heidi and I will be waiting at your house along with a carefully concealed team of deputies positioned throughout the property. Troy will think I'm vulnerable and alone, protected only by the new security systems we've installed."

"No," Trevor said flatly, his jaw set with stubborn determination.

"We'll make the deception even more convincing by parking your truck at the edge of town where it can be easily observed, then having someone other than you drive it away in case Troy is conducting surveillance from a distance," Shea continued as if he hadn't spoken.

"Stop talking as if I'm not sitting right here objecting to every word of this insane plan!" Trevor slammed his hand down on the desktop hard enough to make the coffee mug jump. "This is not happening."

"I'm not asking for your permission, Trevor," Shea said with quiet authority. "We've waited long enough for Troy to make his move on his own terms. It's time to end this nightmare once and for all, and we need to do it on our terms rather than his."

"This is my life we're talking about. My brother. My twenty-year-old unfinished business." Trevor lunged to his feet, pacing behind his chair like a caged animal. "I get a say in how we handle this confrontation."

His face darkened with a mixture of fear and fury. "I cannot and will not let you face him alone, regardless of how many deputies you have hidden around the property. You don't understand what Troy is capable of when he's focused on a specific target."

Shea forced herself to appear calm and composed, folding her hands on her desk in a gesture of professional control. "I won't be alone out there. When Troy comes—and he will come—we'll be ready for him. We'll take him down before he has a chance to hurt anyone else."

"This plan won't work the way you think it will," Trevor argued, his voice rising with desperation. "Troy is too intelligent, too calculating. He's had twenty years in prison to plan every detail of his revenge. He'll have anticipated every possible strategy you could throw at him, including elaborate traps and deception operations."

"We have to try something proactive," Shea insisted, her voice taking on a pleading quality. "Trevor, we can't continue to sit back passively and let him dictate the terms of every encounter. We need to force this confrontation to happen on our timeline and in a location where we have the tactical advantage."

She tilted her head, studying his face with earnest intensity. "I need you to trust me on this. Trust my experience, my training, and my judgment."

Trevor's obvious fear for her safety struck a chord deep inside her chest, in a place where no one had ever reached before. When exactly had their professional relationship crossed the line from colleagues to friends to something much more complex and emotionally significant? Were these intense feelings simply the result of the extreme stress they were facing together, or were they a sign of something deeper that had been building between them for months?

The realization that she might have romantic feelings for Trevor Bolton couldn't have come at a worse time, but the knowledge was undeniable now that she'd acknowledged it.

Trevor sighed heavily and sank back into his chair, running his hands through his hair in a gesture of defeated frustration. "I do trust you, Shea. With my life, with everything that matters to me. If you truly believe this is our best option..."

He looked up to meet her eyes directly. "Okay. Let's do this. But I want detailed contingency plans for every possible scenario, and I want to be in constant radio contact with the entire team."

"Thank you," she said simply, though the words carried the weight of everything she couldn't say aloud.

At dusk, as the sun began to set behind the Arkansas hills, Shea followed Trevor's pickup truck as it made its way slowly down Main Street. Deputy Cutter was behind the wheel, explicitly chosen because his build and general appearance most closely resembled Trevor's from a distance. The truck's windows were tinted dark enough that a casual observer wouldn't be able to see the driver clearly, especially in the fading light.

They drove through the center of town at a deliberately slow pace, ensuring that anyone who was watching would have plenty of time to observe the vehicle and its apparent occupant. Several people on the sidewalks turned to look as they passed, and Shea was confident that word of Trevor's departure would spread quickly through the community's gossip network.

After exiting onto the main highway that led out of Misty Hollow, they drove for several miles before the truck finally pulled over to the shoulder of the road. Shea parked behind it and got out of her patrol car, walking forward to the driver's side window of the pickup.

To any observer, it would appear that she was having an emotional farewell conversation with Trevor, perhaps trying to convince him to stay or wish him well on his journey to safety. In reality, she was giving Cutter specific instructions about the next phase of their deception.

"Drive another ten miles down this highway, then abandon the truck in the parking lot of that truck stop we passed earlier," she told him quietly. "Make sure you're not seen getting out of the vehicle. Deputy Martinez will be waiting there to pick you up and bring you back to Trevor's house through a roundabout route."

With a theatrical slap to the hood of the truck, she stepped back and watched as it accelerated down the highway, disappearing into the gathering darkness. If Troy had been conducting surveillance from somewhere nearby, she hoped her performance had been convincing enough to make him believe that Trevor had fled town to escape the confrontation.

Of course, if Troy truly knew his brother as well as he claimed to, he would realize that Trevor would never abandon her to face the danger alone. But perhaps Troy's arrogance and obsession would blind him to that psychological reality.

She sat in her patrol car for several minutes, maintaining the illusion that she was watching Trevor's departure with mixed emotions. Then she pulled back onto the highway and drove slowly back toward town, taking a circuitous route to Trevor's house to ensure she wasn't being followed.

The house was completely dark as she had requested, with all the curtains drawn and no lights visible from the outside. "Is everyone in position?" she asked softly into the radio microphone clipped to her collar.

"Affirmative," Deputy Butler's voice crackled back through the static. "The package is stashed safely away, and all surveillance equipment is operational."

Shea's trained gaze swept across the property, taking inventory of their defensive preparations. Cameras, thermal scanners, and motion-triggered alerts had been carefully installed throughout the day by a technical team from the state police. She caught a brief glint of reflected light as one of her deputies shifted position under the front porch, then watched as he melted back into the shadows with professional skill.

Everything was in place and ready for Troy's arrival.

She had no doubt that Troy knew about at least some of their security measures. The man had demonstrated repeatedly that he seemed to be one step ahead of their every move, anticipating their strategies and countering them with disturbing effectiveness. He would undoubtedly realize that they were setting a trap for him, but hopefully, his arrogance would convince him that Shea would be essentially alone and vulnerable because of her reliance on the new electronic security systems.

"Come on, Heidi. Stay close to me," she said as she opened the car door and stepped out into the cool evening air.

The German shepherd's ears immediately perked toward the tree line to the west of the house, but she obediently remained at Shea's side as they began walking the perimeter of the property. This was part of Shea's normal nightly routine, something she did every evening regardless of the circumstances. Troy would have observed this pattern during his surveillance, and she needed him to see her continuing with her usual activities, whether Trevor was present or not.

Her heart hammered against her throat as she completed the security walk, hyperaware of every shadow and sound around them. She would perform another perimeter check right before going to bed, just as she always did. For now, all she could do was wait and try to project an image of normalcy despite the tension coiling in her stomach.

Midnight approached with agonizing slowness. The tension in the air was so thick it seemed almost physical, like the oppressive humidity that preceded a violent thunderstorm. Shea sat in front of the main security monitor, her eyes never straying from the screen that displayed feeds from cameras positioned around the property.

The thermal imaging scope occasionally flickered with the heat signatures of small animals moving through the woods—raccoons, possums, perhaps a stray cat or two. Nothing human-sized appeared on any of the screens for hours.

Until almost two in the morning, when a shadow suddenly detached itself from the tree line like a piece of darkness given form. The figure was tall, clearly human, and moved with the purposeful stride of someone who knew exactly where they were going. Even with the poor resolution of the night vision equipment, Shea knew without doubt who it was.

Troy was dressed entirely in black clothing that helped him blend with the shadows. He carried no flashlight, relying instead on his familiarity with the terrain that he had studied extensively during his surveillance operations. After carefully skirting the gravel driveway where his footsteps might be heard, he headed down the side of the house with confident, measured steps.

"I'm going outside to circle behind him," Shea whispered into her radio. "Everyone stay alert and be ready to move. Someone take my position at the monitor and keep track of his movements."

She commanded Heidi to remain inside where she would be safe, then slipped quietly out the front door into the cool night air. This wasn't her first time playing the role of hunter in a deadly game. During that weekend on the mountain when she'd taken down the criminal network that had been terrorizing hikers, she'd learned to move silently through darkness and use the terrain to her advantage.

Slowly and carefully, she drew the tactical knife from the sheath on her belt and rounded the corner of the house, her senses hyperalert for any sign of Troy's presence.

No sign of her quarry was visible.

Suddenly, all the lights in the house flickered once and then went completely dark. From inside, she could hear Heidi barking with obvious agitation, a sound that cut through the night like an alarm.

Shea frowned as she realized the implications. The new security measures they had installed were supposed to be completely independent of the house's main electrical system, powered by their own backup batteries. Yet when she peered through the kitchen window, she could not see the tell-tale blinking red light that should have indicated the room's camera was still operational.

Gripping the handle of her knife hard enough to make her fingers cramp with tension, she continued moving toward the back of the house. An uneasy feeling began building in her chest—the growing suspicion that while she thought she was hunting Troy, he might be following her movements and using her own tactics against her.

The possibility made her double back along her original path, trying to detect any signs that she was being stalked.

"We're completely blind in here, Sheriff," Deputy Butler's voice crackled through her radio, barely audible to avoid giving away his position. "All our electronic surveillance is down."

"I'm aware of the situation," she whispered back. "Get visual confirmation through the windows if possible and be ready to move in for apprehension on my signal."

This was becoming ridiculous. She had seen Troy approaching the house on the thermal imaging just minutes earlier. What kind of elaborate game was he playing this time? Had he somehow anticipated their trap and developed a counterstrategy?

She stopped moving and forced herself to listen carefully to the sounds around her. A gentle breeze rustled through the trees. She could hear the faint movement of some small animal in the underbrush nearby. An owl hooted somewhere in the distance. But there was nothing that signified another human being was circling the house with predatory intent.

Had Troy decided not to approach her after all? The possibility didn't make sense given his established psychological profile and his obsession with completing his mission.

Finally, she positioned herself in the deep shadow cast by the back deck. If Troy was indeed circling the house as she suspected, he would eventually have to pass through this area. Hopefully, he wouldn't detect her presence, and she would have the tactical advantage when he appeared.

The waiting was agony. Every small sound made her heart race, every movement in her peripheral vision caused her to tighten her grip on the knife. Minutes stretched into what felt like hours as she remained motionless in the shadows.

~

Troy hadn't experienced this level of pure enjoyment in longer than he could remember. The act of stalking his prey, circling them like a predator studying its next meal, following the sheriff's movements while she thought she was hunting him—it all gave him almost as much satisfaction as watching the fear bloom in a person's eyes during the final moments before he ended their life.

The security system had been almost laughably easy to disable once he'd constructed a simple electromagnetic pulse device from components he'd stolen from various electronics stores. For someone with his level of intelligence and creativity, the sheriff's elaborate preparations were nothing more than a minor inconvenience.

Soon, very soon, he would have the lovely Sheriff Callahan in his hands. His brother would come running to rescue her—of that Troy had absolutely no doubt. Trevor would think he could overcome Troy through sheer determination and moral righteousness, just like he had managed to do twenty years ago when they were both inexperienced teenagers.

But this time would be fundamentally different. This time, Troy would emerge as the victor. He had planned for every contingency, anticipated every possible move his opponents might make. Failure was not an option.

His strategy was elegantly simple: capture the sheriff, then send his brother a message revealing her location. They would finally meet face to face for the first time since that night in the woods when Trevor had nearly died. The prospect of that long-awaited confrontation made Troy feel almost giddy with anticipation.

Bending low to avoid being seen through the windows, he ducked beneath the kitchen window and continued his circuit of the house. It would completely ruin his carefully laid plans if one of the hidden deputies spotted him before he was ready to make his move.

Which room was his brother hiding in? Of course, Troy had never believed for a moment that Trevor would flee town and abandon the sheriff to face this threat alone. His do-good twin would want to play the hero and come to her rescue when the moment arrived. Then this entire twenty-year saga would finally reach its conclusion. Troy would have completed his sacred count of seven victims, with his brother serving as the perfect finale.

As he stepped around the corner of the house, he

could see a figure standing motionless in the shadows near the back deck. Perfect. Everything was falling into place exactly as he had envisioned.

"Looking for me, Sheriff?" he called out softly, his voice carrying a tone of mocking amusement.

Chapter Twelve

How could she have been so careless? The question hammered through Shea's mind like a physical blow as she slowly turned to face Troy Bolton. Her years of law enforcement training, all her carefully laid plans, all her tactical preparations, none of it had prevented her from walking directly into his trap. Her mind almost went completely blank with shock at how thoroughly she had been outmaneuvered.

Troy stood just a few feet away from her, close enough that she could see the cold satisfaction gleaming in his eyes. He looked exactly like Trevor, yet everything about his posture and expression radiated a malevolent energy that his twin brother had never possessed. It was like looking at a distorted mirror image of someone she cared about deeply.

"Drop the knife and your service weapon," Troy commanded, pulling a compact pistol from his waistband with practiced ease. "Start walking toward the woods, or I kill everyone inside that house. It wouldn't take much to blow the entire place sky-high with all those deputies trapped inside. That's not exactly the way I want to end my dear brother's life, but it'll certainly do the job if you don't obey my instructions immediately."

The threat to Trevor and the other officers left Shea with no viable options. She swallowed hard against a throat that had gone completely dry, then tossed both her tactical knife and service weapon into the nearby bushes, where they disappeared into the darkness. The sound of metal hitting branches seemed to echo through the night like a death knell.

Without another word, she set off toward the tree line, knowing with grim certainty that Trevor and Heidi would eventually find her trail and follow. That knowledge was both comforting and terrifying—comforting because she trusted their abilities completely, terrifying because it would put Trevor exactly where Troy wanted him to be.

The forest floor was soft with decades of accumulated leaves and pine needles, muffling their footsteps as they moved deeper into the woods. The rich scent of pine and decaying organic matter filled the air, while moonlight barely managed to filter through the dense canopy above them, casting jagged shadows that seemed to shift and dance with every breath of wind.

Shea stumbled slightly over a partially buried root

that she hadn't seen in the dim light. Immediately, Troy pressed the cold barrel of his gun against the back of her head, the metal making contact with her skin through her hair.

"Careful, Sheriff," his voice carried an almost playful quality that made her skin crawl. "I'd hate for you to fall and hurt yourself before the real fun starts. We have such interesting plans ahead of us."

She bit back the angry response that wanted to spill from her lips and simply glared at him over her shoulder before resuming her forced march through the forest. Low-hanging branches clawed at her skin and snagged her clothing, while her boots sank into patches of muddy ground that tried to pull them off her feet with each step. Her hands curled into tight fists at her sides, and she found herself hoping that Troy would make the mistake of not restraining her properly. The man would definitely regret underestimating her physical capabilities.

Shea's mind raced constantly, searching for any possible avenue of escape or tactical advantage she might be able to exploit. But Troy had chosen their route through the forest with careful deliberation. There were no roads nearby, no houses or buildings where she might find help, just endless miles of dense woodland that stretched in every direction.

After what felt like hours of walking, though it was probably only thirty or forty minutes, they finally reached a small clearing that had been prepared in advance for Troy's twisted purposes. The ground had been meticulously cleared of weeds and underbrush, creating an open space perhaps twenty feet across. A shovel leaned against a fallen log that had been positioned to serve as a makeshift seat.

"Start digging," Troy ordered, picking up the shovel and tossing it toward her feet. "I need two graves, Sheriff. One for you, and one for my beloved brother when he arrives to attempt your rescue."

Shea hesitated for just a moment too long, her mind reeling at the casual way he discussed their impending deaths.

In an instant, Troy was directly behind her, his fingers curling around her neck with enough pressure to make breathing difficult. His breath was hot and moist against her ear as he spoke in a voice barely above a whisper. "Don't make me ask again, Sheriff. I'd prefer to keep you alive and relatively unharmed until Trevor gets here, but I'm not above making adjustments to my plan if you force my hand."

She shuddered involuntarily at his proximity and the implied threat, then forced herself to pick up the heavy shovel. Each plunge of the blade into the hard-packed earth seemed to seal their fate a little more completely. Each scoop of dirt that she tossed aside felt like it was weighted with the knowledge that she dug her own grave.

The physical exertion was grueling, made worse by the emotional weight of what she was being forced to do. Sweat began to bead on her forehead despite the cool night air, and her shoulders started to ache from the repetitive motion of lifting and throwing dirt.

Eventually, pure fury began to take over her other emotions. She had been played entirely, outmaneuvered by a psychopath who had spent twenty years planning this exact scenario. Her professional pride was wounded almost as much as her fear for Trevor's safety.

Troy resumed his casual position on the fallen log, his gaze locked on her with obvious satisfaction. A smirk played around the corners of his mouth as he watched her work. "You know, the first time I killed something, I think I was about ten years old. I noticed a stray dog wandering around our neighborhood, skinny and hungry, and I convinced my neighbor's kid, Danny, to help me catch the poor mongrel."

He laughed at the memory, the sound echoing eerily through the trees. "Danny didn't want to participate at first. He was afraid the animal would bite him, you understand. But do you know what I discovered that day, Sheriff? I learned that I could literally feed on his fear, draw energy and satisfaction from his terror."

Shea didn't doubt it for a moment. Painful blisters were beginning to form on her palms from gripping the rough wooden handle of the shovel, but she forced herself to keep digging. The hole was getting deeper with each passing minute.

"So I told Danny that we were going to take the

dog home and feed it properly, give it a warm bed to sleep in and all the care it needed," Troy continued, clearly enjoying the opportunity to share his twisted memories. "Instead, once we got it cornered in an old shed, I stabbed it directly in the heart with my father's hunting knife. You should have seen the expression on Danny's face when he realized what I'd done."

Troy laughed again, louder this time. "Have you ever felt that kind of pure power, Sheriff? The absolute control over life and death, the ability to snuff out an existence with a single decisive action?"

Shea had indeed felt something similar during her law enforcement career—the satisfaction of stopping dangerous criminals, the sense of justice served when she put violent offenders behind bars. But she refused to give Troy the satisfaction of engaging with his twisted philosophy. Instead, she focused on the almost musical scraping sound of the shovel against rocks and roots, the weight of each load of dirt she tossed aside. She wanted desperately to shut out his voice, but the man seemed determined to continue sharing his disturbing reminiscences.

"That dog didn't go down easy, though," Troy said with something approaching admiration. "It fought to its very last breath, even with its heart pierced. I found myself respecting its determination to survive against impossible odds."

That was precisely what Shea had to do. Keep fighting until her last breath. She was not going to die in this godforsaken forest, not at the hands of this psychopath. Her arms were beginning to shake from the physical exertion, though she couldn't tell if it was from exhaustion or fear or some combination of both.

Troy was talking again, his voice taking on a nostalgic quality that made her stomach turn. "Poor Danny tried to pretend afterward that the whole thing hadn't happened. He was in complete denial about what he'd witnessed. So I convinced him that the dog had been rabid, that it would have bitten and infected someone if we hadn't dealt with it. The stupid boy started to believe my story the more often I repeated it."

Troy suddenly jumped to his feet and began pacing around the clearing like a caged animal, his energy seeming to build as he relived his early crimes. "You're doing excellent work, Sheriff Callahan. Keep digging at that pace, and we'll have both graves ready by the time my brother arrives."

He kicked casually at a pile of dirt near the edge of the hole she was excavating. "You know, after that incident with the dog, I developed what you might call an itch that needed to be scratched regularly. Do you want to know a secret, Sheriff? Danny was my very first human victim."

Troy shook his head with mock sadness. "No, you wouldn't know about that one because I was clever enough to make it look like a tragic accident. Two young boys out hiking in the mountains, exploring dangerous terrain without proper supervision. One of them tragically plummeted to his death when the rocks under his feet gave way and he went tumbling over a cliff."

Shea's blood ran cold as she realized the implications of what he was telling her. How many victims had Troy claimed over the years that had never been connected to him? How many "accidents" and "disappearances" could be traced back to his twisted compulsions?

"The problem was that I didn't like the fact that no one knew I had killed him," Troy continued, his voice taking on a petulant quality. "There was no recognition, no fear, no acknowledgment of my power and skill. So, I started planning more carefully, developing a methodology that would make my involvement unmistakably clear. I decided that a knife would be the perfect weapon—personal, intimate, requiring skill and courage to use effectively. And I came up with the idea of counting up to seven, the biblical number of completion and perfection."

His expression darkened with sudden anger. "Except my dear brother Trevor messed that up for me twenty years ago. He survived when he was supposed to die, disrupted my perfect plan, and forced me to wait two decades to complete my mission."

Shea clenched her jaw and forced herself not to react visibly to his rambling confession. Every word he spoke was further evidence of his complete lack of conscience or remorse.

"Think about how satisfied you'll feel when you finally lie down in your custom-made final resting place," Troy said with grotesque cheerfulness. "The pleasure of a job well done, the peace that comes from accepting your fate. I do hope you'll take extra special care when you start digging Trevor's grave. I want it to be perfect for him."

She cast him a look of pure hatred, which only made him laugh with obvious delight.

"You'd like to kill me right now, wouldn't you, Sheriff?" He shrugged as if the prospect didn't concern him in the least. "By the time I turned fourteen, I'd had quite enough of practicing on animals. They were no longer provided the same level of satisfaction. The first time I killed an adult human being was truly something special, though it started as a complete accident."

Troy's eyes took on a distant quality as he lost himself in the memory. "This old man yelled at me for walking across his perfectly manicured lawn, really got in my face about respecting other people's property. I had just finished killing a rabbit and was still riding the high from that experience when he started screaming at me. One quick stab to his gut was all it took to shut him up permanently. What an incredible rush that was! I knew immediately that I had to experience that feeling again and again."

Shea's stomach churned with revulsion, but she forced herself to keep working. The grave was nearly deep enough now, though her arms and back were screaming in protest.

"It got so much easier after that first human kill," Troy mused. "Each time, I wondered whether I would finally feel satisfied and be able to stop, but no. The opposite happened. It became easier and more addictive with each victim. Every successful kill made me feel more powerful, more in control of my destiny. My time in prison only proved that I was stronger than I'd ever imagined. I came out of that place more focused and determined than ever before."

He towered over her as she stood in the completed grave, casting a long shadow in the moonlight. "That's quite enough digging for now. Time to start on the next one." He extended his hand as if to help her climb out of the hole.

With a snarl of disgust, Shea completely ignored his offered assistance and hauled herself out of the grave through her own strength. Her knuckles were white where they gripped the shovel's handle, and everything in her wanted to swing the tool like a weapon and bash him in the head with all her remaining strength.

As if reading her murderous thoughts, Troy immediately aimed his pistol directly at her forehead. "Don't even think about trying anything heroic, Sheriff. If you attack me, I promise you that my dear brother will suffer extensively before I finally put him out of his misery. I have so many creative ideas for making his final moments as painful as possible."

~

The instant the lights in the house flickered and died, Trevor emerged from his carefully concealed hiding spot in the back bedroom. He listened with growing horror as Deputy Butler's voice crackled over the radio, reporting that they had completely lost contact with Sheriff Callahan and all their surveillance equipment was non-functional.

"You let him take her?" Trevor demanded, his voice rising with panic and fury as he glanced from one deputy to another. "How did this happen? You all assured me that we had a foolproof plan that couldn't possibly fail!"

He checked the ammunition in his service weapon even though he had loaded it carefully when they first arrived at the house hours earlier. His hands were shaking with adrenaline and barely controlled rage. "I want all of you to stay here and maintain your positions. Heidi and I are going after her right now."

"Maybe we should all go together," Deputy Butler suggested uncertainly. "Safety in numbers and all that."

"No," Trevor said firmly. "Someone needs to remain here in case I'm wrong about where Troy has taken her. If Shea somehow manages to escape and makes it back here while I'm gone, she'll have all our heads if the house isn't properly secured."

Butler nodded reluctantly. "If we don't hear from you within thirty minutes, we're coming after you whether you want backup or not."

"Understood," Trevor replied, already heading for the front door. "Thirty minutes, then you follow."

He marched down the front steps with Heidi close at his side, his jaw set with grim determination. "Find Shea, girl. Track her scent and lead me to her."

Trevor knew with sick certainty that he was probably walking directly into whatever trap Troy had prepared for him. But he absolutely could not let Shea face his psychotic brother alone, regardless of the personal cost. He had to reach her before it was too late. Together, they might be able to overcome Troy's madness, but neither of them would survive trying to face him individually.

Heidi immediately led him to a spot near the tree line where Shea had discarded her weapons. The sight of her service pistol and tactical knife lying abandoned in the bushes made Trevor's heart sink like a stone. Shea would never voluntarily surrender her weapons unless she was under direct threat of death. Troy had taken her, and probably at gunpoint.

"Find her, Heidi," he whispered urgently. "Track her trail and bring me to her."

With a soft woof of acknowledgment, the German shepherd kept her nose close to the ground and set off purposefully toward the dense woods behind the house. The night seemed unnaturally quiet and dark, as if all the natural beauty of the forest had been smothered by the evil that now moved through it.

Trevor clicked on his small penlight and swept the

narrow beam across the path they were following. He could see clear signs of passage—a broken branch here, a dislodged rock there, footprints in patches of soft earth. Troy was making no effort whatsoever to hide their trail. He seemed to be deliberately leaving obvious signs for Trevor to follow.

No, his brother wanted and expected Trevor to pursue them. This was all part of Troy's elaborate plan, leading inexorably toward the confrontation he had been planning for twenty years.

Why had Trevor listened to Shea's strategy in the first place? His brother was far too intelligent and calculating to fall into any conventional trap. Troy would have anticipated and prepared for every possible scenario they could devise. Sometimes, Shea took excessive risks in her determination to catch dangerous criminals, but this time, her boldness might result in both their deaths.

Heidi suddenly picked up her pace, moving from a steady trot to an urgent run. Trevor fought to keep up with the dog's superior speed and stamina, his breath coming in harsh gasps as his feet pounded against the uneven forest floor. Their approach would not be stealthy or secretive, which meant Troy would be waiting for them with Shea positioned as a human shield.

"Heidi, stop," Trevor commanded when he realized they were getting close to their destination. He had to repeat the order three times before the dog whined in frustration but finally obeyed. "You can't go any further, girl. He'll shoot you the moment he sees you coming. Stay here and wait for me."

The dog whined again, clearly unhappy about being left behind when her human companion was in danger.

"Stay," Trevor repeated, giving the firm hand signal he had seen Shea use countless times. "I'll come back for you once this is over."

He continued forward on his own, maintaining a steady jog until he heard the unmistakable sound of his brother's laughter echoing through the trees ahead. The sound made his blood run cold—it was exactly the same laugh he remembered from their childhood, but now it carried an edge of madness that hadn't been there before.

Trevor slowed his approach and began moving with tactical caution, using his training to minimize noise and avoid detection. After glancing back to make sure Heidi had obeyed his command to stay behind, he crouched low behind a thick stand of brush and carefully parted the branches to observe the scene ahead.

Shea was just climbing out of what appeared to be a freshly dug grave, tossing aside a shovel and ignoring the hand that Troy held out to help her. Even from a distance, Trevor could see the exhaustion and defiance in her posture. His brother's smug smile faded when she rejected his assistance, and he immediately aimed his pistol directly at her head in a gesture of unmistakable threat.

Trevor took a deep breath, checked his weapon one final time, and stepped boldly from his concealed position into the moonlit clearing.

Chapter Thirteen

Both Shea and Troy turned simultaneously to face Trevor as he emerged from the tree line, their movements creating a tableau of tension in the moonlit clearing. Shea's eyes widened with a mixture of relief and terror as she instinctively reached for the shovel that lay within arm's reach. But Troy was faster, pressing the cold barrel of his pistol firmly against her forehead with enough pressure to leave an indentation in her skin.

Clouds skittered ominously across the face of the moon, causing the entire clearing to take on an increasingly malevolent atmosphere, though Trevor couldn't be certain whether the oppressive feeling came from the shifting shadows or from the pure evil radiating from his brother's presence. The freshly dug grave yawned open like a gaping wound in the earth, a stark promise of what Troy intended to accomplish before this night was over.

"Step away from her right now," Trevor growled, his voice carrying twenty years of accumulated anger and determination.

Troy's familiar smirk spread across his face—the same expression Trevor remembered from their childhood, but now twisted by decades of madness and obsession. He yanked the shovel away from Shea's grasping fingers and tossed it several feet away, well out of her reach. "Look who finally decided to join our little reunion. You were almost late to this party, dear brother. I was beginning to think you'd run away like a coward."

"Drop the gun, Troy. Now." Trevor's voice was steady despite the adrenaline coursing through his system.

"Or what? You're gonna shoot me?" Troy's sharp, mocking laugh startled a roosting bird somewhere in the darkness above them. "You don't have the guts to pull that trigger. You never did, even when we were kids."

Trevor's finger tightened incrementally on the trigger of his service weapon, and for a moment, he seriously considered ending this nightmare with a single shot. The weight of the gun in his hands felt both familiar and foreign—familiar because of his years of training, foreign because he'd never before contemplated using it against someone who shared his DNA.

His brother's confident smirk faltered for just a

fraction of a second as he recognized the deadly serious expression on Trevor's face. Then Troy moved with lightning speed, pulling Shea directly in front of him like a human shield. He pressed the barrel of his pistol firmly against her temple, hard enough to make her wince with pain. "You can't get to me unless you're willing to go through her first. Are you prepared to sacrifice the woman you care about just to stop me?"

"So, you're a coward on top of all the other horrible traits you possess," Trevor said, giving Shea a subtle shake of his head when he saw her muscles tense in preparation for some kind of escape attempt.

She narrowed her eyes at him, clearly unhappy about being told to stand down and remain passive. Trevor didn't care if she was angry with him; it was better to have her furious but alive than dead at his feet in that obscene grave she'd been forced to dig.

"A coward?" The arrogant smirk returned to Troy's face along with the arch of one eyebrow. "What I do requires tremendous courage and skill. There's nothing cowardly about my methods."

"Really? Killing people who don't expect it, who can't defend themselves properly—that's not brave by any definition I know." Trevor kept his weapon trained steadily on his brother, looking for any opportunity to take a clean shot that wouldn't endanger Shea.

"Those deaths were simply a means to an end, dear brother. Stepping stones designed to bring me to this moment, to you." Troy's grip around Shea's neck tightened visibly, making her breathing more labored. "You do realize by now that our lovely sheriff here is intended to be victim number six, don't you? Which means you should be the one dropping your weapon and surrendering."

Trevor blinked slowly and deliberately, a signal he hoped Shea would recognize from their months of working together. When she responded with one long, meaningful blink of her own, he knew she understood. He raised his gun a millimeter, adjusting his aim slightly.

Like a striking serpent, Troy suddenly lunged forward, shoving Shea roughly to one side as he launched himself toward his twin brother.

Trevor squeezed the trigger without hesitation, but Troy had already begun twisting his body to avoid the shot. The bullet grazed his upper arm, tearing through his black shirt and leaving a vivid red streak across his skin, but failing to stop his forward momentum.

Before Trevor could fire a second shot, his brother collided with him with brutal force. The impact was devastating as their bodies slammed together and crashed to the hard-packed earth. Trevor's service weapon flew from his grasp, skittering across the dirt and disappearing into the shadows beyond his reach.

Dir and gravel peppered Trevor's face as they rolled across the ground, each man struggling desperately for dominance in their deadly embrace. They were evenly matched in size and general strength, but their twenty-year separation had changed them both in fundamental ways.

Troy was fast and driven by psychotic rage, but Trevor had received extensive law enforcement training that included hand-to-hand combat techniques. He managed to flip his brother over, pinning him beneath his weight while raining down a series of punches. His fists connected with solid impacts—one, two, three devastating blows to Troy's face that sent blood spraying from his nose and lips. Crimson droplets splattered across Trevor's face and shirt.

Troy grinned maniacally despite the blood streaming down his face, his teeth now streaked with red. "That all you got, little brother?" Without warning, he rammed his knee upward into Trevor's stomach with vicious force.

Explosive pain erupted through Trevor's midsection as all the air rushed from his lungs in a single agonized gasp. The brutal impact loosened his grip for just half a second—but that was half a second too long.

Troy shoved Trevor off him with surprising strength, then kicked out with both legs to send his brother sprawling across the dirt. Trevor struggled to regain his footing and catch his breath, but Troy was already moving toward him with predatory speed. This time, the gleaming blade of a hunting knife was clutched in his right hand.

"Shoot him, Shea!" Trevor yelled as he rolled

desperately to one side, trying to avoid the descending blade.

"I can't get a clear shot without hitting you!" Shea called back, frustration evident in her voice as she stood at the edge of the clearing with Trevor's retrieved weapon clutched tightly in both hands.

A searing pain ripped through Trevor's side as the razor-sharp blade found its mark, plunging deep into his flesh just below his ribs. His breath hitched involuntarily, and the world seemed to tilt at a crazy angle as white-hot agony spread through his torso like liquid fire.

"One," Troy taunted with obvious satisfaction, twisting the knife cruelly to maximize the damage and make Trevor gasp in renewed pain.

"I don't care if you hit me!" Trevor shouted through gritted teeth. "Just shoot him."

"You should have stayed down twenty years ago, brother. Should have let me fulfill my destiny then instead of forcing me to wait all this time." Troy's voice carried a note of genuine grievance, as if Trevor had somehow wronged him by surviving the original attack.

"The hell with your twisted destiny," Trevor snarled back. He could feel the warm, wet trickle of blood soaking through his shirt, but he refused to surrender. He pushed past the overwhelming pain, drawing on reserves of strength and determination he didn't know he possessed. Not like this. He would not die under his brother's knife like a helpless victim.

Summoning every ounce of strength he could muster, Trevor grabbed Troy's wrist with both hands and yanked the knife free from his flesh. The blade sliced deeply into his palm as he gripped it, but he refused to let go despite the additional pain. Instead, he twisted Troy's arm with vicious force.

A sickening pop echoed through the clearing as Troy's arm bent at an unnatural angle. The sound was followed immediately by his agonized howl as the knife slipped from his suddenly nerveless fingers and clattered to the ground.

Trevor drove his uninjured fist into his brother's already bloody face with all the force he could manage, sending Troy reeling backward. Then another punch and another—each blow fueled by two decades of accumulated pain, rage, and the desperate need to stop this madman once and for all.

Troy staggered under the relentless assault, his legs shaking as he struggled to remain upright. Blood streamed from multiple cuts on his face, and his right arm hung at an awkward angle.

Dizziness threatened to overtake Trevor as blood loss began to take its toll. He shook his head vigorously to clear his vision and forced himself to continue the attack, knowing this might be his only chance to end the nightmare permanently.

Troy's wild gaze darted toward the tree line, and in a final desperate move, he grabbed a handful of loose dirt and flung it directly into Trevor's eyes. The gritty particles temporarily blinded him, and in that moment of confusion, Troy hurled a fist-sized rock at Shea. The projectile struck her in the shoulder hard enough to throw off her aim, causing her shot to go wide of its target.

Before either Trevor or Shea could recover, Troy bolted into the dense woods with the desperate speed of a cornered animal.

"Heidi." Trevor screamed at the top of his lungs, hoping the dog was still within hearing range.

The German shepherd burst from the underbrush where she had been waiting, her powerful muscles propelling her forward like a furry missile.

"Get him. Track him down." Trevor tried to follow Troy's path into the woods, but the searing pain in his side forced him to his knees. His breath came in sharp, uneven gasps as the adrenaline that had sustained him during the fight began to ebb.

"Trevor." Shea dropped to the ground beside him, her hands immediately going to assess his injuries. "You're losing way too much blood." Without hesitation, she stripped off her uniform shirt and began binding it tightly around his midsection, applying pressure to slow the bleeding.

"Leave me here and go after him," Trevor gasped, his vision swimming as shock began to set in. "Don't let him get away again."

"I'm not leaving you to bleed out in this godforsaken clearing," Shea replied firmly, her voice brooking no argument.

The distant roar of an engine starting echoed through the forest, followed by the sound of a vehicle speeding away into the night.

Troy had escaped once again. Wounded and with a broken arm, but still dangerous and still free to continue his reign of terror.

This confrontation was over, but the war was far from finished.

~

"Is backup coming?" Shea asked as she continued to check Trevor for additional wounds beyond the stab wound in his side.

"What time is it now?" Trevor's voice was growing weaker, though he was fighting to stay conscious.

Shea glanced at her watch. "Ten fifteen."

"Yes, they should be here soon. I told Butler to give me thirty minutes before following." His eyes drifted closed despite his efforts to keep them open.

Fresh blood was already soaking through the makeshift bandage she had created from her shirt. Trevor should have his radio somewhere nearby—she needed to call for immediate medical assistance. She quickly searched the disturbed ground around them, finally finding the radio half-buried in a clump of dried leaves where it had been thrown during the struggle.

"This is Sheriff Callahan requesting immediate medical evacuation," she spoke urgently into the device. "Deputy Bolton has sustained a serious stab wound and is losing significant blood. We need a helicopter with paramedics to our location." She rattled off the GPS coordinates as best she could remember them from their earlier planning.

"Copy that, Sheriff," Deputy Butler's voice crackled back through the static. "Medical helicopter is already en route to your location. ETA approximately eight minutes."

"Come on, Trevor," Shea said, gently patting his increasingly pale cheek. "Stay with me. Don't you dare die on me now."

"I don't plan on it," he managed to whisper, his eyes flickering open briefly before closing again.

Heidi came racing back toward them from the forest, her tongue lolling out and her breath coming in heavy pants. She whined softly as she pressed her wet nose against Trevor's face, clearly sensing that her human friend was in serious distress.

"Easy, girl," Trevor mumbled, raising his hand weakly only to let it drop back to his side. "Good dog. You tried your best."

Shea was relieved to see that Troy hadn't harmed the German shepherd during their encounter. The fact that Heidi had returned uninjured meant that Troy was currently unarmed, at least temporarily.

Deputies Butler and Harris emerged from the tree line, having followed Trevor's trail through the forest. Butler took one look at the scene, Trevor bleeding on the ground, Shea kneeling beside him in just her sports bra, the open grave, signs of a violent struggle, and cleared his throat meaningfully.

"What?" Shea demanded, her voice sharp with stress and exhaustion.

"He only stabbed Deputy Bolton once," Butler observed, his tone carefully neutral.

"So?" She narrowed her eyes dangerously.

"You're unharmed and still alive. According to his established pattern, you were supposed to be victim number six, with Deputy Bolton as his final target, number seven." Butler paused, choosing his words carefully. "My guess is that his evil twin deliberately missed all the vital organs. He doesn't want Trevor to die yet—not until he can complete his ritual properly."

Shea frowned as the implications of Butler's observation sank in. Of course. Her fear over Trevor's injury and blood loss had clouded her analytical thinking. Troy's obsession with his specific methodology meant that he needed to kill his victims in the exact order he had planned. Trevor's premature death from blood loss would ruin everything Troy had worked toward for twenty years.

Still, if medical help didn't arrive soon, Troy's careful plans might be derailed by simple logistics. She wouldn't be agitated if that prevented him from completing his mission, though she desperately wanted Trevor to survive.

The distant sound of helicopter rotors grew louder by the second. She sent Harris jogging toward the nearest clearing to flag down the aircraft and guide it to their location. Brilliant searchlights suddenly flooded the area as the medical helicopter settled to the ground, its rotors creating a whirlwind of dirt and debris.

"Want me to fill in this grave?" Butler asked, gesturing toward the hole Shea had been forced to dig.

Relief flooded through her at the practical suggestion. "Absolutely. We don't need any more reminders of this nightmare."

She propped her shoulder under Trevor's arm and helped him struggle to his feet, supporting most of his weight as they made their way toward the waiting aircraft. "Let's get you properly patched up so we can finish this fight."

"You should have shot me if it meant stopping him," Trevor said, his voice barely audible over the helicopter noise.

"Yeah, well." Shea's throat tightened with emotion. She could never have pulled that trigger with Trevor in the line of fire, and now a dangerous killer was running free because of her hesitation. "We'll get him next time."

"He almost got both of us tonight," Trevor pointed out weakly.

"But he didn't succeed," Shea replied firmly, helping the paramedics lift Trevor into the aircraft. "And that's what matters."

She climbed in after them, settling into a jump seat as the helicopter lifted off into the night sky. "Butler, watch Heidi for me," she called down to her deputy. "She deserves a steak dinner when you get back to the house."

Butler gave her a mock salute and stepped back as the aircraft rose into the darkness.

The fifteen-minute flight to Langley Baptist Hospital seemed to take an eternity. Trevor drifted in and out of consciousness during the journey, and each time his eyes closed, Shea's heart threatened to stop beating. The paramedics worked efficiently to stabilize his condition, inserting an IV line and applying pressure dressings to control the bleeding.

One of the paramedics draped a blanket around Shea's shoulders to preserve her modesty, since she had used her uniform shirt as a field dressing for Trevor's wound. "Thank you," she said gratefully.

The paramedic smiled and returned his attention to monitoring Trevor's vital signs as they approached the hospital's landing pad. Shea followed close behind as they rushed Trevor through the emergency department doors and into the controlled chaos of a Level One trauma center.

A doctor immediately took charge of Trevor's care, asking Shea to wait in a family consultation room while they whisked him away for emergency surgery. A nurse brought her a clean scrubs shirt to replace the blanket around her shoulders, along with a cup of coffee that she accepted gratefully despite her trembling hands.

"Deputy Bolton is in excellent hands, Sheriff

Callahan," the nurse said kindly before closing the door to give Shea some privacy.

Shea's shoulders sagged under the accumulated weight and fear of the night's events. Once again, she found herself regretting her failure to take decisive action when she'd had the opportunity. If she had brought that shovel down on Troy's head when he wasn't expecting it, Trevor might not be fighting for his life in an operating room right now. She had failed him when he needed her most.

Her hands trembled despite the warmth of the coffee cup. Her moment of indecision had nearly cost Trevor his life—something she had sworn she would never allow to happen.

Taking a deep breath to regain control of her emotions, she pulled out her phone and called Deputy Harris. "Once I know what's happening with Trevor's condition, I'll need someone to come pick us up from the hospital."

"Do you think Deputy Bolton will be released today?" Harris asked.

"If nothing vital was damaged, then yes, maybe." She certainly hoped so, because she had no intention of leaving Trevor's side, and she didn't relish the prospect of living at the hospital for several days. They had important work to do—tracking down and stopping a madman before he succeeded in completing his deadly mission.

With Troy's arm broken, they would have at least a

week or two of breathing room. He would need time to recover from his injury, which would give Trevor time to heal as well. More importantly, it would give Shea time to develop a new strategy—one that wouldn't allow Troy to catch her by surprise again.

Troy's supreme confidence had given him a cunning intelligence that she hadn't fully appreciated before tonight. His previous victims had been ordinary citizens who had no reason to suspect that a murderer was stalking them. Their deaths hadn't required the kind of elaborate planning that Troy had invested in targeting her and Trevor.

It wouldn't happen again. Her fingers unconsciously crushed the Styrofoam coffee cup in her grip, causing some of the hot liquid to splash over the rim and burn her wrist. She hissed at the pain and wiped the coffee off on her pants leg.

I'm coming for you, Troy Bolton, she thought grimly. Next time, she wouldn't wait for him to make the first move.

~

Troy carefully maneuvered the stolen pickup truck into the shelter of an abandoned barn—a place he remembered visiting as a child with Trevor during their occasional hunting trips with their father. The irony of seeking refuge in a location associated with happier times wasn't lost on him, though such emotional considerations no longer carried any weight in his decision-making process.

He retrieved a bottle of whiskey he had purchased from a drive-through liquor store earlier in the evening, twisting off the cap with his teeth since his right arm was now completely useless. The alcohol burned as it went down, but it was precisely what he needed to dull the excruciating pain radiating from his broken bone.

Once the liquor had taken some of the edge off his agony, he climbed stiffly out of the vehicle and began searching the barn for materials he could use to create a makeshift splint. Trevor had broken his dominant arm, the one he used to wield his knife with deadly precision. His brother would pay dearly for that particular injury when they met again.

Troy took another long swig from the whiskey bottle, feeling the alcohol begin to work its numbing magic. He found several useful items scattered around the abandoned building: a burlap sack, a weathered metal tine from an old pitchfork, and part of a broken wooden handle. The materials were rusty and far from sterile, but they would serve his purposes.

He broke the wooden handle into the appropriate length and used the sharp metal tine to cut the burlap into makeshift bandage strips. Now came the most difficult part of his impromptu medical procedure.

Troy shoved his uninjured left hand deep into a hole in the barn wall to brace himself, then placed a piece of wood between his teeth to prevent himself from biting through his tongue. Taking a deep breath, he leaned backward until the broken bone in his arm shifted back into proper alignment.

A primal scream erupted from deep in his throat, rising to echo through the empty barn like the cry of a wounded animal. The pain was beyond description, white-hot agony that threatened to drive him into unconsciousness. He hung his head forward and concentrated on breathing steadily, in and out, in and out, until the dancing spots in front of his eyes finally disappeared.

Using his teeth and his functional left hand, he carefully secured the wooden splint to his broken arm with the strips of burlap, creating a crude but effective stabilizing device. Another generous swig from the whiskey bottle helped dull the throbbing pain to a more manageable level.

He climbed into the truck bed and lay down on his back, staring up at the barn's sagging roof while he waited for the alcohol to work its magic more completely. At least the broken bone hadn't protruded through his skin. That would have introduced the risk of serious infection, which could have derailed his plans entirely.

A few more swallows of whiskey helped ease the pain even further. He estimated that he would need approximately a week of recovery time before he could properly grip a knife again. Once Sheriff Callahan and his traitorous brother were both dead, he wouldn't care if the bone shifted out of alignment again. He could force a doctor to set it properly at gunpoint, then kill the medical professional afterward to eliminate any witnesses.

To seek proper medical treatment now would alert Trevor to his location and general condition. Troy wanted his brother and the interfering sheriff to spend the next few days wondering what had happened to him, worrying about when and where he might strike next.

He grinned through his alcohol-induced haze, already beginning to formulate plans for their next encounter.

This time, he would ensure they were completely caught off guard.

Chapter Fourteen

Shea helped Butler get Trevor situated on the sofa with the remote and a bottle of water close at hand. "I'm not sure what my next step should be. I kind of thought Troy would come to the hospital and try to finish you off."

"That thought had occurred to me." Trevor shifted and grimaced. "It's been three days. I figure he's holed up somewhere letting the broken arm I gave him heal some." He grinned.

"You feel good about that, don't you?" She smiled.

"Sure do. He got me good with the knife, but he didn't leave unscathed." He rested his head against the sofa back. "Why don't you ask former Sheriff Westbrook what he did when things got to be too much. Or you could call in the FBI."

"I've put a call in to them already. They said if he makes an appearance, to let them know." Once Troy showed up again, the feds wouldn't have time to get to Misty Hollow. "I'll call Westbrook."

She hated leaving Trevor, even with Deputy Butler remaining at the house with him, but she had a job to do. A killer to catch. She thought about leaving Heidi behind, but Trevor refused.

"You need someone to watch your back. She's the best one for the job." He stretched out on the sofa.

Shea fought the urge to kiss his forehead as her mother had done when she was ill as a child. But neither of them were children, but any kiss, even an innocent one on the forehead could be misinterpreted. Instead, she cleared her throat and strode out the door with Heidi at her side.

On the way to the office, she called the former sheriff.

"I've been following the story on the news," he said. "I'll do anything I can to help you."

"Who did you call to help?" She hated to realize Troy was more than she could handle with only a handful of deputies.

"The cowboys of the Rocking W and the Misty Hollow Angels." He chuckled. "That's the town's name for them at least. It's a biker gang led by Dave Wakes. They're indispensable to this town in times of trouble. I'll text you his number. In the meantime, I'll get a hold of Dylan Wyatt at the ranch and see who he can spare. You might want to enforce a curfew until this madman is behind bars…or dead."

"Thank you." As soon as the text came through, she called Wakes and left a voicemail asking him to come into the office at his earliest convenience. Her mind whirled with how she could keep the town safe.

Yes, Troy seemed fixated on Trevor and now Shea, but pushed far enough, he might deviate from his original plan and start killing others again. Shea couldn't risk that. She placed a call to the local newspaper and informed them she'd be doing a press conference in one hour outside the sheriff's office.

First, she gathered her deputies in the conference room. With Trevor down and Butler playing bodyguard, she had four at her disposal. Bombeck, Billings, Cutter, and Harris, newly married. All good men willing to do what it took. She filled them in on her plans. "We're all going to be putting in long hours, patrolling this town in shifts. Any questions?"

Cutter held up a finger. "I'm more than happy to take the night shift. Let Harris work days so he can be home with his new wife." He grinned at the other deputy and made a kissy face.

Harris threw a pencil at him with a grin. "Sure, I'd like to be home with Heather, but I'll do what needs to be done."

Shea split the four into a day shift and a night one. As for herself, she'd grab sleep whenever she could. "I'll have the Rocking W and Wakes' gang helping. We will find Troy Bolton." With a nod, she headed outside for the press conference.

"Until further notice, Misty Hollow will enforce a curfew. Unless you are headed to or from work, all residents must be in their homes by six p.m. We will be patrolling the streets all day and night, setting up roadblocks at all major entrances to this city. If you don't know what the man we're searching for looks like, Deputy Harris has a stack of photos. Do not approach this man. He is very dangerous. Be vigilant, folks."

Refusing to answer any questions about the investigation, Shea turned to go back into the building when she spotted a very large, bald man wearing a flannel shirt and a leather vest. She jerked her head toward the door. "Dave Wakes, I presume," she said as she sat behind her desk.

"Yes, ma'am. Came right over as soon as I got your message. Me and the boys are more than happy to help you keep this town safe." He crossed massive arms. "I'll tell them not to engage, but well, they tend to get a little aggressive toward murderers."

She set her jaw. "I don't want anyone getting killed. I'm serious when I say do not approach this man. Call me immediately if you spot him. How many men do you have?"

"Twenty. We're more than enough."

She nodded, then glanced at the door where Westbrook and another man stood.

"Sheriff, this is Dylan Wyatt. He's brought five of his ranch hands to help." Westbrook introduced them.

"Six if you count me."

"You're retired. Are you sure you want to help?" She was more than happy to accept the experienced man's help.

"Absolutely. This is still my town. As a resident, of course."

Shea shook Wakes' hand, then Wyatt's. Gather your men in the high school auditorium. Do not let the press in. I don't want Troy Bolton knowing what we're up to. I'll meet you there in half an hour."

Before heading over, she called to check on Trevor. Butler answered. "He's sleeping. It's quiet here, Sheriff. Not a thing happening."

"Good." She let him know what she had planned for the town. "Keep me posted on Trevor."

"Yes, ma'am." Butler hung up.

Shea glanced at Heidi. "Let's go, girl." She'd chosen to drive her personal vehicle rather than a squad car in case Troy watched. Squad cars patrolling the streets would be a dead giveaway.

She said the same thing at the high school parking lot. "Please drive your personal vehicles or patrol on foot. Do not gather in groups more than two. We want things to look as normal as possible in case he's watching, but we also don't want to put you in too much danger. Troy will expect me to have the deputies out. If he doesn't learn about the curfew, he won't suspect to see the rest of you out and about. The diner will be open if you need a meal or coffee. The department will pay the cost. Act as natural as possible, but again be aware of your surroundings at all times."

"This ain't our first rodeo," one of the cowboys said. "We got you, Sheriff."

"Thank you." She motioned to Heidi and headed back to her truck.

Shea drove around the town, starting at the outskirts and working her way in. She scanned every yard, alley, and storefront. Each time she passed the diner, different vehicles and motorcycles sat out front giving the illusion the diner was busy with the promised meals. She wasn't sure how she'd pay the bill on a small sheriff department's budget, but she'd figure it out.

Suddenly, two men rushed from the diner and hopped onto adjacent motorcycles, then roared down the street. Shea sped after them, her eyes widening as three men on horseback appeared from the brush and thundered after the bikes. The view might've made her laugh under different circumstances.

The disparate group stopped near a farmhouse. She joined them. "What did you hear?" Why hadn't anyone called her?

"We got a tip that a man was lurking around here," one of the bikers said. "Thought we'd take a look." He tossed her a walkie-talkie. "We're communicating on channel 5."

She caught it and hooked it to her belt. "Spread up and be careful."

Spotting a figure hunkered behind a hay bale, Shea pulled her weapon and crept forward, whispering for Heidi to remain quiet. "Hands where I can see them."

A teenage boy stood, holding his hands high. "I ain't doing nothing wrong."

"The fact you're out past curfew is wrong enough." She slid her weapon into its holster. "What are you doing out here?"

"I, uh…" The boy shrugged. "I thought I could help."

"By putting yourself in danger and breaking curfew? Get in the truck. I'm taking you home." Of all the idiotic things to do with Troy on the loose.

She'd no sooner dropped the boy off at her place than her radio crackled with the spotting of another suspicious character walking the alley behind the drugstore. Shea gripped the steering wheel, her headlights cutting through the dark countryside. She radioed back. "ETA five minutes."

"Roger that," someone replied.

"Never mind," another said. "Just another stupid kid."

Shea frowned. What in Hades was going on?' "If you find another kid out past curfew, take him to the station. Something is fishy."

"Movement out by the silo west of town. Neighbor reports seeing a light."

With a groan, Shea turned the truck around and

headed that way.

The structure loomed, skeletal and rusty. Wind rattled the loose tin. Shea climbed from her truck as two motorcycle riders pulled in behind her, followed a minute later by Wyatt and one of his ranch hands.

"Eyes open," she said, pushing open the door to the silo.

Dust hung heavy in the beam of her flashlight. Beer cans littered the floor along with several camping stools. Something thumped overhead.

Shea swung her light toward a wooden ladder leading to a makeshift loft. Something shifted in the shadows. "Come down, hands up."

After a few tense seconds, a teen clamored down the ladder. "Don't shoot me."

"What are you doing in here?" Shea narrowed her eyes.

"Me and my buddies like to hang out in here."

"Aren't you aware of the curfew?" Shea kept the light on his face. "You're the third kid out tonight. Tell me what's really going on?"

The boy held a hand in front of his eyes. "We're just playing a joke, Sheriff."

"By having me and my department running around on wild goose chases?" Her voice lowered to a dangerous level. "There's a killer on the loose. Do you want to be his next victim?"

"He hasn't been killing kids." He shrugged. "We figured we were safe."

"The rest of the town isn't." She grabbed his arm and shoved him toward Wyatt. "Haul him in. I want the names of all the idiots involved in this prank, then notify the parents about what their kids have been up to."

She didn't have time for this. While they were chasing down false leads, Troy was planning his next move. She wanted to throw every one of the teens in jail. Instead, once Troy was locked up, they'd all be doing many hours of community service.

She stormed to her truck and spun gravel back to the main road. Her knuckles ached from her tight grip on the steering wheel.

Where are you, Troy?

Chapter Fifteen

Fear had taken root and spread like a malignant tumor into every corner of Misty Hollow, permeating the very atmosphere of the once-peaceful community. Residents locked their doors with multiple deadbolts and left their porch lights burning throughout the night, as if artificial illumination could somehow ward off the evil that stalked their streets. After the discovery and arrest of the pranking twins who had wasted precious resources with their juvenile games, the streets remained eerily quiet after dark except for the steady patrols of cowboys on horseback and leather-clad bikers whose engines rumbled through the silence like mechanical heartbeats.

Shea leaned heavily over the conference table, which had become completely cluttered with detailed maps of the surrounding area and the sprawling wilderness of Misty Mountain. Red circles marked every false lead they had pursued over the past week, creating a constellation of wasted effort that made her jaw clench with frustration. Her shoulders ached from hunching over documents for hours at a time, and her eyes burned with the gritty sensation that came from too many sleepless nights spent coordinating searches and fielding panicked phone calls from terrified residents.

She glanced at the sound of knocking on the conference room door and immediately frowned when she saw who was standing there. "What are you doing here? You're supposed to be resting at home."

Trevor stood in the doorway with a steaming cup of coffee in each hand, his familiar grin slightly strained but still genuine. "I thought you might need some help around here. I promise not to overdo anything or put myself in situations that could reopen my wound." He crossed the room and handed her one of the cups, the warmth seeping through the ceramic into her cold fingers.

"Thanks. At this point, I could probably use about ten of these to function normally," she admitted, wrapping both hands around the mug and inhaling the rich aroma.

"What you need is a good long sleep—at least eight hours of uninterrupted rest," Trevor said as he carefully lowered himself into one of the chairs around the table, his movements still slightly guarded to protect his healing injury.

Despite his attempt to hide his discomfort, Shea

caught the brief grimace that crossed his features as he settled into the seat. "You should have stayed home where you could rest properly instead of aggravating your wound by driving over here."

"I was getting incredibly bored sitting around the house with nothing to do but watch daytime television," Trevor replied with a dismissive wave. "Besides, you desperately need someone to help field all these false leads and panicked calls. Mrs. Hathaway phoned the station again this morning, absolutely convinced that she saw Troy sitting on her back porch casually eating a peach like he owned the place."

Shea rubbed her temples where a persistent headache had been building for the past several hours. "That's the third time this week she's called with a similar story. Yesterday she was equally certain that he was in her yard eating a ham and cheese sandwich, and the day before that it was a bag of potato chips."

"She's terrified, just like everyone else in this town," Trevor said, leaning forward and placing a gentle hand on her arm. The contact was warm and reassuring, grounding her in a way that surprised her with its intensity. "I'm here to help you in whatever way I can. Maybe not physically in terms of chasing down suspects, but I can listen to your concerns and serve as a sounding board for new ideas."

Shea nodded gratefully, realizing how much Trevor's presence meant to her during this crisis. He had become her anchor during the long nights when she returned to his house exhausted and discouraged. Through every shaken witness she described to him, through every dead end and false lead that left her feeling incompetent, he had remained steady, unmoving, and utterly loyal to both her and the investigation.

Clearing her throat to cover the emotion that was threatening to overwhelm her, she returned her attention to the maps spread across the table. "I don't want to lose you," she said quietly, the words tumbling out before she could pull them back or consider their implications.

"What did you say? I didn't quite hear you," Trevor replied, though the knowing twinkle in his eyes suggested that he had heard her perfectly well.

She glanced up to meet his gaze directly, seeing understanding and something deeper reflected there. "I said I don't want to lose you, Trevor. Not to Troy, not to anything."

Trevor's expression grew serious. "You're not going to lose me, Shea. I can promise you that."

"I'm being completely serious here," she continued, her voice cracking slightly with the strain of voicing her deepest fears. "I have this really bad feeling growing stronger every day. Troy is going to make his final move when we least expect it, when we've finally let our guard down just enough for him to slip through our defenses."

"Then we make sure we never let our guard down for even a moment," Trevor replied firmly. "We stay vigilant for as long as it takes to end this nightmare. We'll find him, Shea. Together."

The conference room door burst open without warning, and Doris rushed in with her face flushed red from exertion and obvious stress. "Do you hear all that noise? Every single phone line in the building is ringing at the same time. I desperately need help answering calls or I'm going to lose my mind."

"Answering phones is something I can handle without putting too much strain on my injury," Trevor said, pushing himself to his feet with determination. "I'll help filter out the false leads and paranoid sightings from anything that might be useful."

"Thank you both," Shea and Doris said in perfect unison, their relief evident. Phone duty shouldn't put any dangerous pressure on Trevor's healing wound, and it would free up Shea to focus on more complex aspects of the investigation. "Make sure to send some of the more credible-sounding calls directly to me," Shea added. "I could use a break from staring at these maps."

While Trevor headed out to his desk in the main bullpen area, Shea slid the conference room telephone closer to her position and began answering the endless stream of calls that continued to pour in from frightened residents.

"There was someone lurking outside my bedroom window last night," reported one elderly woman whose voice shook with terror.

"I heard heavy footsteps on my roof around three

in the morning," claimed another caller.

"My German shepherd won't stop growling and staring at the woods behind our property," added a third.

She methodically jotted down the name, address, and phone number associated with every single call, even the ones that seemed paranoid or unlikely. It would take far more time than they realistically had available for her regular deputies to personally check out each reported sighting or suspicious incident. She would have to rely heavily on the volunteer cowboys and bikers to investigate many of these leads. While they might not have formal law enforcement training or experience, they possessed enough common sense and local knowledge to determine whether a particular lead held any genuine merit or was simply the product of fear-induced imagination.

Needing a brief break from the constant stream of panicked voices, she pushed herself to her feet and stepped outside the sheriff's office into the afternoon sunlight. What she saw on Main Street made her heart sink even further. Vehicles loaded down with personal belongings and household items were driving slowly through town as families packed up their lives and moved away from Misty Hollow entirely. Other residents darted nervously from store to store, casting furtive glances in every direction as if expecting Troy to appear around every corner or emerge from every shadowy doorway.

Her mouth fell open in shock as she watched Trevor's pickup truck speed away from the back of the building and roar down Main Street with apparent urgency. He caught sight of her standing there and tapped his ear to indicate he was responding to a phone call, then disappeared around a corner before she could react.

Without a second thought, she raced to her patrol car and immediately called him using the vehicle's Bluetooth system. "Please tell me you're not pursuing a potentially dangerous lead in your current medical condition."

"I am following up on something that sounds legitimate," Trevor's voice came through the speakers with determination. "The last call I received was from a woman who claimed Troy was actually at her location right now. She described him in enough accurate detail to warrant checking it out immediately."

"Don't speed off and lose me in traffic," Shea commanded, trying to keep her voice calm despite her rising panic. "I need that address right now."

As Trevor rattled off the street address, she frantically typed it into her GPS navigation system, keeping one hand on the steering wheel while her eyes flicked constantly between the GPS screen and the road ahead. When she looked up from the device to focus on driving, Trevor's truck was nowhere in sight.

Shea slammed her fist against the steering wheel hard enough to make her knuckles ache. She wanted to throttle him for taking such a reckless risk. When she still couldn't spot his vehicle after several minutes of searching, she grabbed her radio and tried to raise him. "Trevor, are you on scene yet? Please respond."

Nothing but static answered her.

She tried again with increasing desperation. "Trevor, please confirm your status."

Still complete silence from his end.

When she finally reached the GPS coordinates he had provided, she found herself staring at a clearly uninhabited, ramshackle house with a partially caved-in roof and windows that had been boarded up for what appeared to be years. Trevor's truck sat in the overgrown driveway with the driver's side door hanging wide open, which sent ice water through her veins.

"Trevor!" she shouted, drawing her service weapon as she approached the abandoned structure. Shea moved carefully toward the house, her boots crunching loudly on broken glass and dried leaves that littered the front yard. With her heart lodged firmly in her throat, she pushed open the front door that was hanging precariously on rusted hinges.

She burst into the dim interior and nearly tripped over Trevor, who was sitting on the floor holding his head in obvious pain.

Blood trickled down the side of his face from what appeared to be a significant head wound. "He was here," Trevor groaned, his voice slightly slurred. "Troy was here."

'Are you injured anywhere else besides your head?" Shea demanded, kneeling beside him to assess his condition while keeping her weapon ready.

"No, I don't think so," Trevor replied, sitting up slowly and wincing at the movement. "He came out of nowhere and hit me with something solid. I could see that his arm is still in some kind of makeshift sling, which put him at a disadvantage in terms of mobility. He struck me with whatever he was using as a splint and then ran immediately—"

A floorboard creaked ominously somewhere overhead, cutting off his explanation mid-sentence.

"Stay down and don't move," Shea whispered, creeping cautiously toward the staircase that led to the upper floor. On the wall beside the stairs, smeared in what appeared to be fresh blood, were the words "I SEE YOU, SHERIFF" written in Troy's familiar handwriting.

A heavy thump sounded from directly above them, followed by the sound of something dragging across the floor. Her throat tight with growing dread, Shea took the wooden steps two at a time, her weapon raised and ready. The upstairs hallway reeked of decay and mildew, and the stagnant air immediately triggered her asthma. Her lungs seized and her breathing became labored. She quickly pulled her rescue inhaler from her pocket and took two puffs of medication before continuing her search.

She burst into the first bedroom with her gun

raised, but found nothing except tattered curtains fluttering in the breeze from an open window. Moving quickly to the window, she peered out just in time to see Troy staggering away from the house, favoring his injured arm but moving with surprising speed. He paused at the edge of the woods, turned back toward the house, waved mockingly in her direction, and then disappeared into the dense forest.

The radio clipped to her duty belt suddenly crackled to life. "Sheriff, you need to get over to Lucy's Diner as soon as possible," Doris's voice reported with obvious stress. "The townspeople are gathering there, and they're in an uproar. They're not happy that no one has seen you responding to any of the calls that have been coming in all day."

Shea stifled a groan of frustration. The last thing she needed right now was an angry mob questioning her competence. "I'm on my way there now."

Back at her patrol car, she helped Trevor clean the blood from his face using bottled water and tissues from her first aid kit. The head wound looked painful but not life-threatening. "You need to go home and rest," she told him firmly.

"No," Trevor replied with stubborn determination. "You're going to need moral support when you face that crowd. They're scared and looking for someone to blame." He gingerly touched the growing lump on his head and winced. "Good thing I inherited a thick skull from Dad's side of the family. Troy hit me with the wooden stick he was using as a makeshift splint for his broken arm."

The interior of Lucy's Diner was packed wall-to-wall with agitated residents. Every head turned as Shea and Trevor entered together, and numerous pairs of eyes immediately focused on the apparent head injury Trevor was sporting.

"If the sheriff can't even protect her deputy," someone called out from the back of the room, "what chance do the rest of us ordinary citizens have?"

"My ten-year-old daughter is so terrified that she's sleeping with a kitchen knife hidden under her pillow," a distraught woman shouted.

"I'm starting to think you're in way over your head with this situation, Sheriff," another voice added. "Maybe it's time to call in the state police or federal agents."

Maybe they were right, Shea thought with a sinking heart. Perhaps she was completely out of her depth and endangering everyone by trying to handle Troy Bolton with insufficient resources. She opened her mouth to defend her actions, but Trevor beat her to it.

"Now hold on just a minute, folks," Trevor said, his voice carrying the authority that came from years of respected service to the community. "The only reason I'm still alive and standing here today is because of Sheriff Callahan's competence and dedication. There isn't anyone better qualified for this job anywhere in the state."

His features hardened as he surveyed the crowd. "Look at how she's recruited additional help from volunteers who know this area intimately. You all trusted Sheriff Westbrook implicitly when he held this position, and he recommended Shea for the job when he retired. He wouldn't have done that if he didn't have complete confidence in her abilities."

Several people in the crowd looked away from Trevor's stern gaze, clearly feeling chastened by his words. "Troy Bolton isn't going to stop his killing spree until he gets exactly what he wants, and what he wants is me. He's no longer actively hunting any of you as potential victims. He's reached the final phase of his countdown, which means his focus has narrowed to very specific targets."

Trevor paused to let that information sink in. "So how about you all take a deep breath, go back to your homes, and let the sheriff do her job instead of undermining her efforts with this kind of panic?"

Shea stepped forward to address the crowd directly. "I know every single one of you is scared right now. I'm frightened too, but letting that fear turn us against each other is exactly what Troy Bolton wants to achieve. He feeds on chaos and terror."

Murmurs of agreement began to ripple through the assembled residents.

"Troy attacked Deputy Bolton again today and left me a threatening message written in blood on the wall of an abandoned house," she continued. "But the important thing to understand is that he isn't hunting any of you anymore. His obsession has narrowed to a very small number of specific targets."

"So, what exactly are you planning to do about this situation?" a man called out from the back of the crowded room.

"Whatever it takes to end this nightmare permanently," Shea replied, enunciating each word with steel-hard determination. "But I need all of you to let me do my job without constant interference. I need you to trust me and my judgment."

She paused to survey the faces looking back at her. "God help me not to disappoint any of you or let you down when you need me most."

"All right then, Sheriff," the diner's chef said as he stepped out from behind the kitchen counter. "What do you need from us?"

"I need your continued vigilance and cooperation. I need everyone to keep their eyes open and stay alert. But please stop calling the station with false alarms and imaginary sightings," Shea said firmly. "You all know exactly what Troy Bolton looks like from the photographs that have been circulated. Only call us with a positive identification or genuinely suspicious activity."

She looked around the room. "Continue to observe the curfew strictly. If we all work together as a unified community, Troy will have nowhere to hide and nowhere to run."

The room erupted in sustained applause, and Shea felt some of the tension leave her shoulders.

~

"Well, that ended up going much better than I expected," Trevor said as they walked toward his house. "I couldn't be prouder of the way you handled those frightened people."

"It was touch and go there for a minute," Shea replied. "Thanks for backing me up when they started getting hostile. Your support means everything to me."

She entered his house first, then stepped aside for Heidi to conduct her usual security sweep to make sure no one was waiting in hiding. When the German shepherd didn't give any warning signals, Shea and Trevor headed for the kitchen.

"It's going to feel wonderful to go to bed at a decent hour tonight," Shea said with genuine anticipation. "I could easily sleep for ten hours straight."

"Let me heat some soup for dinner," Trevor offered, pulling cans of potato soup from the pantry. "It's not much of a gourmet meal, but it'll fill us up. Then we can crash in front of the television and try to decompress. If we fall asleep on the couch, so be it."

"Let's find something boring to watch," Shea suggested, removing her duty belt and holster and setting them within easy reach on the kitchen table. "Can you promise me something important?"

"Of course," Trevor replied, glancing over his

shoulder from the stove.

"Don't ever do what you did today again. Don't respond to calls without me."

Trevor frowned. "You mean follow up on leads?"

"Yes, exactly that. Not without me as backup. It would have taken only a minute for you to wait and let me get in your truck with you. Maybe if we'd gone together, Troy wouldn't have been able to ambush you."

"Or maybe he would have had both of us exactly where he wanted us," Trevor countered. "Once Troy gets his hands on you, this whole thing is over. He knows I'll do anything to save you, which means he'll have his number six and seven victims. Without you as bait, he can't complete his twisted mission."

Uncertainty flickered in Shea's eyes. "I can't let you face him alone when the final confrontation comes."

"I won't face him completely alone, but you can't be there until the timing is right," Trevor said as he dumped the soup into a saucepan and turned on the burner. "Not until there's zero chance of him escaping or using you as leverage against me."

He gestured toward the cupboard. "There are some crackers in there if you want them."

"What's our actual plan then?" Shea asked, setting the box of saltines on the table.

"We wait for him to make contact directly. I don't expect that to happen for at least another day or two. His broken arm will have to heal significantly more before he's physically capable of the kind of fight he's planning."

"Then now is the perfect time to find him while he's still vulnerable," Shea said with growing excitement. "He'll be much easier to apprehend if he's dealing with pain and limited mobility. Let's get everyone we can find scouring Misty Mountain starting first thing tomorrow morning. Troy can't stay hidden forever, and he's got to eat regularly, which means your brother will need access to a store eventually."

"He'll drive to some remote location outside our jurisdiction," Trevor predicted. "Some backwoods place where they might not have seen his picture on the news broadcasts. You and I should focus our search on those types of isolated establishments."

Shea nodded enthusiastically. "It feels good to have a solid, proactive plan finally. To know how we can put some real pressure on him instead of just reacting to his moves. We'll flush him out of hiding like the dangerous snake he is."

~

Troy sat hunched in the shadows of a half-collapsed hunting shack deep in the wilderness, his injured arm throbbing with constant pain that had become his unwelcome companion. The ache had intensified after he'd used the makeshift splint to bash Trevor's skull, but the satisfaction of drawing blood from his brother had been worth the additional agony. The pain was now a constant presence in his life, but so was the burning hunger for revenge that consumed his thoughts.

If his injury hadn't weakened him, he would have stayed at that abandoned house and finished off both the interfering sheriff and his traitorous brother. But patience was a virtue he had learned to cultivate during his years of imprisonment.

Not yet, he reminded himself. He still needed more time for his arm to heal properly.

He had been systematically watching and listening to his enemies' activities, keeping track of the sheriff's movements and her deputies' patrol patterns using a ham radio he had stolen from a house where the occupants were away on vacation. The device allowed him to monitor their radio communications and stay one step ahead of their search efforts.

The entire town was saturated with the kind of fear that nourished his twisted soul. Fear that he had personally created and cultivated. The knowledge filled him with a renewed sense of purpose and power. He literally fed on their terror, yearned for it like an addict craved his next fix.

On the wall directly in front of him, he had carefully nailed a detailed map of Misty Hollow that he had stolen from the library. He had marked all the familiar and significant locations with red ink—the sheriff's house, his brother's property, the sheriff's office, the school, the diner where people gathered to voice their fears.

But it was the name he had scratched deep into the wooden wall that commanded most of his attention. "Shea," carved in letters three inches tall.

He picked up his hunting knife and carefully carved his brother's name directly underneath hers in equally large letters. "Trevor."

"She'll see soon enough," he whispered to the empty room, his voice carrying the promise of violence to come. "They all will witness my final triumph."

Chapter Sixteen

With the vast wilderness of Misty Mountain being systematically searched by teams of volunteers, experienced ranch hands from the Rocking W, and members of Dave Wakes' motorcycle gang, Shea and Trevor had decided to take a completely different tactical approach to tracking down Troy Bolton. In Shea's personal pickup truck, with Heidi lying alertly in the back bed, they had planned to spend the day visiting the scattered collection of mom-and-pop stores that dotted the remote areas of the mountain like forgotten relics of a simpler time.

These were the establishments that served the hill people, the families and individuals who had chosen to live far from civilization's conveniences and complications. The owners of these tiny roadside businesses knew everyone and everything that happened within their sphere of influence on Misty Mountain. If Troy had been moving through their territory, seeking supplies or shelter, someone would have noticed.

Shea's truck rattled and bounced down a narrow logging road that hadn't been adequately maintained in years, the suspension working overtime to absorb the impact of deep ruts and scattered rocks. Ancient sunlight filtered through the dense forest canopy above them, casting constantly shifting beams of golden light across the dusty dirt road. Trevor held a hand-drawn map in his lap, marked with dozens of X's indicating every location that was rumored to have a roof and a functional cash register, no matter how primitive the operation might be.

Their first stop was a rustic log cabin that appeared to have been built sometime in the 1940s, complete with a single gas pump that leaned at a precarious angle and looked like it might topple over in the next strong wind. A hand-painted wooden sign reading "Rupert's Fuel & Bait" hung from a crooked post, the lettering so faded and weathered that it was barely legible. The entire establishment resembled something from a bygone era, forgotten by progress and overlooked by time.

Leaving Heidi to maintain watch from her position in the truck bed, Shea approached the cabin and pushed open a screen door that had seen better decades. A faint jingle from an overhead bell announced their arrival to whoever might be inside, the sound unexpectedly cheerful in the wilderness setting.

She jumped slightly when the spring-loaded screen door slammed shut behind Trevor with a loud bang that echoed through the small interior.

An elderly man with graying hair that looked like it hadn't encountered a comb in at least a decade stood behind a counter that was cluttered with an eclectic collection of dusty fishing lures, packages of beef jerky, and a locked display case containing various sizes of hunting and utility knives. His weathered face bore the deep lines that came from a lifetime of outdoor work and mountain living.

"Howdy, folks," he said in the slow, measured way of people who weren't accustomed to unexpected visitors. "What can I do for you today?"

Shea introduced herself and Trevor, showing her badge to establish their official credentials. "We're looking for someone who might have passed through this area within the last couple of days." She handed him a flier bearing Troy's official prison mugshot. "Have you seen this man?"

The old man—presumably Rupert—adjusted a pair of wire-rimmed glasses that had been repaired multiple times with electrical tape and studied the photograph with the careful attention it deserved. "Nope, can't say that I have." He paused, then looked more closely at the image. "Definitely not... oh, wait just a minute here. Would this fellow happen to be sporting a broken arm or some kind of injury to his upper body?"

"Yes, that's exactly right," Shea replied, shooting a hopeful glance toward Trevor. Finally, they had found someone who had actually encountered Troy.

"Well then, yes, he came in here right as I was getting ready to close up shop a few nights ago," Rupert said, his expression growing more serious. "Bought himself a heavy-duty flashlight and several packages of dried food—the kind backpackers use. Didn't say much of anything during the transaction, just pointed at what he wanted and paid cash."

The old man shook his head with obvious discomfort. "But I'll tell you what really stuck with me about that encounter. This fellow had what I call shark eyes—you know, completely dead and emotionless. Made my skin crawl something fierce. I kept my hand on the loaded shotgun I keep under this counter the entire time he was in my store."

"Did you happen to see which direction he headed when he left your establishment?" Trevor asked, trying to keep the urgency out of his voice.

"Nope, I'm afraid I didn't," Rupert replied, then squinted more closely at Trevor's face. "You know, you favor that man quite a bit. Y'all related somehow?"

Trevor's jaw tightened almost imperceptibly. "Something like that."

Shea quickly handed the store owner one of her business cards. "Please call me immediately if you see him again, and whatever you do, be extremely careful around him. This man is very dangerous and has already killed multiple people."

"Is he the one I've been hearing about on the ham radio networks?" Rupert asked, referring to the informal communication system that many rural residents used to stay in contact with each other and the outside world.

"Yes, sir, that's him," Shea confirmed.

The old man tucked his tongue thoughtfully into his cheek and nodded slowly. "Well then, I think it's time for me to take an extended vacation. I'll close up shop and reopen once you folks have caught this dangerous individual." He followed them to the door and made a point of turning the deadbolt and hanging a "Closed" sign in the window behind them.

"At least now we know for certain that Troy is somewhere in this general area," Trevor said as he climbed into the passenger side of Shea's truck. "But unfortunately, it's a vast area with countless places where someone could hide indefinitely. There are natural caves, abandoned buildings from old mining operations, hunting cabins that haven't been used in years..."

They would never be able to search every possible hiding spot before Troy decided to end his cat-and-mouse game and come for his final victims. "We'll keep looking systematically," Shea said with determination she didn't entirely feel. Maybe they would get lucky and find Troy dead from an infection related to his broken arm. She immediately felt guilty for entertaining such a thought. Regardless of his crimes, Troy was still technically a human being, even if barely.

A sickness had clearly taken root in Trevor's brother—a fundamental malfunction of his basic humanity that she didn't believe could be cured through any known medical or psychiatric intervention. Troy appeared to be evil to his very core, most likely born with whatever genetic or developmental abnormality had created his complete lack of empathy and conscience. Which meant that in some sense, he couldn't help being what he had become. A maximum-security psychiatric prison was probably where he belonged for the rest of his natural life.

Further up the mountain ridge, their second stop was an establishment called "Betty's Bait, Tackle, and Mercantile" that looked like it had been frozen in time somewhere around 1950. A cracked and faded Coca-Cola advertising sign swung lazily on a rusted chain in the afternoon breeze. When they stepped inside, the interior smelled of wood polish, pipe tobacco, and the sharp tang of pickle brine from large jars sitting on the counter.

A middle-aged woman with steel-gray hair and sharp, intelligent eyes stood behind the counter, immediately alert to their presence. "I ain't seen you folks around here before," she said in a tone that wasn't quite suspicious but wary.

Shea repeated her introductions and official credentials, then handed the woman Troy's photograph.

"We're searching for this individual. Has he been in your store recently?"

"Yep, sure has," the woman replied without hesitation. "Came in exactly three nights ago, right at closing time when I was getting ready to lock up. Bought several cans of food and multiple bottles of water, paid in cash just like your other fellow said."

She reached under the counter and retrieved something wrapped in brown paper. "He also said that if anyone came looking for him, I should give them this." She handed Trevor a photograph. "Said you'd know exactly what it meant."

Trevor studied the image, his expression growing grim. "It's our childhood home," he said, showing the picture to Shea. The photograph showed a modest two-story house with a white picket fence and a large oak tree in the front yard—the kind of idyllic family home that belonged in a Norman Rockwell painting.

Betty shook her head with obvious distaste. "I knew the moment he walked into my store exactly who he was. I'd seen his picture on the television news broadcasts. If he had told me to stand on my head and sing the national anthem, I would have done it without question. There ain't no way I'm going to do anything that might get myself killed by a maniac like that."

She leaned across the counter and lowered her voice to a conspiratorial whisper. "I'm telling you, anger just rolled off that man in waves like heat from a furnace. That kind of deep, consuming anger is something truly dangerous. I didn't even make him pay for the food he took—I just wanted him out of my store as quickly as possible."

"You did the right thing, ma'am," Shea assured her, handing over a business card identical to the one she'd given Rupert. "If you see him again, don't try to confront him or detain him. Just call me immediately and try to avoid any contact with him."

"Sheriff, if I see that devil coming down the road again, I'm running in the opposite direction as fast as these old legs can carry me," Betty declared emphatically.

"Did you happen to notice which direction he went when he left your store?" Trevor asked.

Betty pointed toward a trail that led higher up the mountain, disappearing into the dense forest that covered the upper elevations.

Their final planned stop was a ramshackle auto repair shop that had been built inside what appeared to be a converted barn. The structure appeared to be on the verge of collapse in the next strong storm, but it was still apparently functional. Inside, an impressive wall of hunting rifles sat locked behind protective mesh wire, and behind a counter constructed from wooden shipping pallets, a man in grimy overalls was cleaning his fingernails with a large hunting knife.

"Ain't seen him around here," the man said before they had even finished showing him Troy's photograph. He barely glanced at the image and made no eye contact whatsoever with either Shea or Trevor, which immediately raised red flags about his credibility.

"But I will say that someone was here sometime during the night," he continued, still focused on his fingernails. "You'll find fresh tracks outside if you know where to look for them."

Realizing that this individual either couldn't or wouldn't provide any useful information, Shea thanked him curtly and marched outside with Trevor following close behind. They spent several minutes walking the perimeter of the property, carefully examining the ground for any signs of recent activity.

Finally, Shea knelt beside a faint but distinct shoe print in the mud underneath an outdoor water faucet. The impression wasn't complete, but it was fresh— probably made within the last twelve hours based on the condition of the surrounding soil.

"Could be his footprint, I suppose," Shea said, though she wasn't entirely convinced. "The size looks about right."

Trevor crouched down to examine the print more closely, then stood up slowly, exhaling in frustration. "How does any of this fit into his psychological game? I can understand his need to acquire food and water— those are basic survival necessities. But why leave me that childhood photograph? Why visit an auto repair shop in the middle of absolute nowhere that doesn't appear to sell anything he would need?"

He shook his head in bewilderment. "None of it

makes any logical sense."

"Maybe that's exactly the point," Shea suggested. "He wants to keep us confused and off-balance. I don't think his actions are supposed to make rational sense to us. Troy is operating according to his twisted internal logic."

~

The silence between Trevor and Shea grew heavier and more oppressive as they drove back toward town along the winding mountain roads. Shea glanced in his direction frequently, as if she wanted to understand the complex thoughts that were churning through his mind. When he could successfully decipher those thoughts himself, he would be happy to share them with her.

"He's deliberately taunting you with these little games," she observed, tilting her head to study his profile. "Every move he makes is designed to get under your skin psychologically."

"I know that," Trevor replied, his voice tight with controlled frustration.

"How are you holding up through all this—both physically in terms of your healing injuries and mentally in terms of the emotional pressure?" Shea asked with genuine concern.

"I'm fine," Trevor said, though his jaw ached from clenching his teeth so tightly for the past several hours.

"Well, at least while he's leading us on these elaborate wild goose chases around the county, he isn't actively killing anyone," Shea pointed out, trying to find some positive aspect to their situation.

"There's that," Trevor agreed. They were getting closer to Troy's location, inch by painstaking inch, but that was exactly what his brother wanted them to do. Get close enough to think they were making progress, then watch him slip away to start the process all over again from a new location.

Back at the sheriff's station, Shea stood in front of a large pull-down map of the entire area and carefully marked off all the places the two of them had visited during their day-long search. She also added colored circles around larger areas when radio calls came in reporting that the various teams patrolling different sections of the mountain had cleared those zones without finding any trace of their quarry.

Trevor crossed his arms and studied the map with intense concentration, trying to spot patterns or gaps in their search coverage. Where are you hiding, you bastard? He couldn't envision his brother simply running ahead of the organized search parties like a common fugitive, but then again, he was beginning to realize that he didn't know Troy nearly as well as he had thought. Maybe playing an elaborate game of hide-and-seek with armed pursuers was precisely the kind of twisted entertainment that Troy found enjoyable.

How much longer would Troy continue this psychological torture before he stopped playing games and killed someone else? The uncertainty was almost as maddening as the threat itself.

The healing stitches in Trevor's side pulled painfully, and he gingerly lowered himself into a nearby chair to ease the discomfort. His gaze wandered across the map until it landed on a particular spot that had a circle drawn around it, indicating that the area had been searched. "Wait a minute. Why hasn't anyone gone to investigate the large lake near that circled area?"

Shea glanced in his direction. "A helicopter made two complete passes over that entire region. The pilot reported that he didn't see any signs of human activity."

"There's an abandoned campground right on the shore of that lake," Trevor said, his interest growing. "The main host's cabin burned down several years ago in an accidental fire, but last I heard, the old barn was still standing and structurally sound."

"Is it worth investigating?" Shea asked. "There's no one available to send on another search mission right now."

"I'm up for checking it out personally," Trevor said, pushing his physical discomfort aside through sheer force of will. He would rest later, after his brother was finally behind bars where he belonged.

Shea didn't look convinced that Trevor was in any condition for more fieldwork, but she didn't try to talk him out of accompanying her. "How far is it from here?"

"Forty, maybe forty-five minutes if we take the

direct route through the forest service roads," Trevor estimated.

"Good. That gives you time to take a nap during the drive," Shea said with a faint smile tugging at her lips. 'I've already copied the GPS coordinates from the map. You look like you're about to collapse from exhaustion."

"I told you, I'm fine," Trevor protested, though his body was telling a different story.

"Sure, you are," Shea replied with skepticism. "We'll scour this one location, and then you're going straight home to rest properly. No argument."

To his surprise, Trevor found that he had no trouble falling asleep while Shea navigated the rough roads leading to the old campground. The steady vibration of the truck and the security of having her as his driver allowed him to relax his vigilance for a few precious minutes, finally.

He had stayed at this campground once during his Boy Scout days, back when Troy had still pretended to be a normal kid participating in normal childhood activities. The place looked dramatically different now—abandoned, overgrown, and somehow sad in the way that forgotten places often appeared.

"I should have thought of this location much earlier," Trevor said as they climbed out of the truck. "Troy would know about this place. We were in the same Boy Scout troop for two years before his behavior became too disruptive for the troop leaders to handle."

"I can't imagine him as a child, much less as a Boy Scout," Shea said, standing in front of the truck and staring at the dilapidated barn that dominated the overgrown clearing.

"This was once a genuinely beautiful place," Trevor explained, feeling a pang of nostalgia for simpler times. "There used to be a sprawling log cabin with multiple rooms that could accommodate church retreats and summer day camps. It sat right near the lake shore until it was destroyed in a kitchen fire. The elderly owners didn't have the financial resources to rebuild, or maybe they just lost the desire to continue operating the campground. They were both getting up there in age."

He moved cautiously toward the barn, stepped carefully inside the dim interior, and waited for his eyes to adjust to the reduced lighting. "I think we've definitely come to the right place this time."

Clear evidence of recent habitation was scattered across the dust-covered floor: a sleeping bag that still held the impression of a human body, empty food cans and water bottles, candy bar wrappers, and various other pieces of camping gear. A small kerosene burner sat next to where Troy had obviously been sleeping, probably used for heating food and providing minimal warmth during cool mountain nights.

Trevor knelt down and pressed his hand against the sleeping bag. The fabric was cool to the touch, but not completely cold. "He hasn't been here for several hours, but not more than that."

Shea moved to examine the rest of the barn's interior. "I think I found what he used to create a splint for his broken arm," she said, nudging a broken shovel handle with the toe of her boot. "There's also an empty whiskey bottle over here."

"Probably used the alcohol to numb the pain while he reset the bone," Trevor said, his hands automatically folding into tight fists at the thought of his brother's self-treatment. Once again, they had arrived too late to apprehend him.

"Should we hide somewhere in here and wait for him to come back?" Trevor suggested. "This is obviously his current base of operations."

"We could definitely try that approach," Shea agreed. "There are plenty of empty horse stalls where we could conceal ourselves effectively. I can move the truck to a location where he won't spot it immediately, then contact the office to let them know our exact location in case we need emergency backup."

Trevor's phone suddenly buzzed with an incoming call. He pulled the device from his pocket and glanced at the screen display. Unknown number—which could only mean one thing. "Deputy Bolton speaking."

Static filled the connection for several seconds, then a chillingly familiar voice came through clearly. "How's the reminiscing going, dear brother?"

Trevor spun around to face Shea and mouthed the words "He's watching us" while pointing toward the barn's open doorway.

"I think it's time we ended this elaborate game, don't you?" Troy's voice carried a tone of mock friendliness that made Trevor's skin crawl. "You know exactly where this whole thing started twenty years ago, don't you?"

Trevor could hear the sound of wind on the connection, indicating that Troy was outside and probably very close to their current location. He stepped cautiously from the barn as a cool breeze kicked up, stirring the leaves and making every shadow seem potentially threatening.

"Meet me where it all started two decades ago," Troy continued, his voice taking on a more serious and commanding tone. "And Trevor? If you don't show up alone and on time, I'll start killing random people in town just for the fun of it. I'm growing very tired of this particular game, and I'm ready to begin a new and much more entertaining one."

The line went dead with an ominous click.

"What exactly did he say?" Shea asked, joining Trevor outside the barn with her hand resting on her service weapon.

Trevor took a deep breath, knowing that his next words would determine the course of everything that followed. "He wants me to go home," he said carefully.

"When does he want you there?" Shea asked.

Trevor turned away slightly so she wouldn't be able to see the lie forming in his eyes. "He didn't specify an exact time," he said, though they both knew that Troy had undoubtedly been precise about his expectations and timeline.

The truth was that Troy wanted him home immediately, and Trevor was already calculating how long it would take him to drive there and what kind of head start he could get before Shea figured out what he planned to do.

Chapter Seventeen

Shortly after midnight, when the house had settled into what appeared to be peaceful silence, Trevor quietly flushed the toilet without actually using it, then carefully snuck out of the house through the back door. He hoped desperately that Shea would assume he had returned to bed after using the restroom and wouldn't discover his absence until morning. She would undoubtedly come after him once she realized what he had done—of that he had absolutely no doubt. But maybe, if luck was on his side for once, he would have finished his deadly business with Troy before she could arrive and put herself in mortal danger.

Moving with the stealth that his law enforcement training had taught him, Trevor put his pickup truck in neutral. He pushed it silently down the gravel driveway before hopping behind the wheel and starting the engine only when he was far enough away that the sound wouldn't wake anyone in the house. As he drove through the empty streets toward the interstate, he accepted the grim reality that only one of the Bolton twins would be walking out of their childhood home alive. He wasn't foolish enough to think he could somehow overpower Troy, handcuff him, and haul him peacefully to the police station like a common criminal. No, his psychotic twin would rather die fighting than submit to capture, and he would gladly take Trevor with him into whatever hell awaited them both.

Trevor's only goal that night was to keep Shea from dying at the hands of his brother. If that meant sacrificing his own life in the process, then so be it. She had too much to offer the world, too much good left to accomplish, to have her light snuffed out by a madman's obsession.

Two hours of hard driving later, fighting fatigue and the constant throb of his healing wounds, Trevor pulled slowly onto the familiar street where he had grown up during what now seemed like someone else's childhood. The Bolton family home loomed before him in the darkness, tired and rotting like a diseased tooth in the mouth of the neighborhood. No one had been willing to purchase the house of a serial killer after his parents' deaths, and the structure had been left to decay slowly under the weight of its terrible history.

The very air around the property felt heavy with accumulated evil as Trevor climbed the sagging porch steps that had once supported the feet of two innocent children playing together. His heart hammered so loudly in his ears that he was certain Troy would be able to hear it from inside the house. The wooden boards of the porch creaked ominously under his weight, each sound seeming to announce his arrival like a funeral bell.

He placed one hand on his service weapon for reassurance, then forced himself to exhale slowly and steadily as he pushed open the front door and stepped across the threshold into the suffocating darkness of his past.

Decades of abandonment had left their mark on the interior. Dust hung thick in the stagnant air like a shroud, and the entire house reeked of decay and mildew. As his eyes gradually adjusted to the dim light filtering through broken windows, Trevor could make out the remnants of furniture that had been left behind when the house was abandoned—broken chairs, a collapsed dining table, peeling wallpaper that curled away from the walls like diseased skin.

His gaze inevitably settled on his father's old recliner, the same chair where the man had sat every evening after work to read his newspaper and watch television with his family. Now the chair was nothing but a skeleton of its former self, with stuffing hanging out of multiple tears in the arms and seat like exposed intestines. Sitting casually in that chair, as if he owned the place, was Troy.

A hunting knife sat balanced carefully across his knee, its blade catching occasional glints of moonlight from the window. A crooked, knowing smile stretched his lips in an expression that held no warmth whatsoever. "I was beginning to think you'd decided not to show up after all, but then I remembered how you always used to follow me around when we were kids. At least until you decided you were too good for your brother."

"I'm here now," Trevor said, his voice steady despite the fear coursing through his system. "Let's finish this once and for all."

Troy held up one hand in a mockingly casual gesture. "Not so fast, dear brother. We haven't seen each other in twenty years. Let's take a few minutes to catch up properly." His eyes glinted with malevolent intelligence in the pale moonlight streaming through the window. "First things first, though. Drop that gun you're carrying. I've got someone positioned with a clear shot at your lovely sheriff if you don't comply with my instructions immediately."

Trevor's blood turned to ice water. "You're bluffing. There's no way you could have coordinated something like that."

"Am I bluffing?" Troy asked with a casual shrug that somehow managed to be deeply threatening. "Is that a gamble you're willing to take with Sheriff Callahan's life?"

After a moment of agonizing hesitation, Trevor slowly bent down and placed his service weapon on the dusty floor, the metal making a soft clicking sound against the hardwood.

"Excellent. Now kick it away from yourself so we don't have any unfortunate accidents."

A well-aimed nudge of Trevor's foot sent the gun skidding across the floor until it came to rest against the far wall, well out of his reach.

"Much better," Troy said with obvious satisfaction. "Now I'd like you to listen carefully to what I have to say before your backup arrives to try and take me away. We may not have much time together."

Trevor squared his shoulders and remained silent, not wanting to hear whatever twisted justification his brother was about to offer for his crimes.

"Six victims, Trevor," Troy began, his disturbing smile never wavering. "That's how many I successfully eliminated before my unfortunate incarceration. I remember each of their faces with perfect clarity, especially the fear that filled their eyes in those final moments. Each and every one of them."

He paused, as if savoring the memories. "They were all boys on the verge of manhood, but despite what you've always believed, dear brother, they weren't innocent victims. They were monsters in the making, future predators who would have gone on to hurt countless others if I hadn't stopped them. You have no idea what I could see in their eyes when I looked closely enough."

A low chuckle escaped from Troy's throat. "I see that same darkness now when I look into your eyes.

You want to kill me, don't you? You want to wrap your hands around my throat and squeeze until I stop breathing."

"You hunted those boys like they were nothing more than prey animals," Trevor said, his voice thick with disgust.

"I don't really expect someone like you to understand the complexities of what I was doing," Troy replied with condescending patience. "After all, we were both quite young at the time. But I'm sure you remember that day in our garage with the neighbor kid, don't you?"

Trevor felt his resolve waver slightly as a long-buried memory began to tug at the edges of his consciousness. There had been an incident when they were very small—maybe five years old—involving an older boy from down the street who had...

"Ah, I can see you're beginning to remember," Troy said with obvious satisfaction. "I came to your rescue that day when that eight-year-old was touching you inappropriately, and I beat him almost senseless for daring to lay his filthy hands on my brother. He ran home crying with his face covered in blood, but nothing ever came of it. I promised you that day that I would kill anyone who posed a threat to our family."

Troy's expression grew more serious. "It turns out that I genuinely enjoyed the act of violence, the power that came with taking control of a situation. But you turned your back on me after that, didn't you? You made sure our parents showered all their love and attention on you while treating me like I was some kind of dangerous animal that needed to be contained."

He stood up slowly, the knife still gripped firmly in his right hand. "You were always the good son, the one who could do no wrong. Me? I was cast in the role of the evil twin from the very beginning. But a parent is supposed to love their child unconditionally, regardless of their flaws or mistakes."

Trevor stared at his brother in amazement. "You became a cold-blooded killer who murdered innocent children. How could anyone love something like that?"

"I was their firstborn son!" Troy snarled, his carefully maintained composure finally cracking. "I entered this world seven minutes before you did, which should have made me the favored one. I should have killed you while we were still sharing the womb and saved everyone a lot of trouble."

"You can try to kill me now if you want," Trevor said with more bravado than he felt. "You failed once twenty years ago, and you'll fail again tonight."

"Oh, you think you can reach that gun before I get to you?" Troy asked, his teeth flashing in a predatory grin. "By all means, go ahead and try. It'll be entertaining to watch you scramble around desperately before I put you out of your misery."

Without hesitation, Trevor lunged desperately for his weapon, knowing it was probably a futile gesture but unable to stand there and wait for death.

Troy tackled him before he could cover even half the distance, and they crashed together into an empty bookcase that had once held their mother's collection of romance novels. The impact sent them both sprawling, and Trevor felt the burning sensation of the knife blade slashing across his shoulder, opening up a deep gash that immediately began soaking his shirt with blood.

He bit back a cry of pain and drew back his fist, then delivered a solid punch that caught Troy squarely in the jaw. The blow barely seemed to faze his brother, who moved with the mechanical efficiency of someone who had spent years fighting for survival in the brutal environment of maximum-security prison. Troy had become something inhuman during his incarceration—a predator who killed without emotion or hesitation.

Troy slammed Trevor violently into the wall with enough force to crack the drywall behind him. The impact drove all the air from Trevor's lungs and left him gasping helplessly.

"You never were much of a fighter," Troy taunted as Trevor struggled to catch his breath. "Always the scared little boy hiding behind mommy's skirt."

Trevor scrambled desperately away from his attacker, diving awkwardly over the remains of their family's old coffee table in another futile attempt to reach his discarded weapon. Troy tackled him from behind before he could complete the maneuver and drove his knee viciously into Trevor's spine, sending waves of agony through his already injured torso.

"Did you think you could come here and stop me?" Troy laughed, the sound completely devoid of human warmth. "You don't have the guts to hurt anyone, much less kill them. You're the same pathetic weakling you were when we were teenagers."

He flipped Trevor over onto his back and raised the knife above his head, then pressed the razor-sharp blade against his brother's exposed throat. "This is almost too easy, dear brother. I expected more of a challenge from someone with your law enforcement training."

"Just do it and get it over with," Trevor sneered, trying to project defiance even as he felt the cold metal biting into his skin. "They're coming for you, you know. You didn't cover your tracks as well as you think you did. You never could."

Troy paused, his right eye beginning to twitch with what might have been uncertainty or rage. "I didn't come here planning to run away. I came to finish what I started twenty years ago. But there's a problem—the sheriff isn't here yet to play her assigned part in my grand finale. You aren't supposed to be victim number six. '

"So what?" Trevor asked, genuinely confused. "Why does it matter what number I am in your sick countdown?"

Troy's expression grew almost philosophical. "Don't you understand? We entered this world together as twins, sharing the same womb, breathing the same air. It's only fitting that we should leave it together as well. That's the kind of poetic justice that gives meaning to everything I've done."

"Spending eternity with you is the last thing I want," Trevor snarled, bucking violently under his brother's weight in a desperate attempt to dislodge him. The movement caused the knife to nick his throat, and he felt a warm trickle of blood begin to flow.

"Shut up," Troy hissed, grabbing a handful of Trevor's hair and slamming his head against the hardwood floor with enough force to make stars explode behind his eyes.

Trevor's vision blurred and darkened around the edges as consciousness began to slip away from him.

~

Heidi's urgent whining penetrated the fog of sleep that had finally claimed Shea after hours of restless tossing and turning. The German shepherd was standing beside the bed, her wet nose pressed against Shea's face and her entire body radiating anxiety.

"What is it, girl?" Shea mumbled, glancing blearily at the bedside clock. One o'clock in the morning. She lay still for a moment and listened carefully to the sounds of the house, trying to identify what had triggered the dog's distress. Something didn't feel right about the oppressive silence that surrounded them.

Moving as quietly as possible, she grabbed her service weapon from the nightstand drawer and stepped cautiously into the hallway. Trevor's bedroom door was hanging wide open, which immediately sent alarm bells ringing in her mind. "Trevor?" she called softly, not wanting to wake him if he was having trouble sleeping.

She entered his room and found it empty, the bed covers thrown back as if he had left in a hurry. Her heart sank as she realized what had happened. She whirled around and darted back to her room, throwing on her uniform with hands that trembled slightly from adrenaline and fear.

Trevor had gone to face his brother alone, exactly as she had feared he would. Despite all their discussions about working together, despite his promises to include her in any final confrontation, he had chosen to sacrifice himself rather than allow her to share the danger.

She thundered outside to her patrol truck, pausing only to give Heidi a command that broke her heart. "Stay here, girl. You can't come with me this time." She wouldn't risk the loyal dog's life, no matter how much she could use the backup.

As she sped toward the interstate with her emergency lights flashing, she placed an urgent call to the Pea Ridge police department. "This is Sheriff Shea Callahan from Misty Hollow. I have reason to believe that escaped fugitive Troy Bolton is currently holding my deputy hostage at their childhood home address. I'm en route from Misty Hollow, but it will take me at least an hour and a half to reach your jurisdiction. I'm requesting immediate assistance from any available units."

She rattled off the address from memory, hoping desperately that the arrival of local law enforcement might make Troy hesitate before killing Trevor. After all, according to his twisted methodology, he was supposed to wait for her arrival to complete his countdown properly, wasn't he?

Her heart felt like it had lodged permanently in her throat as she activated her siren and pushed the truck to its maximum safe speed. She could make the drive to Pea Ridge in an hour and a half under ideal conditions, maybe faster given that traffic was virtually nonexistent at this hour. When she and Trevor had made the trip earlier to question neighbors about his childhood, it had taken them a leisurely two hours. But they hadn't been racing against time and death.

Please, God, she prayed silently, give this truck wings and let me get there before it's too late.

She blazed past cars that obediently pulled to the shoulder of the interstate and wove expertly between those drivers who either didn't notice her emergency signals or chose to ignore them. Her knuckles ached from gripping the steering wheel with white-knuckled intensity, but she didn't dare relax her hold.

The terrible possibility that Troy might deviate from his original plan haunted her thoughts during the long drive. Trevor could already be dead, his body growing cold while Troy disappeared into the night to begin hunting new victims. Unless... unless Troy had no intention of surviving past this final confrontation. He could be planning a murder-suicide that would claim both brothers along with Shea herself when she arrived. The thought made her blood run cold with terror.

By the time she finally reached the Pea Ridge city limits, she had barely managed to keep her frayed nerves under control. Three patrol cars were parked outside the dilapidated Bolton family home, their red and blue emergency lights painting the abandoned structure in alternating colors of urgency.

"Has there been any activity?" she asked the lead detective as she approached the makeshift command post they had established on the street.

"We know your deputy is still alive," the man reported grimly. "The suspect confirmed that much when we attempted to establish communication, but as to his current condition..." The detective shrugged helplessly. "We have no way of knowing. The subject says he's waiting for you to arrive."

Shea nodded, her stomach churning with dread. "I'm the final piece of his puzzle. Without me, he can't complete whatever sick game he's been playing."

"What's our tactical approach going to be?" the detective asked.

"You and your officers wait here and maintain your perimeter," Shea said, her voice steady despite the fear coursing through her system. "I have to go inside alone."

"With all due respect, Sheriff, but that's completely insane," the detective protested. "You'll be walking directly into a trap with no backup and no way for us to assist you if things go wrong."

"I have to make sure my deputy survives this," Shea replied with iron determination. "But feel free to position a sniper with a clear view of the interior if possible. Don't hesitate to take the shot if you get a clean opportunity that won't endanger Trevor."

She squared her shoulders, checked her weapon one final time, and approached the front door of the house where evil had been born and nurtured for so many years.

Chapter Eighteen

Shea squared her shoulders and cast one final glance at the Pea Ridge police officers who had positioned themselves strategically behind their patrol cars, weapons drawn and ready to provide backup if the situation deteriorated beyond her control. Their presence was both reassuring and terrifying—reassuring because she knew they would do everything possible to help her, terrifying because their involvement meant this confrontation could easily turn into a bloodbath that would claim multiple lives before it was over.

She gave them a resolute nod to indicate she was ready, then approached the front door of the house where so much evil had been born and nurtured over the years. Her service weapon felt both familiar and foreign in her grip as she pushed open the weathered door, her heart hammering so loudly in her ears that she was sure Troy would be able to hear it from wherever he was waiting inside.

The interior of the abandoned house was even worse than she had imagined. What remained of the furniture that had once made this place a family home now lay scattered in pieces across the dusty floor— shattered remnants of chairs, a collapsed dining table, broken picture frames that had once held happy family photographs. In the center of this domestic devastation stood Troy Bolton, holding Trevor's limp and bloodied body in front of him like a human shield.

Blood had soaked through the front of Trevor's shirt in multiple places, and his head lolled forward at an unnatural angle that made Shea's stomach clench with fear. But his chest was still rising and falling with shallow breaths, which meant he was alive despite his injuries. That knowledge was the only thing that kept her from completely losing control of her emotions.

Rage and terror formed a tight knot in her chest as she leveled her weapon directly at Troy's head, trying to find an angle that wouldn't endanger Trevor. "Let him go right now, or I will put a bullet through your skull."

Troy's grin was a horrible thing to see, made even more disturbing by the blood that was smeared across his face and the rapidly swelling bruise that was closing his left eye. "Look who finally decided to show up for the grand finale. The mighty Sheriff Callahan herself, come to save the day." He tilted his head mockingly and adjusted his grip on Trevor's unconscious form. "But why would I let my dear brother go when he's providing such excellent protection? If you shoot me, that bullet has to pass through him first. Those are very bad odds for someone you claim to care about."

His grin widened to reveal teeth that were stained with his blood. "But I'm feeling generous tonight, so let's make this interesting. Just you and me, no guns, no weapons, no backup. A fair fight to determine who walks out of here alive. If you win, you both get to leave this place breathing. If you lose..." He shrugged casually. "Well, we both know what happens then."

Shea stared at him for a long moment, her mind racing through the tactical options available to her. None of them were good. Troy was using Trevor's body as a shield so effectively that she couldn't get a clean shot, and even if she could, Trevor was positioned in such a way that any bullet would have to pass through him to reach his brother.

She switched her gaze to Trevor's pale face, noting the fresh cuts and bruises that marked where Troy had beaten him unconscious. The only realistic chance either of them had for survival was if she could somehow defeat Troy in hand-to-hand combat—something that seemed almost impossible given his superior size, strength, and complete lack of moral constraints.

But impossible or not, it was their only option.

With a heavy thud that seemed to echo through the empty house like a funeral bell, she dropped her service weapon to the floor and kicked it away from herself.

"Fine. But I want your word that this will be a fair fight—no weapons, no tricks, no outside interference."

She lifted her radio to her lips. "All units, hold your positions. Sniper, stand down and do not engage under any circumstances."

"Sheriff, that's not advisable," came the immediate response from outside. "We can't provide assistance if—"

"That's a direct order," Shea interrupted firmly. "Stand down and maintain perimeter only."

Still wearing that horrible grin, Troy carefully set his hunting knife on the windowsill where it caught the moonlight like a promise of death. "No weapons, Sheriff. Just you, me, and whoever proves to be the stronger."

"Not a chance we're letting you face him alone," the voice on her radio protested.

"I said that's a direct order. Stand down immediately."

Troy suddenly flung Trevor's unconscious body away from him with casual brutality, sending him crashing into the wall where he slumped like a broken doll. Shea barely had time to register Trevor's impact before Troy was rushing toward her, his right fist already swinging in a wild haymaker that she managed to duck at the last possible second.

The punch grazed her left cheekbone hard enough to send stars exploding across her vision, but she managed to stay on her feet and strike back immediately. Years of law enforcement training kicked in as she aimed low and connected solidly with his ribs, then followed up with a knee strike to his thigh that made him grunt with pain.

"You hit like a little girl," Troy growled, wrapping his powerful arms around her waist and using his superior weight to slam her backward into the remains of the old coffee table. The impact sent up a cloud of dust and debris, and she heard something—probably a lamp—shatter against the wall.

Troy delivered a devastating punch to her solar plexus that drove all the air from her lungs and left her gasping helplessly. She stumbled backward, trying to create some distance between them, but she could already feel the familiar and terrifying tightness beginning to form in her chest.

No. Not now. Not when Trevor's life depended on her ability to fight.

Her lungs began to make the distinctive squeaking sound that she recognized as the precursor to a full-blown asthma attack. The stress and physical exertion were triggering the condition that had plagued her since childhood, and she knew she had only minutes before her breathing would become completely compromised.

She dropped to one knee and frantically dug into her pocket for the rescue inhaler that she always carried, her fingers trembling as she searched for the small device that could mean the difference between life and death.

Troy began laughing—a sound that held no humor whatsoever—and casually slapped the inhaler from her hand before she could use it. The plastic device skittered across the floor and came to rest near the fireplace, well out of her reach.

"It seems our brave sheriff has a critical weakness beyond her obvious affection for my brother," Troy said with malicious satisfaction. "How unfortunate for you."

"Not fighting fair," Shea managed to gasp between labored breaths. "No honor in taking advantage of a medical condition."

Something she couldn't quite identify flickered briefly in Troy's eyes, perhaps a ghost of the conscience he had once possessed before evil consumed him completely. He paused in his circling and tilted his head as if considering her words.

"You do realize that my face is going to be the last thing you see as you draw your final breath, don't you?" he said, but his voice had lost some of its earlier mockery. After a moment of apparent internal debate, he retrieved her inhaler from where it had fallen and extended it toward her. "But I suppose you have a point about fairness. I want you to die by my hands, not because of an illness that I didn't cause."

She accepted the inhaler with hands that shook from both adrenaline and oxygen deprivation, then took two desperate puffs of the medication that would hopefully open her constricted airways. The familiar taste of the albuterol was like a lifeline as she slipped the device back into her pocket.

"Thank you," she said, though the words felt strange when directed at someone who was trying to kill her.

With her gaze locked on Troy's battered face, she struggled back to her feet, using the wall for support. "Just give me a minute to catch my breath," she said, planting both hands on her knees and waiting for her respiratory system to respond to the medication.

Out of the corner of her eye, she noticed Trevor beginning to stir from where he sat slumped against the wall, his head moving slightly as consciousness started to return. She couldn't let Troy realize that his brother was waking up—the element of surprise might be their only advantage.

Adopting a defensive fighting stance that she had learned during her police academy training, she shot a quick glance toward the hunting knife that Troy had placed on the windowsill. What would it take to reach that weapon? Could she create enough of a distraction to grab it and turn the tables on her attacker?

She returned her full attention to Troy and nodded grimly. "All right. Let's finish this."

She managed to dodge his next punch and landed a solid hit of her own to his jaw, putting all her weight behind the blow. The impact sent a shock of pain up her arm, but she had the satisfaction of seeing Troy's head snap back from the force of her strike.

Her lungs were still producing that ominous

wheezing sound with each breath, serving as a painful reminder that a full-blown asthma attack could still incapacitate her at any moment. The medication would help, but it wasn't a miracle cure—she still had to be careful not to overexert herself.

She landed another solid punch that made Troy stagger backward several steps. "You are as tough as people say," he admitted, dancing around her like a professional prize fighter sizing up his opponent. "Oh yes, I did extensive research on you, Sheriff Callahan. Your reputation for taking down dangerous criminals is quite impressive."

"You won't get away with this," Shea said, trying to keep him talking while she looked for an opening.

"I don't plan to escape," Troy replied with disturbing calmness. "I entered this world just a few minutes before my dear brother, and I fully intend to leave it a few minutes after he does. Unfortunately, neither of you will be alive to witness my departure."

Everything in Shea wished she could live to see Troy Bolton finally meet his end, but she focused her energy on the immediate challenge of surviving the next few minutes. "We'll see about that."

Without warning, Troy whipped around and delivered a devastating roundhouse kick to her stomach with enough force to lift her completely off her feet. She crashed to her knees, her breath leaving her in an explosive rush that left her seeing spots.

Her vision blurred as oxygen deprivation began to

affect her brain function, and she knew she was running out of time.

~

Through the haze of pain and semi-consciousness, Trevor forced his eyes open just in time to see Shea collapsing under Troy's brutal attack. The sight of her falling to the floor sent a surge of rage through his battered body that was stronger than any physical pain he had ever experienced.

With a growl that seemed to come from the depths of his soul, he launched himself at his brother, tackling Troy to the ground with all the force he could muster. They crashed together and tumbled across the dusty floor in a tangle of limbs, fists flying as twenty years of accumulated hatred and hurt fueled Trevor's desperate assault.

Out of the corner of his eye, he could see Shea scuttling backward toward the wall, gasping for breath as she struggled with her asthma attack. She managed to speak into her radio, probably calling for medical assistance, but Trevor couldn't make out her words over the sounds of their violent struggle.

Troy landed a punch that sent Trevor crashing into the wall hard enough to crack the old plaster, but adrenaline and determination brought him back to the fight almost immediately. He grabbed his brother by the collar of his blood-stained shirt and used his momentum to push Troy backward across the room.

"You think you're better than me?" Troy snarled,

spittle flying from his lips as he fought to break free from Trevor's grip. "You think being a deputy sheriff makes you some kind of hero?"

"No," Trevor replied, his voice steady despite the chaos around them. "But I'm done being afraid of you. I'm done letting you control my life with threats and violence."

The struggle continued with neither man able to gain a decisive advantage. Both were injured, both were exhausted, but both were fighting for their lives and the lives of people they cared about. Troy's foot suddenly slipped on a piece of broken glass, causing him to lose his balance. His hand flailed desperately as he tried to regain his footing, but it was too late.

His eyes went wide with what might have been surprise or fear as he fell backward, his head snapping against the sharp corner of the stone fireplace mantel with a dull, wet crack that seemed to echo through the room like a gunshot.

Suddenly, absolute silence filled the house.

Trevor froze and stared in horror at the growing pool of blood that was spreading across the floor beneath his brother's motionless head. "No," he whispered, his voice breaking with anguish. "I didn't mean for this to happen. I didn't want him to die."

Shea managed to slap the floor twice with her palm, the sound sharp enough to draw Trevor's attention away from his brother's body. She was still struggling to breathe, but she was alive and conscious.

He immediately dropped to his knees beside her, noting that her skin had gone pale and clammy with the classic signs of respiratory distress. "Where's your inhaler? You need medication right now."

"Pocket," she managed to gasp. "Won't work well. Too severe."

He dug the plastic device out of her pocket anyway and thrust it into her trembling hands. "It will work, Shea. I know it will. You need to try." He pulled her into his lap, drawing her back against his chest so she could feel his steady breathing. "Take two puffs and try to match my respiratory rhythm. One, two, three..."

She took two desperate puffs of the medication, sucking in air with obvious difficulty.

Her radio crackled with an urgent voice from outside. "Sheriff? What's your status in there? We heard sounds of a struggle."

Trevor reached for the radio and keyed the microphone. "Suspect is down. Send medical assistance immediately. We're both alive but need paramedics."

"He's gone," Trevor whispered, his gaze returning to Troy's still form. "My brother is dead."

"You saved my life," Shea said, turning in his arms to cup his face with both hands. "And you saved countless future victims. Troy can't hurt anyone else ever again."

Trevor's gaze drifted to the faded family portrait that still hung inexplicably on the wall, apparently no one had bothered to remove it during all the years the house had stood empty. He studied the faces of two young boys who had grown up under the same roof, shared the same DNA, breathed the same air, but had somehow become entirely different people.

Police officers swarmed into the room, their boots crunching on broken glass and debris. One of them immediately shoved bottles of water into both Shea's and Trevor's hands. "Ambulance is already on its way," the officer reported. "ETA approximately five minutes."

"Sheriff, I'm Detective Dawson," a large man announced as he loomed over them with a notepad in his hand. "I'll need to take formal statements from both of you about what happened here tonight."

"I never fired my weapon," Shea said, her breathing slowly returning to normal as the medication took effect. "Neither of us used firearms during the confrontation."

Detective Dawson frowned as he scribbled notes. "Neither one of you discharged your weapons? Are you certain about that?"

"Yes," Trevor said, taking over the explanation to give Shea more time to recover her strength. "That wasn't the game Troy wanted to play. He insisted on hand-to-hand combat only. His death was accidental— he hit his head on the fireplace mantel when he lost his footing during our struggle."

Trevor's throat clogged with emotion as he spoke the words aloud for the first time.

Detective Dawson continued writing. "We'll need

to review all the evidence and get a full reconstruction of events, but the sniper outside confirms that he never had a clean shot at any point during the incident. Both of you are extremely lucky to be alive. Things could have been significantly worse."

"They almost were," Trevor said softly, his voice barely audible.

Later that evening, after Trevor had received stitches for his various cuts and Shea had been given a steroid injection to prevent further respiratory complications, they found themselves sitting on Trevor's front porch with glasses of iced tea in their hands. The familiar ritual of sharing a quiet drink felt surreal after everything they had been through.

Trevor stared through tear-filled eyes at the amber liquid in his glass, unable to focus on anything except the events of the past few hours.

Shea reached over and took his free hand in hers, her fingers warm and steady against his skin. "Are you going to be okay?"

He gave a humorless laugh that held no joy whatsoever. "I killed my own brother tonight. I honestly don't know how I'm supposed to be okay with that fact."

She didn't answer immediately. Instead, she gazed out at the moonlit field beyond his house, where silver light kissed the tips of the tall grass and painted everything in shades of black and white. "Troy was going to kill both of us," she said finally. "You stopped him from committing murder. And after he finished with us, he would have continued killing innocent people, playing different versions of his sick games until someone else stopped him."

Trevor shook his head, his voice cracking with grief and guilt. "I spent my entire life trying to prove that I wasn't like him, that I was different from my psychopathic twin brother. But in the end, I did exactly what he would have done. I took a human life."

"No," Shea said firmly, giving his hand a gentle squeeze. "Troy hurt and killed people for sport because he genuinely enjoyed inflicting pain and terror. The fact that you acted to save lives, that his death causes you this much anguish—that's exactly what makes you completely different from him."

They sat together in comfortable silence as the night deepened around them, just the two of them and the peaceful darkness. For the first time in weeks, Trevor had no reason to fear what might be lurking in the shadows or waiting to attack when he least expected it.

He turned to study Shea's profile in the moonlight, noting the exhaustion etched in her features and the bruises that were already beginning to form from her fight with Troy. "I would do it again if it meant saving your life," he said quietly. "I would make the same choice every time."

They remained on the porch until dawn began to creep across the horizon, painting the sky in brilliant streaks of orange and violet that promised a new day free from the shadow of Troy Bolton's evil. When the sun showed above the tree line, Shea finally stood and stretched, still keeping hold of his hand.

"It's been an incredibly long day and night," she said gently. "We both need real sleep and time to process everything that's happened. I'll stay here with you until tomorrow to make sure you're all right, but then I think you should take some time off work to deal with your grief properly."

She squeezed his fingers one more time. "Take a few days off, Trevor. You've earned it, and you need time to heal—both physically and emotionally."

As they walked toward the house together, Trevor felt something he hadn't experienced in twenty years: the absolute certainty that he was finally, truly safe from his brother's evil influence. Troy Bolton was dead, and the nightmare that had shaped Trevor's entire adult life was finally over.

Chapter Nineteen

Trevor stopped by the station during lunch when he was supposed to be off duty, bringing her a sandwich. "You probably forgot to eat again."

Shea glanced up from her desk. "You're supposed to stay away from here for a few days."

"I'm bored." He gave her a sad smile and handed her the food. "Ham, cheese, and honey mustard. Just as you like it."

"Thank you."

He leaned against the door jamb. "I'm not the only one who needs some downtime. How about supper tonight?"

Her mouth dried. "You mean like a date?"

"Sure, you could say that. Burgers at Rusty's. Meet you at seven?"

"A biker bar?" She frowned.

"They serve great food and have live music. Say yes. You need this as much as I do."

What would it mean going on a date with him? Did she want to move past a friendship? A working relationship to a more personal one? She never thought anyone would interest her in that way. For years, she'd focused solely on her career. Despite her misgivings, she nodded. "Sure. I'll see you at seven." She prayed she wasn't making a huge mistake.

Dressed in skinny jeans and a black tee, Shea stood outside the bar unsure of how to act out of uniform. Doing her best to ignore the curious glances shot her way by those entering the bar, she searched the road for signs of Trevor's truck.

On cue his truck turned into the parking lot and rumbled to a stop. Smiling, he exited the truck, his gaze scanning her from head to toe. "You clean up nice, Sheriff."

She arched a brow. "Sure you want to be seen with me outside of work?"

"I fought a guy to save you." He crooked his arm. "It's safe to say I'm committed."

She rolled her eyes to take some of the seriousness out of his comment. Commitment? She wasn't sure she was ready. He put his hand on the small of her back, an intimate gesture that sent bolts of electricity through her and guided her into the dim recesses of the bar.

They ended up in a quiet booth at the back and ordered cheeseburgers smothered with mushrooms. They were as delicious as Trevor had promised.

After they ate, Shea tossed her napkin on her plate and captured Trevor's gaze. "I don't know how to do this."

"Do what?"

"This." She waved a hand. "Relationships. Letting people pass the wall I've built."

"You have friends."

"That's different."

"Is it?" His mouth crooked as he reached across the table, his calloused fingers brushing here. "We've got time to figure this out, Shea."

"What if I'm too broken?"

"Nonsense. You're the most together person I've ever met." He rose to his feet and pulled her up beside him as the band started a slow country song. "Let's dance."

"I don't dance."

"You do now." He pulled her close and swung her onto the dance floor and taught her the two-step. The next song was slower, and he tugged her ever so close, resting his chin on her head.

Shea sighed and closed her eyes. Maybe she could do this.

The End

Enjoy the first chapter of the next book, Drowned in Silence.

Prologue

The killer slipped through the trees like a wisp of smoke, each step rehearsed, each breath measured. The killer cannot make a mistake.

Tonight is the night. After days of observation and planning, the killer sees the victim, right where she should be. Abby Pearson hums along the shoreline, alone as usual. Foolish girl? Doesn't she know how dangerous it is?

The killer springs forward and blocks the girl's retreat. Abby gasps, confusion filling her eyes as she recognizes the face in front of her. Her brow furrows. Then, sensing that the usually friendly face now means her harm, she whirls to run. The killer clamps a gloved hand over her mouth. The pungent odor of ether soaked into the glove, filled the air. Not enough to keep her unconscious for long. The killer thirsts to feel the life drain from the girl's body.

The struggle is short. Abby slumps to the ground.

Gripping her under both arms, the killer dragged her to a waiting rowboat moored at the edge of the lake, concealed from the main trail by tall reeds. The killer pulled the girl into the water.

The coolness of the water revives Abby. The killer smiles and submerges her face below the surface of the lake. Abby's hands claw at the killer's arms, panic making her strength desperate. The killer holds her under, relishing in the frantic struggle—the bubbles, the trembling of her body. The girl's fight slows, then ceases. The moment her body goes slack, the killer steps back. The silence settles, cold and absolute.

After a few seconds of no movement, the killer drags the body into the boat and places the girl on her back. After smoothing her wet hair away from her face, the killer folded the girl's arms over her stomach. To the casual observer, Abby seems nothing more than a girl dozing, not a victim of violence.

The killer placed a small card under the folded hands before placing a silver heart necklace next to her side. "Foolish girl doesn't know the dangers of walking alone at night."

A gentle push of the killer's foot sends the boat away from the reeds. It drifted a short way along the misty water's edge before stopping the length of the rope, mooring it to the bank. As the boat drifted, the killer picked up a bucket on the shore and washed away the footprints.

Satisfied, the killer melted back into the trees, pausing once to watch the fog envelope the boat. A secret for now, but the dawn will reveal the horror waiting for the unsuspecting hiker.

Chapter One

Sheriff Shea Callahan crouched next to the rowboat that had drifted to shore, moored by a weathered rope. Her gaze flickered over details. The angle of the body, the scrape on her cheek, from the side of the boat maybe? She sighed and, planting her palms firm against her thighs, pushed to stand.

She noted the drag marks that suggested the body had been moved. A flash of white from the water's edge drew her attention. With a gloved hand, she pulled a white sneaker with daisies printed on the canvas from the weeds and placed it in a bag.

Deputy Trevor Bolton stood a few feet away, black rubber gloves on his hands as he sketched a rough diagram of the scene. "Identification," he nodded to a cell phone next to the body. "Says she's Abby Pearson. The parents have not been notified yet. Said their daughter went hiking last night. When she didn't return, they figured she'd spent the night with a friend. I bagged a necklace from next to her body."

The silver chain caught the morning light as Trevor held up the evidence bag, a small heart pendant visible through the plastic. Shea recognized it immediately— half the girls at the high school wore identical ones from the local jewelry store's discount bin.

"I see where the body was dragged, but what's

strange is the fact that there are no footprints." Gaze on the ground, Shea moved away from the water's edge. A few strands of dark hair, Abby's, trembled from a low-hanging tree branch.

"Washed away." Trevor nudged a bucket half buried in the mud. "This was thought out, planned."

Shea knelt beside the bucket, studying its position. "Or covered up. Look at this—the mud's been disturbed around the rim, but there's no reason for that if it was just sitting here." She photographed the scene from multiple angles, her camera clicking steadily in the morning stillness.

"The killer could be watching us right now. Getting a thrill from the proceedings." Shea turned and surveyed the early morning forest. Mist still clung to the trees, creating ghostly shapes between the pines. "I want to talk to the ones who discovered the body."

"Two young boys." He jerked his head toward a battered Chevy pickup. "They're pretty shaken up."

The truck sat at an angle, as if the driver had pulled over hastily. Fishing rods jutted from the bed, and a tackle box rested on the tailgate. The boys sat in the front seat—one with his head in his hands, the other staring blankly at the lake.

Shea approached the two boys and spoke through the window. "I'm Sheriff Callahan. Can I have your names and what happened this morning?"

"That's our boat," one of them said, his words catching in his throat. His face was pale, freckles standing out like scattered pennies across his nose.

"He's Seth Reynolds," the other one said. "I'm Caleb Whittaker. We go fishing every Saturday morning. When we got here…we found…Abby."

"You knew her?"

They nodded in unison. "She's in our class. We're Juniors at the high school," Caleb said. "She sat behind me in history. Always borrowed a pen." His voice cracked on the last word.

'Does Abby usually go walking alone at night?"

Seth shrugged, wiping his nose with the back of his hand. "It's no secret that she likes to walk around the lake. Said it helps her think. We've got finals coming up, and she was stressed about college applications. Her mom wants her to go to the state university, but Abby wanted to study art somewhere smaller."

"The bucket yours?"

The boys nodded. "We use it for our catch," Caleb said. "Been using the same one for three years. My dad gave it to us when we started coming out here."

"Can you think of anyone who might have wanted to harm Abby?"

They shook their heads in unison, the movement mechanical, shocked.

"She was quiet, kind of shy, but well-liked." Caleb swallowed hard, his Adam's apple bobbing in his neck. "She helped tutor kids in art class. Never had a mean word to say about anyone."

"We'll have to take the boat and bucket as

evidence. You'll get it back when we've finished our investigation." Shea handed them each a business card. "Call me if you think of anything that might be helpful, no matter how small."

Shea headed down the walking trail that circled the lake. In the distance, morning campfires flickered to life, sending thin columns of smoke into the gray sky. It had rained earlier yesterday, and she hoped the killer wouldn't have washed away any evidence on the trail. The path was soft underfoot, muddy in places where water had pooled.

She spotted footprints. One set matched the tread on Abby's shoe, the other the type you would find on the sole of hiking boots. She frowned. The boot prints weren't much larger than Abby's—either a small man or a woman.

About fifty feet from the lake, the tracks stopped at the base of a large pine. Shea brushed away the dead needles, finding a faint impression as if someone had crouched there. Waiting. The pine's thick trunk would have provided perfect cover, giving a clear view of the trail while remaining hidden.

She stood, tension tightening in her shoulders as she continued her search. There. A broken limb on a bush. Leaves disturbed. This was where Abby had fallen. The ground showed signs of a struggle—torn earth, scattered leaves, a small piece of blue fabric caught on a thorn.

How had the killer subdued her? Had the girl

known her assailant and not suspected an attack? The struggle indicated Abby had fought back when she realized the danger.

She glanced back at the lake. The flashing lights of her patrol car highlighted the body of Abby, covered by a white sheet, Shea always kept in the back of her car. The sight never got easier, especially when the victim was so young. When the coroner from Langley arrived, Dr. Linda Fuller, Shea returned to the water's edge.

Dr. Fuller was a woman in her fifties with graying hair pulled back in a practical bun. She worked with quiet efficiency, her movements precise and respectful. "What do we have here?" she asked, pulling on latex gloves.

"Seventeen-year-old female, found in the boat this morning by two classmates. Appears to have been moved post-mortem."

The coroner glanced up. "I'm not busy. If you want to follow me back to the morgue, I can do the autopsy right now."

"Not being busy is a good thing." Shea exhaled slowly. In a county of their size, Dr. Fuller staying busy usually meant bad things were happening. "We'll follow you."

At the morgue, Shea and Trevor stood in the observation window. The sterile room felt cold despite the afternoon sun streaming through high windows. Arms folded, jaw tight, Trevor started to pace.

As Dr. Fuller worked, she called out her findings.

"Time of death between ten and eleven p.m. Cause of death is drowning." She glanced at Shea through the glass. "I found a trace of ether in her nose. Not enough to knock her out for more than a few minutes, just enough to disorient her." She returned to the task at hand. "Defensive wounds, scrapes, and bruises showed she fought back. Skin beneath her fingernails."

"She fought," Shea said softly. "Good girl. Hopefully, the skin under her nails belongs to the killer, and the DNA is in our database."

"That would be too easy." Trevor stopped pacing and stared out the window. "Nothing's ever that simple in this job."

"Let's go question some campers. Maybe someone heard something."

"You okay?" It had been five months since their encounter with Troy, Trevor's murderous twin, and Trevor had only been back to work for two of those months. Some cases still hit him harder than others.

"I'm fine. It's a shame when a young life is snuffed out." He marched out of the building, leaving her with the feeling that he was anything but fine. His shoulders were rigid, his movements sharp with barely contained anger.

At the Misty Hollow campground, they split up; Shea took the campers, while Trevor went to question those in the cabins, including both rental and permanent residents. The campground sprawled along the eastern shore of the lake, a mix of RV sites, tent areas, and small wooden cabins nestled among the trees.

First stop, a small convenience store that sold ice, bait, and anything a camper might have forgotten to bring. The building was weathered cedar with a screen door that squeaked when she pushed it open. A bell above the door announced her arrival.

The clerk, a young man in his early twenties with shoulder-length hair and multiple piercings, welcomed her, his eyes widening at the sight of her uniform. Shea introduced herself. "A body was found this morning on the other side of the lake. I'm wondering whether you might've seen or heard anything."

He shook his head, nervously adjusting his name tag that read 'MIKE.' "I just got here. The store is closed at night. The owner is in the back room. Want me to get him?"

"Please." Shea pasted on a smile, glancing around the cramped store. Shelves lined with canned goods, fishing supplies, and camping necessities created narrow aisles—a handwritten sign advertised night crawlers and minnows.

The boy rushed through a door marked "EMPLOYEES ONLY," returning a few seconds later with a middle-aged man wiping grease from his hands with a red shop rag. "Can I help you?"

Shea repeated her question.

"I don't know if this is relevant or not, but right before closing, a man wearing a hoodie came in and bought duct tape and cough syrup." The owner, whose name tag identified him as "EARL," scratched his beard thoughtfully.

"Cough syrup? Did you get a good look at his face?"

The man shrugged. "Sorry. He kept his head down. Paid with cash, exact change. Seemed like he wanted to get out of here quick. Thing is, we don't get many folks buying that combination of items, you know? Made me wonder what he was up to."

"What kind of cough syrup?"

"The generic stuff with dextromethorphan. Kids sometimes buy it to get high. This guy had soft hands, like he hadn't worked a hard day his whole life."

Shea thanked him and left the store. Maybe ten sites were occupied by campers. With it being Saturday morning, she expected more to arrive throughout the day. She went from site to site and found out nothing useful. Most campers had retired early, tired from hiking or fishing. By ten, they had extinguished fires and gone to bed. Only one family commented on their dog barking around ten, but they hushed it quickly, not wanting to disturb other campers.

An elderly couple in a pristine RV mentioned seeing a vehicle with only one working headlight driving slowly through the campground around ten-thirty. Still, they couldn't provide any other details.

They had nothing to go on but a man in a hoodie who'd purchased tape and cough syrup. Abby hadn't been killed or bound with either of those items, but the purchases felt significant somehow. Shea went in search of Trevor, following a winding path through the cabin area.

~

Trevor knocked on the door of a small cabin painted forest green with white trim. A woman wearing a frilly white apron decorated with red apples opened the door with a smile. "I wasn't expecting visitors so early."

"I'm Deputy Bolton, ma'am. May I ask you a few questions?" He showed her his ID, noting how her friendly demeanor shifted to concern as she read his badge.

"Absolutely. I'm Mrs. Brown." She pulled the door closed and invited him to have a seat in one of the rockers on her porch. The chairs were well-worn but comfortable, positioned to take advantage of the lake view.

He gazed across the lake, noting how the morning mist had finally lifted, revealing the far shore where they'd found Abby's body. "Beautiful view you've got."

"The primary reason my husband, may he rest in peace, built this place. Now, what can I do for you?" Her voice carried a slight tremor, the kind that came with age and worry.

"A body was found this morning on the other side of the lake. Do you recall anything out of the ordinary last night, around ten p.m.?"

Her brow furrowed as she rocked slowly, the chair

creaking rhythmically. "I did see headlights moving real slow. Thought maybe it was someone looking for a good spot to go night fishing. It happens. The strange thing is, they never turned off their vehicle. Not for a good twenty to thirty minutes, then the vehicle left quicker than it arrived."

"Are you usually awake at that time of night?"

She chuckled, though the sound held little humor. "When you get to be my age, sleep is a luxury not often granted. I sit out here most evenings until sleep beckons. Sometimes that's midnight, sometimes later."

"Did you notice anything else about the vehicle? Size, color, make?"

"Too dark and too far away. But it was definitely larger than a car, a pickup truck, or maybe an SUV. The headlights sat high off the ground, although only one headlight worked."

Seeing Shea approaching along the lake path, Trevor handed the woman a business card. "Thank you for your time, Mrs. Brown. If you remember anything else, please call."

He went to meet Shea halfway, noting the frustrated set to her shoulders. "Find out anything?"

"Nothing useful. You?"

He told her about the vehicle Mrs. Brown had seen. "No way of knowing the make or model from this distance. We can try to find tire tracks."

She nodded, glancing back toward the convenience store. "Man in a hoodie bought duct tape and cough syrup right before closing. Owner said he kept his head down, had soft hands."

"Doesn't match what we found at the scene, but it's suspicious timing."

"Lead the way."

After studying the area, the older woman had said she'd seen the lights, so he drove them to the other side of the lake. It didn't take long to find a small patch of dirt used for launching boats into the water from trucks. The area was rutted from years of use, with a concrete ramp extending into the lake.

Large tire tracks marred the wet ground. The tread looked like half the ones found in Misty Hollow and surrounding areas—a common pattern that wouldn't narrow their search much.

Trevor approached the water in one direction, while Shea moved in the opposite way, both searching methodically along the shoreline. A sliver of white poked from under a rock near the water's edge. After pulling on a glove, he slipped the paper free. The water smeared the words, but they were still readable. "Shea."

She hurried to his side, her boots squelching in the mud. "What did you find?"

He handed her the paper, watching her face as she read the message. The words were written in block letters with blue ink, partially dissolved but clear enough to make out.

"She shouldn't have gone out alone after dark."

Dear Reader,

I hope you enjoyed Trevor's story. If so, please leave a review or a rating on Amazon. Reviews are the lifeblood for authors.

God bless,

Cynthia

www.cynthiahickey.com
Cynthia Hickey is a multi-published and best-selling author of cozy mysteries and romantic suspense/thrillers. She has taught writing at many conferences and small writing retreats. She and her husband run the publishing press, Winged Publications. They live in Arizona and Arkansas, becoming snowbirds with three dogs. They have ten grandchildren who keep them busy and tell everyone they know that "Nana is a writer."

Connect with me on FaceBook
Twitter
Sign up for my newsletter and receive a free short story
www.cynthiahickey.com

Follow me on <u>Amazon</u>
And <u>Bookbub</u>
Shop my bookstore <u>on shopify</u>. For better price and autographed books.

Enjoy other books by Cynthia Hickey

Cowboys of Misty Hollow
<u>Cowboy Jeopardy</u>
<u>Cowboy Peril</u>
<u>Cowboy Hazard</u>
<u>Cowgirl Blaze</u>
<u>Cowboy Uncertainty</u>
<u>Cowboy Christmas Crisis</u>
<u>Cowboy Pitfall</u>

The Sheriff of Misty Hollow
<u>Girls' Weekend Survival</u>
<u>The Threat</u>

Misty Hollow
<u>Secrets of Misty Hollow</u>
<u>Deceptive Peace</u>
<u>Calm Surface</u>
<u>Lightning Never Strikes Twice</u>
<u>Lethal Inheritance</u>
<u>Bitter Isolation</u>
<u>Say I Don't</u>
<u>Christmas Stalker</u>

<u>Bridge to Safety</u>
<u>When Night Falls</u>
<u>A Place to Hide</u>
<u>Mountain Refuge</u>

Stay in Misty Hollow for a while. Get the entire series <u>here</u>!

The Seven Deadly Sins series
<u>Deadly Pride</u>
<u>Deadly Covet</u>
<u>Deadly Lust</u>
<u>Deadly Glutton</u>
<u>Deadly Envy</u>
<u>Deadly Sloth</u>
<u>Deadly Anger</u>

The Tail Waggin' Mysteries
<u>Cat-Eyed Witness</u>
<u>The Dog Who Found a Body</u>
<u>Troublesome Twosome</u>
<u>Four-Legged Suspect</u>
<u>Unwanted Christmas Guest</u>
<u>Wedding Day Cat Burglar</u>

Brothers Steele
<u>Sharp as Steele</u>
<u>Carved in Steele</u>
<u>Forged in Steele</u>
<u>Brothers Steele</u> (All three in one)

The Brothers of Copper Pass
Wyatt's Warrant
Dirk's Defense
Stetson's Secret
Houston's Hope
Dallas's Dare
Seth's Sacrifice
Malcolm's Misunderstanding
The Brothers of Copper Pass Boxed Set

Time Travel
The Portal

Tiny House Mysteries
No Small Caper
Caper Goes Missing
Caper Finds a Clue
Caper's Dark Adventure
A Strange Game for Caper
Caper Steals Christmas
Caper Finds a Treasure
Tiny House Mysteries boxed set

Wife for Hire – Private Investigators
Saving Sarah
Lesson for Lacey
Mission for Meghan
Long Way for Lainie

<u>Aimed at Amy</u>
<u>Wife for Hire</u> (all five in one)

A Hollywood Murder
<u>Killer Pose, book 1</u>
<u>Killer Snapshot, book 2</u>
<u>Shoot to Kill, book 3</u>
<u>Kodak Kill Shot, book 4</u>
<u>To Snap a Killer</u>
<u>Hollywood Murder Mysteries</u>

Shady Acres Mysteries
<u>Beware the Orchids, book 1</u>
<u>Path to Nowhere</u>
<u>Poison Foliage</u>
<u>Poinsettia Madness</u>
<u>Deadly Greenhouse Gases</u>
<u>Vine Entrapment</u>
<u>Shady Acres Boxed Set</u>

CLEAN BUT GRITTY Romantic Suspense

Highland Springs

<u>Murder Live</u>
<u>Say Bye to Mommy</u>
<u>To Breathe Again</u>
<u>Highland Springs Murders</u> (all 3 in one)

Colors of Evil Series

Shades of Crimson
Coral Shadows

The Pretty Must Die Series

Ripped in Red, book 1
Pierced in Pink, book 2
Wounded in White, book 3
Worthy, The Complete Story

Lisa Paxton Mystery Series

Eenie Meenie Miny Mo
Jack Be Nimble
Hickory Dickory Dock
Boxed Set

Hearts of Courage
A Heart of Valor
The Game
Suspicious Minds
After the Storm
Local Betrayal
Hearts of Courage Boxed Set

Overcoming Evil series
Mistaken Assassin
Captured Innocence
Mountain of Fear

Exposure at Sea
A Secret to Die for
Collision Course
Romantic Suspense of 5 books in 1

INSPIRATIONAL

Nosy Neighbor Series
Anything For A Mystery, Book 1
A Killer Plot, Book 2
Skin Care Can Be Murder, Book 3
Death By Baking, Book 4
Jogging Is Bad For Your Health, Book 5
Poison Bubbles, Book 6
A Good Party Can Kill You, Book 7
Nosy Neighbor collection

Christmas with Stormi Nelson

The Summer Meadows Series
Fudge-Laced Felonies, Book 1
Candy-Coated Secrets, Book 2
Chocolate-Covered Crime, Book 3
Maui Macadamia Madness, Book 4
All four novels in one collection

The River Valley Mystery Series
Deadly Neighbors, Book 1
Advance Notice, Book 2

<u>**The Librarian's Last Chapter**</u>**, Book 3**
<u>**All three novels in one collection**</u>